THE BANGTA

Keith McCafferty is the survival and outdoor skills editor of *Field &
Stream* and the author of *The Royal Wulff Murders*, *The Gray Ghost
Murders*, *Dead Man's Fancy*, *Crazy Mountain Kiss* (which won the 2016
Spur Award for Best Western Contemporary Novel), *Buffalo Jump
Blues*, *Cold Hearted River*, and *A Death in Eden*. Winner of the Traver
Award for angling literature, he is a two-time National Magazine
awards finalist. He lives with his wife in Bozeman, Montana.

Praise for Keith McCaffery

"If you're not reading Keith McCafferty because you don't fly fish or
because you don't like mysteries or westerns, you need to get started
because he's just flat-out terrific."
> —Craig Johnson, author of the Walt Longmire novels,
> the basis for the Netflix drama *Longmire*

"Like Brad Smith and Elmore Leonard, McCafferty does a marvelous
job of manipulating mood. . . . A must for Craig Johnson and C.J. Box
fans." —*Booklist* (starred review)

"[Keith McCafferty] writes with heart and command of the story that
sparkles on every page."
> —Michael McGarrity, *New York Times* bestselling author of
> *Backlands*

"Fresh, quirky, and yet utterly believable."
> —Nevada Barr, *New York Times* bestselling author of
> the Anna Pigeon mysteries

"McCafferty nails the delicate balance between humor and heft in a
genuine way."
> —P. J. Tracy, *New York Times* bestselling author of *Off the Grid*

"Rich in history, local color, and unique characters." —*Kirkus Reviews*

ALSO BY KEITH MCCAFFERTY

THE
BANGTAIL
GHOST

Keith McCafferty

A
SEAN STRANAHAN
MYSTERY

PENGUIN BOOKS

PENGUIN BOOKS
An imprint of Penguin Random House LLC
penguinrandomhouse.com

First published in the United States of America by Viking,
an imprint of Penguin Random House LLC, 2020
Published in Penguin Books 2021

ISBN 9780525562078 (paperback)

THE LIBRARY OF CONGRESS HAS CATALOGED THE
HARDCOVER EDITION AS FOLLOWS:
Names: McCafferty, Keith, author.
Title: The bangtail ghost : a Sean Stranahan mystery / Keith McCafferty.
Description: First edition. | [New York] : Viking, [2020]
Identifiers: LCCN 2020011854 (print) | LCCN 2020011855 (ebook) |
ISBN 9780525562054 (hardcover) | ISBN 9780525562061 (ebook)
Subjects: GSAFD: Mystery fiction.
Classification: LCC PS3613.C334 B36 2020 (print) |
LCC PS3613.C334 (ebook) | DDC 813/.6—dc23
LC record available at https://lccn.loc.gov/2020011854
LC ebook record available at https://lccn.loc.gov/2020011855

Printed in the United States of America
1st Printing

Designed by Alexis Farabaugh

For Kathryn Court and Dominick Abel

AUTHOR'S NOTE

A few years ago, I was asked to sign books at Malmstrom Air Force Base in Great Falls, Montana. I was subjected to the mandatory rigmarole of being fingerprinted and photographed, and then was directed to follow an escort car to the commissary, where I was greeted by the first of several enormous banners advertising my visit. I was assured that many people were looking forward to meeting me and would be lining up to buy books. I practiced my signature and waited. I bled a little more ink onto a piece of paper and waited some more.

The customers never materialized. In fact, almost no one came through the doors in two hours. Finally I was informed that a mountain lion had been spotted on the base and a "Remain in Place" order handed down to all personnel and nonmilitary guests. I was escorted back to my car by armed guards, then led to a back gate because the main entrance was closed. After I left, the entire base went into lockdown. Here was a facility with enough firepower to bring down a small European nation and, if you include the ordnance in the missile silos in the surrounding area, start World War III. All brought to a dead halt by what was probably a just a badly frightened cat.

I have been drawn to cats since childhood—to the point of traveling halfway around the world to fulfill a dream of seeing tigers in the wild—and so I was naturally rooting for the mountain lion spotted at the air force base. Alas, paranoia ruled, and the poor lion, which I was told had been hiding in a culvert pipe, was found and executed the following day. The incident made me think about humankind's primal, if often misguided, fear and superstition with regard to large carnivores, the so-called monsters of God that have the audacity to remind us of our place in nature's hierarchy by occasionally indulging in a meal of human flesh. I wondered how a community would react in a similar situation if the cat in question was thought to have killed human beings. And so from this kernel of thought a story grew: *The Bangtail Ghost*.

The word *ghost* is the appropriate, in fact almost inevitable choice to describe mountain lions, which are almost never seen and yet are known by more names—including *catamount*, *cougar*, *painter*, *panther*, and *puma*, the scientifically correct name—than any other animal on earth.

Leslie Patten, a wildlife author of my acquaintance, undertook a five-year journey to try to catch a glimpse of a mountain lion, hiking thousands of miles in the mountains of Wyoming. *Ghost Walker*, the journal of her quest, is among the best-researched books on mountain lions I've read. Yet she has never seen a lion in the wild. I know houndsmen who have treed hundreds of big cats but have never seen a single one without the aid of their dogs. To have seen seven lions without the benefit of a cold nose to pick up the scent, as I have, is a blessing, I am convinced, bestowed upon me by the cats themselves. That is, if you can call being growled at from a distance of ten feet a blessing. One of those seven lions you will meet in the opening chapter of this book. The story is quite an accurate description of the encounter, with one unnerving difference: There were two sets of jade-green eyes reflecting the light of my headlamp that night, not one.

One more ghost among the shadows of the night.

PART ONE

BLOOD IN THE TRACK

CHAPTER ONE

Fallen Star

To Sean Stranahan, the light that glimmered on and off looked like a star that had fallen to Earth and was slowly, haltingly, but inexorably climbing the mountainside to reclaim its position in heaven. It was there, and it wasn't, and then there it was again, each time a little higher. When the star quit moving, it had nearly reached the black sharpness that defined the ridgeline a half mile to the west, and simply pulsed, like a heartbeat. That was where the national forest ended and the wilderness began, where the starry night ended and clouds rode the moon.

Sean watched the light flicker out. A hunter, he thought. Or perhaps it really was a star, playing hide-and-seek with the horizon. Eyes played tricks at night. He adjusted the hip belt of his backpack and began to whistle a Hank Williams tune that Martha sometimes played on her harmonica. It was Martha who had shot the cow elk that he was lugging out of the mountains. Fifty pounds of boned-out elk quarter. Second load of the day. Winter meat. Spring and summer, too. She'd have come with him if Petal, her Appaloosa mare, hadn't stepped on her foot the day before.

Sean stopped whistling. He'd heard something, a drawn-out scream that seemed to float down from the ridge where he had seen the lights. The scream sounded human, as if someone were in mortal agony or lamenting a dead child. Yet Sean knew that ears, like eyes, were unreliable witnesses, and he told himself it could be anything. Maybe the sound was made by friction, two trees that tilted against each other, rubbing shoulders in the wind. He'd heard trees make eerie sounds before.

But here there was no wind, not even a breath of breeze to stir the big flakes of snow that fell straight down, like in a fairy tale, and that Sean could taste on his lips. His first impulse was to try to rescue whoever was screaming. But the canyon that separated him from the ridge was steeply walled, with masses of deadfall interrupted by sheer cliffs, and to try to hike down there at night was asking for a broken leg, or worse.

It was probably nothing anyway.

Sean started back down the trail, no longer whistling, his senses heightened, his pace a little faster than it should have been. He had gone perhaps a quarter of a mile when a scent invaded his nostrils, a heavy, putrid odor trapped under the low canopy of the pines. It smelled the way an elk's gut pile smells after six days in the sun. He stood still, his heart beating under the binoculars that hung down his chest. Maybe it wasn't a kill. Maybe it was a bear, whose odor is not much better. Instinctively, Sean's hand moved to the trigger of his pepper spray.

The growl started low in the throat and rose, then fell and rose again. This was no bear. Nor was it wind. Sean strained his eyes, but all was darkness. Then a shadow moved, a ghostlike visage that was a shade lighter than the night. Sean saw just enough of a shape to think it was a cat. It was crouched a few yards away, the fat scythe of its tail flipping from one side to the other. In a bound the animal was on the hillside above him. Another growl, then silence.

Sean had a moment when he seemed to float away, seeing his predicament as if from above. He was remembering a night earlier in the autumn when he was hiking out of the Gallatin Range and two German shepherds came running at him, growling as if possessed by demons. Too exhausted to be afraid, Sean had wheeled on a heel and shouted, "Get out of here!" The dogs abruptly turned tail. He tried the command now, the words the same but his voice unable to convey the requisite note of authority. Sean smiled in spite of himself. Then the growling started again, the smile was gone, and he was back on Earth.

Sean had been saving the battery of his headlamp, but now he switched it on and swept the beam up the slope. The eyes that reflected back at him burned with green fire. Sean felt the hairs on his neck tickle against his jacket collar. For a few moments he seemed not to breathe. Then the eyes were gone.

He turned his head to cast the light, catching the eyes again, piercing in their intensity. Sean began to walk down the trail, the cat—for he could think of nothing else it could be—prowling the hillside above him, following abreast, growling. After the initial shock, the reflective eyes had a curiously calming effect, for they gave away the animal's position.

Sean snapped the safety off the pepper spray. He could trigger a blast in the direction of the eyes, but why take the chance of provoking an attack? Besides, he'd bought the spray when he first moved to Montana. It was years out of date, the canister dented, and as it had

ridden in the glove compartment of his '76 Land Cruiser summer
and winter, the contents had been subjected to temperatures that
ranged from ninety-five degrees to minus forty. It might not work at
all. It was only after one mile became two, with the cat still following, that Sean's unease turned to fear. The near-continuous growling had diminished. The eyes fired back at him less often when he
swept his light. No odor, nor had there been since it had begun to
follow. Now all was silence, all was darkness.

And it could have been anywhere.

Sean had reached the toe of the ridge, where a creek ran with
snowmelt. On his way in that afternoon, he had forded the creek
farther up, where it was narrow and three logs spanned it. But now,
in trying to keep to open ground, Sean had strayed from the trail.
To reach the Forest Service road where he'd parked his rig, he'd have
to wade the stream. Tentatively, he took a step onto the pane of ice
near the bank. His boot broke through and he felt the ice of the water as it rushed over his boot top. He took another step. Now the
water was flooding over the tops of both boots. One more step, using a stick he'd found on the bank as a wading staff. The stick slipped
on anchor ice covering submerged rocks and Sean half fell, then,
attempting to regain his balance, abruptly sat down in the stream.

The shock of immersion disoriented him. He knew he looked vulnerable and struggled to his feet. *Where is the cat?* He slogged to the
far bank, his boots heavy, sloshing water, his legs staggering under
the weight of the pack. *Don't panic,* he told himself. *Where is the
damned cat?*

Sean began to walk, twisting his neck this way and that, the light
on his hat flaring up into the trees. He hadn't heard the animal or
seen its shape since before reaching the creek. After what might
have been twenty minutes—it seemed much longer—he saw the

Land Cruiser bulking against the pines. Sean fished his keys from his pocket. His fingers were numb from cold and he fumbled the key ring into the snow. He shrugged the heavy pack off and knelt down and dug with both hands, his heart jackhammering in his chest. There. The keys glinted. He unlocked the door and hefted his pack inside, then climbed into the cab. He turned the key and listened to the motor cough, then just sat there, his body shaking. As the adrenaline rush slowly subsided, he told himself that he hadn't really been that afraid, only alert.

It was a clarification he would repeat to Martha, after he hung the quarter of venison in her barn and they were sitting down to a late-night leftovers dinner. Got some exercise, that was all, he told her. Exciting, I'll give it that. My fault really. Should have settled for hauling one quarter out and gone back in tomorrow. Taking the last load out in the dark, not a good idea. Too many things that go bump in the night up there. The cat? Never really saw it clearly. More like a ghost than an animal. The scream, that was the weird thing.

"Where was your rifle all this time?"

"In the rig. I was hauling meat, not hunting."

"You could have dropped your backpack. That might have distracted it."

"I thought about it, but it would make me look smaller without it. And I thought if it attacked, the pack would protect my back and the back of my neck. Anyway, I had so much adrenaline flushing through my system that I hardly felt the weight."

"Interesting," Martha said. "Go on."

He told her about falling into the stream. "That's why I'm shaking."

Martha nodded. "I can see you're shaking." Then, under her breath, "Men."

"What?"

"Is it so hard to admit you were afraid? It's just me, Martha. We live together now. We'll be married in a few months. We don't keep things from each other. I've been down that road. It ends in divorce."

"He cheated on you."

"That's not what I'm talking about. You know, I take the badge off when I'm home. You can talk to me a little. I can't divine what you're thinking." She kissed him. "Go clean up."

"I'll do the dishes first. You're still hobbling."

"It looks bad, but I don't think anything's broken. Could be worse. I love you, you know. Even if you were afraid." And she smiled and he smiled, and they fell back into their easy ways.

The cold inside of Sean ached, and was still there after a hot shower an hour later. Martha was sitting up in the bed when he came out of the bathroom. She had lit a candle. Sean saw a tumbler of amber liquor on the nightstand. The two dogs and both cats were on the far side of the door.

"Is that the whiskey from Willie's Distillery?"

"It is. I know only one way better to warm you up."

"Being?"

"We'll get to it. But first, tell me honestly, you were afraid up there, right? I would be."

"What would I have been afraid of?"

"Oh, I don't know. Maybe a mountain lion that looked like a ghost. Or the other way around. Something along those lines."

"All I ever really saw were its shadow and its eyes. Anyway, a mountain lion hasn't killed anyone in Montana in years."

"Nonetheless."

"Okay. A little, I suppose. How afraid do you want me to have been?"

"Be serious. You weren't afraid up there in the dark, just you and whatever? Maybe just a little bit?"

"I was scared."

"You're not just saying that to get a sip of whiskey?"

"Maybe."

"How scared were you, really?" She held out the glass to him, pulled it back as he reached for it, then pushed it forward again. Sean took the glass and swallowed, the fire of the liquor spreading through his body.

"A little more than a little."

Martha tugged up her nightgown so it gathered at her waist.

"Maybe more than that," he said.

"How much more?"

"I was scared to death," Sean said.

She pulled the nightgown over her head and shook out her hair. "That's better," she said. "Scared to death, I believe. Scared to death gets you the other way to warm up."

CHAPTER TWO

The Fire in Her Eyes

The strangest part of dying was the tickling. It felt like a small bird had caught its claws in her throat and was beating its wings. The sensation reminded her of an old boyfriend who had a gunslinger mustache. Every night, he would wash the wax out and work in conditioner to make the hairs soft. Kissing him was erotic once she let herself go, only ticklish on nights when she just went along, happy to bend to his pleasure for the feeling of being close to someone, to hear the words "I love you," even if they were said reflexively, as a sigh.

His name was Wyatt—he was in his early twenties; she liked them young then, before she didn't like them at all—and she couldn't remember why they had split apart. She had chosen to veil large chunks of the "Tucson years," as she called them, while painting other parts in a soft, glowing light like the blush of dawn over the Chiricahuas. Wyatt had been a fine young man in life. He became an even better man now as a snapshot in her memory, when her breathing became labored.

How far had she been carried? She could remember nothing after leaving the trailer, not even switching on her headlamp. In one moment she was shuffling along, the snow so cold that it creaked under her boots, and in another she had come back from some unnamed ether with a tremendous pressure on her throat. She was being carried up the slope of a ridge, her hair hanging down, her head knocking against the downfall, her hands and her boots dragging in the snow. Somehow the band of the headlamp had stayed on her forehead, and its cold white fire cast circles that swirled up through the trees. She could barely breathe, and yet it didn't hurt.

I must be in shock, she thought.

Finally the clamped weight on her throat eased. As she lay in the snow, she heard a deep breathing that at first she mistook for her own, followed by a soft, throaty sound, like a muffled outboard motor coughing to life and then choking out. She turned her head to the sound and that was when she saw the eyes. They glowed in the reflection of her headlamp with a green tint, like the gemstone known as Arizona peridot, the poor man's emerald. She had worked at a rock shop once, in that half-forgotten, half-misremembered life of adobe and sand and saguaro cactus, where everything had gone right for a while before everything went wrong.

Instinctively, she lashed out toward the glowing orbs and her hand contacted a nap of fibers like the bristles of a boar-hair brush.

"What are you?" she tried to say. "Who are you?"

She heard an angry coughing sound, followed by what sounded like a scream from the canyon below. Hers? It seemed nothing of this Earth. Then the pressure on her throat came back, this time with a searing heat, and she hit at the hard stiffness as she became dreamy until, finally, she was only stroking the stiff hairs with her fingertips, as if tracing a lover's skin in the dark.

What was his name?

She couldn't remember, though his face had come back. She saw him clearly. Then he receded, like she was looking at his image through the wrong end of a telescope.

"Wyatt?" The word formed on her lips. She felt happy to have remembered his name. There was a pulsing of light behind her eyelids as her headlamp flickered rapidly and went out.

She opened her eyes to the engulfing blackness. No, that wasn't her world anymore. She closed her eyes to try to find him again, and as she did, she felt the fluttering against her throat stop as the bird took flight.

CHAPTER THREE

At One with Eagles

Sean groped for the phone vibrating on the nightstand. It was
Sam Meslik, the outfitter Sean worked for, guiding fly fishermen
being one of his several jobs that kept the wolves at bay.

"Sam," he said. No hellos. There never were.

"You know where the hunting rigs park up Johnny Gulch Road?"

"I know it. I was up that way last night."

"You were?"

"A little to the south. Long story."

"Well, ah . . . you can tell me about that later. I'm up here now and
there's blood in the snow."

"It's elk season."

"Yeah, well, I don't think this is elk blood."

"You want to elaborate?"

"There's blood in the *fucking* snow. Meet me at the trailhead. Bring
your fiancée." He clicked off.

Sean reached across the sleeping Siamese cat and snoring Aussie shepherd to rub Martha Ettinger's shoulder.

"It's four in the morning," Martha said.

IT WAS FIVE and change when the headlights of Martha's Cherokee shone on Meslik's three-quarter-ton parked at the trailhead. No other rigs, just an old Airstream trailer that must have been hauled in before the first heavy snowfall and wouldn't be going anywhere until the weather changed.

Sam clambered out of his truck. "I had one all but roped to a tree. This ruined my hunt," he said.

"You did the right thing by calling," Martha said. "I didn't think you'd get reception here."

"Smaller state every day. Won't be long before a man can't take a piss without using his free hand to answer his phone. Actually, I had to drive about a mile to pick up a bar. Last day of the fucking season, too. And I'm being a Boy Scout."

"You're becoming a contributing member of society despite your-self."

Sam grunted.

"So what's up?" Sean said.

The big man fingered his beard. "I don't know, but I stepped into shit, sure as we're standing here. That's supposed to be your de-partment, Kemosabe. Anyway, I got a real bad feeling about it." He pointed to the trailer. "Tracks start at the door. I didn't touch nothing."

"But you went inside?" Martha said.

"Fuck, yeah. It was unlocked. I thought somebody might be hurt in there. But the way I read it, whoever it was stepped outside and started walking toward the outhouse. I saw where somebody fell and I saw blood and I did my civic duty."

He turned to Martha. "She's a pro, you ask me."

"What makes you think it's a she?"

"Go see for yourself."

"I will, but right now I want to see this blood."

"You're the one with the badge."

Until the next election, anyway, Martha thought. She rubbed the hammer of her holstered revolver, one in a long line of nervous habits.

She wore the badge, all right. But in the mountains, she often found herself deferring to the trackers. For nearly a decade, the best tracker on the force had been Harold Little Feather, whom she had met when he was teaching a field course at the Montana Law Enforcement Academy in Helena and she was a cadet. But Harold had been lured from county employ to the State Investigative Services, which left Sean Stranahan, a licensed private investigator who had contracted out to the sheriff's department on several occasions, as the only person associated with the county who was better than your average elk hunter at reading sign.

Martha unholstered her Carnivore tracking light and handed it over.

"Does this mean I'm on the county nickel?" Sean said.

"You're employed until we get to the end of these tracks."

Sean switched the light on. He could discern five boot trails, two double trails up and back, as well as one single trail with no return trip to the trailer. Sam's track was easiest to distinguish because the impressions were freshest and he had the biggest boots. Shining the light ahead of him, Sean saw a stack of pine quarter-rounds partly covered by a tarp. Stuck into a splitting block was an ax, the steel glinting in the LED cluster.

From this woodpile all the trails angled toward the silhouette of the outhouse, and Sean had progressed no more than twenty feet when he saw where a person had fallen or been taken down in the snow. A drag mark led to the west. One set of tracks reversed direction, heading back toward the trailer. Sam Meslik's continued to follow the drag for another thirty yards. Then they, too, turned around, the impressions going out superimposed on the tracks coming in.

Sean waited for Sam and Martha to come up behind him. "This is as far as you followed," Sean said. He pointed with the flashlight beam.

"Hereabouts," Sam said.

"You saw blood, you said."

"I kicked a few spots out that were under the snow."

"Where?"

"Back by the woodpile."

"You're sure?"

"No, it was food dye from my daughter's Easter egg coloring kit. Yes, I'm sure. Blood is blood."

"Okay. Wait here." Sean switched his headlamp to its tracking mode. Blood drops caught in the beam of the red and blue LED clusters would appear radioactive, seeming to jump off the ground. He saw no such reaction on the surface snow, but there wouldn't be, as the snowfall had continued on and off through the night. He kicked around as he backtracked. There it was. Blood, all right. Not a lot, more of a sprinkling, like first stars in a clear sky.

He walked back to Martha and Sam. The three stood in silence, looking at the drag mark that led into the deeper forest. There was death here, as palpable as a pulse.

"I'll check out the trailer," Martha said. "Give us a few more minutes for the sky to get lighter."

"I'll slip a few stogies into Thumper," Sam said.

Martha glanced at him.

"His rifle," Sean said.

Martha shook her head. "Whatever's up ahead is official business. I don't want to be responsible for any fallout because of public participation."

"Bullshit," Sam said. "If it wasn't for me, you two would still be breathing dog farts in your feather bed. I was a medic in Iraq One. I trained on the M16 and shot a .338 Lapua with the snipers. I could have qualified if I'd made it a career choice, but I got a soft heart. I drew the line at killing anyone who was picking his nose a half a mile away."

"Nonetheless," Martha said.

"Then I guess I won't tell you what it is I hadn't got around to telling you."

"What's that?"

"You just gave up your right to know."

"This isn't a game."

Sean interrupted them. "Martha, let him come. I'm happy to have his rifle."

Martha muttered, "Et tu, Brute?" under her breath.

"I didn't catch that," Sam said.

"I said okay. What was it you didn't get around to telling me?"

"When I was driving up here there was a guy driving out, got his truck stuck in a snowbank about half a mile back, the dumb fuck. I winched him out."

"What was his name?"

Sam shook his head. "All I know is he was driving a Ford Ranger, the fucking training bra of trucks, and he was sweating in zero fucking degrees. Of course, he'd been trying to dig himself out for an hour, or that's what he said."

"Wasn't he going the wrong way? At four in the morning you're driving in to hunt, not driving out."

"He said he'd got lost and spent the night walking in circles."

Sean flashed to the lights he'd seen the night before. This might explain them.

"Describe him?" Martha said.

Sam shook his head. "I don't know. Regular guy. Medium height, I guess. Medium build. Beard."

"Hair?"

"It was under a hat, but there were, like, strands hanging down. So I'd say longish."

"The beard. Was it a lumberjack beard, hipster beard, metrosexual stubble?"

"I don't recall. He had facial hair, sort of medium."

"So your description is regular guy. Medium height, medium build, medium beard, training bra of trucks."

"Hey, you asked. It was fucking dark out."

"All right, get your gun," Martha said. "Sean, get my 06 out of the Cherokee. Cartridges are in the glove compartment. I'll be ten minutes."

LIKE SAM HAD SAID, there was no one home. Martha's cursory search revealed a chipped Formica table on a post that was bolted to the floor, a sheepherder's stove that was an addition to the original propane range, and an unmade bed with a string of twinkle lights suspended from an oval track affixed to the ceiling. At the head of the bed was a small stand with an ashtray, a coffee cup, and a paperback novel. Martha opened the drawer. Condoms, a tube of personal lubricant, a soft pack of Virginia Slims, NicoDerm patches.

She saw a roller bag in a corner and hoisted it onto the bed without touching the handles. She rifled through it, revealing jeans encrusted with butt bling, clingy tops cut to showcase what was under them, panties with hearts, and a slinky Japanese kimono embroidered with three-toed dragons. In with the frillies were country woman clothes—canvas overalls, sensible underwear, and a University of Arizona crewneck sweatshirt embroidered with a wildcat. No signs of violence, nor evidence that a man had ever got beyond the door. But the unmentionables pointed to the likelihood.

Martha opened the door of the sheepherder's stove. The embers were down to ashes, but the metal was still warm. She walked back out into the pastel palette of dawn, powder-blue wafers of sky layered on top of pink streaks in alternating bands. Montana, yawning awake.

"Well?" Sean said.

"A woman. Petite, small feet, fair-haired, by the hairs in her hairbrush. Maybe more generous on the top half than nature intended. Uses coral lipstick, paints her nails black."

"Just the type you see so many of in elk country," Sam said.

Martha ignored the comment. "Odd thing is no vehicle. Somebody dropped her off here, so that means someone's coming back."

"She's gotta be a pro."

Martha shot Sam a look. "You're repeating yourself."

"Like it isn't the first thing comes into your mind, too. Christmas lights around the bed, come on." He shrugged. "Maybe she's one of

Ginny Gin Jenny's girls. It's her MO, a trailer parked at the end of the road. You know, the Elk Camp Madam."

"I've made her acquaintance," Martha said. "But right now I'm more interested in what's standing at the end of this drag. Or isn't. Sean, it's your show."

Sean hesitated, then looked at Sam. "About that long story I mentioned," he said. And told him about the lights he had seen on the mountainside and his encounter with the lion.

"Pussycat, huh?" Sam said. "And you think the lights might have been hers?"

"They seemed to flash from the ridge." He pointed north and west.

"You think a lion could have dragged her up that ridge? Have to be pretty damned strong."

"I guess we'll find out," Sean said.

Sam chambered a cartridge and moved the three-position safety to safe. "Tell Mother I died with my Muck boots on," he said.

THEY HAD TWO RIFLES and one canister of bear spray among them. Sean took the lead, unarmed but for the grizzly juice, Martha two steps behind, her .30-06 at port arms, Sam three yards to her right side, the bore of his .350 Magnum pointing down.

One hundred yards into the forest, a teardrop of blood here, a teardrop there. Another fifty yards, the blood drops closer together, in places a fine drizzle, then nothing. Now they were climbing, grasping tree trunks to haul themselves up, the forest graying, no sound but the shuffling of their boots and their combined breathing.

Sean stopped. Earlier, he had picked up a few long hairs snagged on deadfall, confirmation that the drag they were following was almost certainly made by the body of the woman who had occupied the trailer.

Now his attention was drawn to a strip of something that looked vaguely like a Band-Aid. It was clinging to a tree branch, three or four inches long and paper-thin, raw-looking, and, in the coming light, nearly translucent. There were two shorter strands also stringing from the branch. Sean broke the branch off short and held it up for Sam and Martha to see.

"What is it?" Martha kept her voice down.

"It's the skin off her fingers. She grabbed hold of the branch and hung on so tight that it ripped the skin off."

"Then . . . she was still alive?"

"To this point."

"Fuck me," Sam said.

With the gain in elevation, the snow was deeper here and the occasional tracks were loosely filled pockmarks or indentations, the identity of the maker conjecture at best. Still very little blood.

Reading the white book. That's what Harold Little Feather called tracking in winter. Sean thought of Harold for a moment. For three years Sean had lived in an eighteen-pole tipi of Sioux design that Harold had lent him, and at one time or another they had both been in love with the woman who was standing beside him, her thumb resting on the safety of her Winchester rifle. Thinking of Harold was a sure sign that his concentration was flagging. You could only keep that razor edge of focus for so long before you needed a break.

"Rest a minute." Sean mouthed the words. The steam from their breathing hung over them in a cloud.

As they stood there, Sean bending from his waist with his hands on his knees, Sam twisting his torso to get the cricks out, Martha sucking at her cheeks, an eagle lifted from the ridge, then another. The pair flew silently over their heads. They exchanged glances. They knew what the presence of eagles meant.

"I got a feeling it isn't going to be pretty," Sam said under his breath.

It wasn't. Although the remains of the woman's body were partially shrouded by a blue terry-cloth bathrobe and lay under a covering of snow, muting the carnage, it was still difficult to look at. On the crest of the ridge a spray pattern of blood showed where an artery had been torn and the woman had taken her last breaths. From there the body had been dragged twenty yards to the place where it was eaten. Martha's eyes were drawn to a boot. The rabbit-fur collar was bloodstained and it took a moment for her to realize that a foot was still inside the boot. Somehow this bothered her more than the mangling of the body. She bent down and scraped away some of the snow covering the bathrobe, revealing a pattern of calico kittens playing with yarn balls.

She stood up and put her hands on her hips. All around the body were delicate feather patterns where the eagles had touched their wings to the snow. They had been busy with their beaks for quite some time, Martha thought, for several of the impressions were drifted in, where others were freshly made. Still, she doubted they had consumed more than a few pounds of flesh. She saw something red that wasn't blood and fished a headlamp with a bright forehead strap from the snow. She slipped the end of a stick through the band and picked it up. The switch was in the "on" position, but the batteries had died. Headlamps no longer faded as they lost juice, but flickered rapidly and abruptly went out. She looked at Sean. "This was that star you saw."

Sean recalled the lights and realized that he had been witness, if at some remove, to this woman's last moments on Earth. He became aware of Martha speaking.

"We get back to the trailhead, I'll call Fish, Wildlife and Parks. They have a special response team to investigate this kind of thing. I'll get a houndsman on the horn, too."

Sean shook his head. "I haven't gone back up where the lion confronted me, but I'm pretty sure it had an old kill there. I could smell it. Now why would it leave a fresh kill to visit an older kill on the other side of the canyon?"

"Maybe what you were smelling was the cat," Martha said.

Sam was shaking his head. "I've chased lion. The hounds can smell them but you can't. They don't give off much odor, compared to, say, a bear or a wolf."

Martha grunted. "Maybe that scream you heard wasn't a cat at all."

"What else could it have been?"

"I don't know. The wind. The windmills of your mind."

"You think I made it up?"

"No." She pulled at her lip. "But I think when we start trying to second-guess each other, it's time to make the calls to people who might have answers."

Sean nodded. He unknotted the red silk scarf he was wearing and tied it to a tree limb, a hunter's trick to keep scavengers at bay.

"You want," Sam said, "I could piss on the perimeter. Haven't lost an ounce of venison to a bear or coyote yet."

"You want to pee in the snow, you go right ahead," Martha said. "Just don't let it touch the body."

"Okay. But you'll have to turn your back. I wouldn't want you to swoon or go all girlie on me."

"I'm guessing that's not going to happen," Martha said. She managed a smile in spite of herself. It was the first attempt by any of them at levity in two hours, though Sam would be true to his word.

When Sean and Martha started back down the ridge and were out of sight, he said, softly so that only the departed soul of the woman might hear, "You're with the eagles now, my darling." He kissed two fingers of his right hand and blew her a kiss. Then he unbuttoned the fly of his wool army-surplus trousers and burned his name in a loopy yellow script into the snow.

CHAPTER FOUR

Rocket Girl

The house was a fish out of water for the setting, a split-level mid-century modern with a backward-slanting roof and casement windows offering a spectacular view of the Madison Range, if only a sliver of the river itself. It was a lot of concrete and steel in a development dominated by cabins built tongue-and-groove, but the house, Sean thought, had been constructed before the onslaught of second homes choked the valley, back when the concept of covenants still made most people think of church. He parked and climbed out of his Land Cruiser.

Finding the residence had been surprisingly easy, thanks to Sam's eyes. After descending the ridge, Sean and Sam had explored the grounds around the trailer while Martha called for troops on the radio. It was a search they'd had neither time nor light to do on the way in, and Sean had hoped they might find cat tracks and settle the identity of the killer once and for all. But the snow had been falling off and on all night and was deep enough to keep its secrets, and he was pondering his next step when he'd heard Sam's "aha" grunt. He'd found him behind the trailer, sporting a smile that revealed the V-shaped notches in his front teeth.

"See how the snow's been shoveled out to make a clear lane all the way around the trailer? It was piled into this bank. He hit it when he backed his truck around to drive out. See?"

The indented letters of the license plate were clearly visible where the plate had pressed into the packed snow: MAESTRO 5.

"You figure it's the hunter you winched out? His rig?"

"Good chance."

Martha had walked over while they were examining the snowbank. "The number," she said. "Is that a five or a six?"

"I can't do all your job for you," Sam said. "I have to leave you with some shred of dignity."

But he'd done enough of it, and Martha had the name and address of the truck's owner plus the model and registration within the hour. By then the techs were searching the trailer and three men from the Wildlife Human Attack Response Team, called by the acronym WHART, had arrived to investigate the scene of the kill and remove the human remains. Martha was still waiting on the houndsmen when Sean left to visit the address that the license plate had led them to.

He pressed the buzzer beside the door, waited a minute, then knocked.

Down the hill on the lawn, two children were taking turns ramming a snowman with a Flexible Flyer sled. They eyeballed Sean incuriously, as they might glance for a few moments at a deer that wandered into the yard. Sean had driven in over two sets of tire tracks, one coming in, the mud and snow it disturbed stiff, one going back out sometime later, the snow softer. The only vehicle was a late-model RAV4 in electric blue with a cracked headlight and a dent on the left front panel. The training bra of trucks was nowhere to be seen. Sean went back to his rig and listened to the engine tick down as a girl with a mess of curls detached herself from the snowman demolition zone to walk up the hill.

"Did you come to tune the piano?" she asked.

"Do I look like a piano tuner?"

"Sort of," the girl said. She looked to be eight or so. "I don't know. Are you? When it's winter, the humidity is too low and the keys go flat. The ideal is forty-two percent, but it's like twenty-two now. But Daddy says we can't afford one."

"What can't you afford?"

"A humidifier." Her tone said he should know this, whether he was the piano tuner or not. "That's what I want for Christmas. Or before, if we get some money."

"Then you play?" Sean asked. Another silly question.

"Of course."

"How about him?" He gestured down the hill toward the boy.

She nodded. "Jimmy's okay, but not as good as me. I'd have a chance at being a career pianist if my fingers were longer. Daddy says it's his fault. He has short fingers. It's like a family curse."

"What do you play?"

"I can play 'Piano Man.'"

"Then you like Billy Joel."

"Oh, yes. Billy Joel and Elton John are my favorites."

"What do you play of Elton John?"

"Sir Elton to you."

"But you just called him Elton."

"That's because that's what he told me to call him."

"You met Elton John?"

"Yes, when he played in Missoula. I got to go backstage because I won the six-and-under division of the Treasure State Music Competition for popular song."

"What did you play?"

"'Rocket Man.' Elton gave me a pair of sunglasses. Mommy had them framed. They have blue sequins. They're on the mantel. Would you like to see them?"

"I would, but the reason I came here was to talk to your father. His name is Leonard Johnson, right?" That was the name on the registration for the license plate.

"Lenny. Or Lenny Two J. 'Cause our last name's Johnson and his middle name is James."

"So that means you're . . . ?" Sean paused, waiting for her to fill in the blank.

"I'm Lorca Johnson," she said. "Like *orca* but with an *L* in front."

"Is your father home, Lorca?"

"No, he took the truck into town to get a haircut."

"Is your mother home?"

"No. She went with him to get groceries."

"Why didn't she take the blue car?"

"Because Daddy drove in with the headlights out and ran into it by accident. It bent the radiator."

"You mean last night?"

"This morning, when he came back from hunting. He said he didn't put the lights on so not to wake us up, 'cause it was early, and that's why he hit the car. Mommy's mad at him. She called him an imbecile. I looked it up. It's a kind of insult. She's always mad at him for something."

"What's your father do?"

"He conducts the orchestra."

"In Ennis."

"No, there's no orchestra in Ennis. In Bridger."

He remembered the letters on the vanity license plate. MAESTRO 5.

"He lost his job," the girl said.

"Oh? Why was that?"

"We're not allowed to talk about it, but he sleeps in the music room now. You can hear him playing the violin. 'In that way lies madness.' That's what G-Ma says."

Beyond her, Sean saw the brother trudging up the hill, towing the sled. Behind him, the snowman lay in ruins.

"Who's looking after you?" Sean asked. "Nobody answered when I rang the bell."

"G-Ma is. But the buzzer doesn't work. She wouldn't hear it, anyway. When we go outside she sits in the window, but she always falls asleep. She says it doesn't matter because we're all in the bubble and her aura is looking out for us."

The brother had arrived. Winded, he set his hands on his hips. Same curls as his sister. Coonskin hat, minus the tail. "You're not supposed to talk to strangers," he said.

"He's not a stranger," the girl said. And to Sean, "You're not, are you?"

"No, but I don't want you to get into trouble. Do you think you could do me a favor? Could you give your father my card?"

Sean fumbled a card from the glove compartment of the Land Cruiser. He had two cards. One read BLUE RIBBON WATERCOLORS, the lettering embossed above a pastel landscape with a river. The other read USUAL SUSPECT INVESTIGATIONS and featured an Atlantic salmon fly pattern of the same name. It included Sean's investigator's license number and contact information. Martha had once told him that the fly, however good the illustration, was an amateurish touch. It made him seem less of a serious person. Sean had replied that that was the point. He really wasn't looking for work.

After a moment's hesitation, he picked out one of his artist cards and drew a circle around the street address of his second-floor studio in the Bridger Mountain Cultural Center.

"Tell your dad I'd like to ask him how his hunting went up Johnny Gulch."

"He didn't get one," the boy said.

"Still, I'd like to talk to him. Tell him he'll want to see me." He handed the card to the girl, who bent her face over it.

"Did you paint that?"

"I did."

"It's pretty."

"Let me see," the boy said, and when he grabbed for the card, she held it out of reach over her head.

"I'll tell Mommy you were talking to a stranger," he said.

"I'll say you were first."

"But you're older. You'll be the one gets in trouble."

This seemed to register and she handed him the card. "You won't be able to read it, anyway."

And to Sean, "I hope the tuner comes today."

He left them standing in the bubble under G-Ma's aura, the boy's brow furrowing as he mouthed the words on the card, the girl ruing the tragedy of an out-of-tune piano, hoping for humidity.

AFTER LEAVING THE HOUSE, Sean drove south on the river road to a pullout by a field with a fox den. The foxes drew photographers from across the country in the summer. Now the mounds of the den were covered in white, the fence posts snowcapped, magpies perched on the skeletal branches of a cottonwood snag. The trails of foxes wound geometric patterns in the snow. It was the kind of two-toned landscape people walked through with their heads in their collars, but Sean loved it. It reminded him of the Andrew Wyeth exhibit that he had gone to in Seattle. The American master's famous dry-brush technique would have found a perfect subject here.

From the pullout, Sean could see the upper level of the house and a part of the drive, and decided to wait awhile and see if the truck came back. He drew out his sketchbook and sharpened a 3B pencil with his pocketknife. He put the pencil lead to the paper without knowing what he was going to sketch, but such was his way in many endeavors, and his pencil had not yet found a subject when his cellphone vibrated.

It was Martha. "You go first," she said.

"The girl says the air is too dry." Sean filled her in on his visit to the mid-century modern.

"You think that was wise, giving the kid your card? If Johnson has something to hide, he'll hide it."

"Or go back to find it. People panic when they think someone's on to them."

"Does that mean you're going back to the trailer?"

"Unless you object. Like you said, somebody dropped her off, so presumably somebody was coming back. Could be this Johnson. Could be someone else. But I won't go if that's crossing some kind of official line."

"Before you go down that rabbit hole, I ought to tell you that the WHART guys found partial tracks that we missed, pugmarks as they're called, also places where a lion dragged its tail in the snow and hairs scraped off where it rubbed up against trees. So we're

dealing with a cat, no question. But the reason I called is the Dusan
brothers sicced their Walker hounds on the trail, and the lion turned
and killed one, knocked it off a cliff. They called in on the sat phone
about an hour ago."

Sean let that sink in. "Does this mean you don't want my help
anymore?"

"Well, I'm not sure where the crime is—human crime. I don't know
if I can justify loosening the county's drawstrings to meet your per
diem."

"This is shit-hits-the-fan news, Martha. You're going to devote
more manpower dealing with the public fallout than you will catching the lion. You need all the help you can get, starting with IDing
the body."

"And you think this guy Lenny what's-his-name—"

"Lenny Two J."

"You think he can provide the answer."

"I know he's getting a haircut this morning."

"A haircut?"

"That's what his daughter says. Here's a guy who told Sam he'd got
lost and walked all night long. You'd think after an ordeal like that,
the natural response would be to collapse. But only a few hours later
he's driving into town for a haircut."

"He's changing his appearance."

"That's my thinking. As far as he knows, Sam's the only one who
can put him in the proximity of the trailer. He doesn't know about
his license plate hitting the snowbank and giving him away. It was
dark. They were working with flashlights to get the truck unstuck.
All Sam remembers is a guy who's medium height. He can't even
remember the color of the truck. What we're left with is longish hair

and a nondescript beard. Trim and a shave and who do you have? No one Sam could remember, that's who."

There was a hesitation on the other end of line. Sean could imagine Martha considering, scratching at her chin.

"Do you have a plan? I mean, besides going back to the trailer?"

"I set a trap for him."

"The business card?"

Sean nodded, then realized she couldn't see him and said yes. "If I don't catch him returning to the trailer, I'll catch him knocking on my door. He'll want to know what I know. He won't be able to stay away."

"You sound sure about that."

"Always certain, often right."

He heard Martha chuckle softly.

When she spoke, her voice was slow, measured, her coming-to-a-decision tone. "Consider yourself on the county dime until we get an ID. Keep me in the loop. And be careful."

"You always say that."

"If you think I say it too often now, wait until you're my husband."

Sean admired the comeback, said good-bye, and got out of the Land Cruiser to stretch. There was a splash of color as a fox came into view from a screen of willows. It was a cross fox with a russet-colored body and a sooty tail tipped white. The fox caught sight of Sean and stopped, its ears cocked forward. It halved the distance between them and again stopped. It was close enough that Sean could see the cunning in its eyes.

"You're supposed to be smart," he told it. "What should I do?"

The fox began to walk across the field in a pattern that resembled a big question mark. Every dozen feet it would put its nose to the snow and cant its head. Then it would slowly bring its hind feet forward, so that they could act as springs, and it would jump straight up into the air and, jackknifing down, plunge headfirst into the snow, until only its tail was visible. Each time it dove, it came up with a mouse in its jaws and wolfed it down. Then it looked back at Sean, as if seeking his applause.

Well, that's what I'll be trying to do, too, Sean thought. *Walk a question mark with my ears cocked and my nose in the wind, ready to take the plunge.*

CHAPTER FIVE

Little Black Book

At the trailhead, Sean saw that the crime scene tape had been taken down and a heavy chain looped through the rusted tongue of the trailer and padlocked to a pine tree. The only rig at the trailhead was a black Toyota Tundra with a camper shell parked in a sea of dog tracks. Sean heard a voice, more of a human bark than a decipherable word, and the houndsmen came into view, a pair of skinny longbeards who looked like Confederate soldiers stepping out of a sepia-toned photograph. One was staggering under the weight of the dead hound on his shoulders. The dogs, three not counting the dead one, were of a type—deep-chested, built like triangles with waists that tapered to fists. They had their tails down, their heads down, their ears down, each in its own gloom of exhaled breath. As they approached, one of the hounds uttered a low growl and the man carrying the dog said something to it in what could have been a foreign language—"Har now, har."

Sean said he'd heard what happened and sure was sorry.

"Not as sorry as I am," the man said. He knelt down to take the hound off his shoulders and laid it on the snow. Sean could see the claw marks deep across the dog's muzzle and forehead, half the face peeled away from the bone. The houndsman tried to place the loose skin back in position, but the dog was stiff with rigor mortis and his hands were trembling. He gave up and came up to his knees, his eyes far away.

The other man turned to Sean and said, "Ike's taking it mighty hard. Dog like Blue, he never done a wrong thing in his life. Just a shame is what it is. A lion, he's no more dangerous than a house cat, 'less you back him into a place he can't see his way out but take a swipe. Something about this one, though—the dogs were off the whole durned day. Following ladylike, when they should have been bawling, should have been hammering that track. They knew this was a bad-un."

Ike stood up and nodded. "They weren't but half what a hound ought to be. I blame myself for not pulling them off."

"Did you get a look at it?" Sean asked.

The question was ignored as the two men lifted the dead hound and placed it inside the camper. Ike followed after it. He leaned back against a hay bale, putting his hands around his knees. Two of the Walkers joined him, burrowing their noses under his bent knees and his arms. The other man, who'd introduced himself to Sean as Jedediah, shut the camper shell lift gate and climbed into the cab of the truck with the remaining hound sitting shotgun. He ran bony fingers over the dog's copper-colored ears. He turned the key and powered down the window.

"You asked if we saw the lion. No, sir, we didn't."

"Do you have a card, a way I can get in touch?" Sean said. "I'm helping the sheriff on this one."

"This one being exactly what? Ain't no mystery here. Cat got her. You can take it to the bank." But he rummaged in the glove compartment and found a card. He inked a line through the phone number, updated it, and handed it through the open window. It had DUSAN BROTHERS OUTFITTING written in a banner. The card advertised elk, deer, bear, and lion hunts.

"We don't message the way the young-uns do. You got to call the number." He shook his head. "I suppose you think we're shirking our end of the deal, not follering through. But the cat, once he got cornered in the cliffs and fought his way out, he's got his big-boy britches on. He got a taste for it now. If we put the pack back on him, why, it would be a sin is what it would be. Wouldn't be fair to the dogs. You think that's a coward's way out, it ain't. Just survival smarts is all. You go on and tell your woman sheriff she can make reparations as she sees fit."

"How much was a dog like Blue worth?"

"You can't put a dollar tag on a dog like that." He powered up the window.

Sean watched the truck grumble away with its priceless cargo and stood there thinking, as the mountains filled back up with their brooding silence. He found the key under the chopping block, where Martha had told him it would be, and let himself into the trailer. He glanced around to take inventory, but there wasn't much to see and it took him all of thirty seconds to conclude that Sam's assertion of the woman being a prostitute was probably correct.

The techs had stripped the bed, leaving a bare double mattress that mice had nipped, exposing the ticking. A gauzy curtain hung

from faux wrought-iron curtain rods in the shape of arrows. If that
wasn't enough to hint at the bed's broader purpose, the twinkle
lights suspended from the curtain rods served as confirmation. It
was a love nest—that was the pretty way to put it. Sean noted a small
portable generator with an extension cord that would reach the
plug-in for the lights, or anywhere in the trailer, for that matter. He
switched on the lights and watched the colors pulse over the bare
mattress.

Out of idle curiosity, he picked up the coffee cup on the small
nightstand. He read the words stenciled on the cup. THINK ONLY OF
THE PAST AS ITS REMEMBRANCE GIVES YOU PLEASURE.—JANE AUS-
TEN, 1775–1817.

He picked up the paperback beside it, which continued the theme.
Jane and the Unpleasantness at Scargrave Manor, by Stephanie Bar-
ron. A work of fiction, with Austen as a sleuth in Georgian England.
Sean hadn't known who Austen was when he'd noticed a copy of
Sense and Sensibility on the Ponderosa pine stump that served as
Martha's home desk. He'd made the mistake of admitting his ignorance. Martha had responded by pressing his wrist against the
stump and whacking him across the knuckles with a ruler. He had
half of *Pride and Prejudice* under his hat by the following weekend,
and as a bonus to not getting smacked again, had found he was en-
joying the novel. Austen had a wicked wit, once you got past the
suffocating veil of manners.

Sean flipped through the novel. There was a postcard bookmark,
a Georgia O'Keeffe painting, one of her sensuous desert landscapes
called *Red Hills and Bones.* O'Keeffe was one of Sean's favorite art-
ists. On the back of the postcard were a few words written in a masculine hand:

MY BONES ACHE FOR YOUR TOUCH. ALL YOU NEED TO DO
IS ASK AND I'LL BE THERE.

W.

No postmark, no address, no name. The card commemorated an O'Keeffe exhibition three years ago at a gallery in Santa Fe.

The book was furred from use and several pages had stuck together. Sean fingered them absently. Two of the pages seemed a little thick. He ran a fingernail between the stuck pages and peeled them apart. Between the pages were two paper-thin sheets of onionskin written on with a pencil and cut to fit inside the page margins. The secret compartment, for that was most assuredly what it was, was almost unnoticeable, even with the book in hand.

Sean plugged in the lamp that squatted on the Formica table. He put on the dollar-store magnifying glasses he carried for tying on tiny mayfly imitations while trout fishing. The writing on the onionskin was in two hands, the first notations printed, only the last few entries on the mostly blank second sheet in longhand, the tiny letters precisely drawn, suggestive of calligraphy.

He read the first three lines of notation.

    10/27–8 P.M.—PATRICK—IMP
    10/28–7 P.M.—ANON—6 P.M.—BHB
    10/28–10 P.M.—RAY—SP

There were thirty-three entries over a span of four weeks, starting the last weekend in October. Sean knew that Saturday had been the opening day of the elk season. The largest number of entries for one day was four, and there were days in the middle of the week not awarded a notation. It was a little black book. The names, Sean intuited, were those given by the hunters playing hooky from their marital vows. The letters were cryptic. Shorthand for specific sex acts? He would need a key to break the code, but was pretty sure he had the gist.

Sean replaced the pages and put the book in a resealable plastic bag. He smiled, thinking of the last entry.

11/23–8 P.M.—LENNY—BHB

"Lenny Two J," Sean said under his breath. "You naughty boy."

CHAPTER SIX

Wearing Her Colors

He almost talked himself out of going. The boot prints made by the WHART team were clear, both going to and returning from the kill site. There would be nothing left on the ridge but blood, and no reason for a cat already traumatized by hounds to return. Not to mention it had a full belly. Still, it was an opportunity Sean might not have again, and if nothing else, he wanted to test his courage.

No, he thought, testing his courage wasn't the real issue. What he wanted to do was feel the darkness surround him so that he could experience, as much as was possible, what the woman must have felt before she died. It was something that Martha had taught him by her example. She always attended the autopsies, gathered the backgrounds of victims, and, as much as was possible, walked in their final footsteps. It was what made them human to her. You joined teams with the dead, she'd once told him. You wore their colors. They walked with you, and the better you understood their terrors, the harder you worked for them, and the more likely you were to discover the truth.

And yet, as he slung his .300 Savage rifle from his shoulder and began to hike, it was not trepidation that he felt. Part of the reason was that until yesterday, his only previous experience with a mountain lion had been anything but terrifying. Even in the creeping shadows, thinking back to it brought a smile. A young woman Sean knew had knocked on the door of his art studio with a proposition. Her boyfriend's birthday was coming up, and she wanted to surprise him with a painting of herself in her birthday suit. She'd heard that the studio next door was rented by a wildlife photographer who kept several animals, including an otter and a mountain lion, that he rented out to other wildlife photographers on shoots. Did Sean think the photographer might agree to taking photos of her with the cat, and then Sean could paint her from the photos? She wasn't getting any younger, and her body was never going to look better than it did now. Besides, it would be a hoot and her boyfriend would love it.

Sean had approached the photographer with her proposition and the day arrived. The photographer walked the cat up the stairs of the cultural center on a leash, its paws padding the halls at midnight. The woman arrived a few minutes later. Her eyes got big when she saw the cat, but she had armored herself with a belt of Yukon Jack and did not express second thoughts.

"Just don't give me cockeyed nipples," she told Sean.

The idea was that Sean would sketch as the photographer shot photos. There were two hiccups to the plan. The first was that the cat became interested in the crease of skin above the line of the woman's trimmed pubic hair, and started to run its rough tongue where it didn't belong. She tried to be a good sport about it, saying, "If I'd known this was going to happen, I'd have got a Brazilian."

But she was clearly shaken up. The other problem was that the cat wouldn't face the photographer. Normally, give it a pellet of dried duck meat and it was as shameless as a Victoria's Secret model, but on this occasion it was more interested in the woman than the camera.

Then Sean had a brainstorm. Another artist at the cultural center sometimes entertained his son with videos on his computer. The doors were thin enough for Sean to hear the songs of the old Disney classics, and if he'd heard Baloo sing "The Bare Necessities" once, he had heard it a hundred times.

"I've got an idea," he said, and ran down the stairs to the center's office, letting himself in the door with a key he'd wheedled out of the manager. He found the master key that unlocked all the building's shops and galleries. Five minutes later he had inserted the DVD into his laptop and was fast-forwarding through *The Jungle Book*, pausing when he got to the first scene that was full of monkey calls and other jungle sounds. He cranked up the volume, the mountain lion swiveled its head to look dead into the lens of the camera, pulling its upper lip in a silent snarl, and the shoot was deemed a success, even if the woman emerged from the ordeal looking shell-shocked. Her expression in the oil Sean painted was Come hither, the lion's was Stay back or I'll bite, and Sean was happy with the outcome. He'd finished the painting and the young woman would be by to pick it up.

Thinking back to that incident had taken him as far as the top of the ridge. Sean surveyed the scene for a long minute: the blood-stained tracks of the WHART team, the heaped-up branches that had covered the kill. After scraping the snow off a big pine tree with his glove, he sat down with his back to the trunk and piled up branches to the height of his chest. Some thirty paces in front of him was where the lion had eaten its victim. To his right, the wall of the canyon into which the hounds had followed the cat fell steeply away, and beyond the opposite canyon rim were the cresting ridges of the mountain range. Snarled on the crags, a sunset worthy of Charlie Russell's paintbrush deepened—brilliant streaks of orange becoming fire, becoming burgundy.

Then, with the snuffing of the last candle of the twilight, the night closed upon him. Trees faded to black, and all the world became engulfed in a vast, echoing silence. Sean had warmed himself climbing to the ridge, but that warmth left him now, and, shivering, burying his face in his coat collar, he took the cold deep into his bones. The fear he sought settled over him like a dark cloud, and as he became afraid, he was able to make the bones and flesh and blood of the victim into a whole person, whereas before he had not been able to see beyond a mangled corpse.

When the time had passed that the cat might return, or rather when he assumed it had, for Sean had no experience in such matters, he got to his feet and stretched, whirling his arms, trying to bring blood back into fingertips. In the three long hours he had sat motionless, he had seen one living creature, an ermine whose slender body, pale in the moonlight, looked to be writing letters on the snow in a disappearing ink.

CHAPTER SEVEN

Preempting the Blues

"Y ou must be going to a cut," the man said, as he used steel tongs to drop doughnuts into a white paper bag.

Martha looked at him. Grady McSweeny was tall and angular, had mutton-chop sideburns, and wore an apron over a blousy painter's shirt. An Irish flat cap in green and red tartan perched at a rakish angle on his head.

"How do you know that?"

"Paper said you always stop for doughnuts and coffee at my place on your way to the morgue. 'Never go to an autopsy on an empty stomach'—I believe that was the quote."

"Don't believe everything you read."

"Are you?"

Martha's "humpff" was a reluctant yes.

The newspaper story had run two months before, after Martha had announced her run for a third term as Hyalite County sheriff.

The hook was that she was one of a handful of female sheriffs in the entire country who had actually been elected, not appointed interim after a husband's untimely demise. Martha had been unguarded, not Martha being Martha at all, and Gail Stocker, the reporter for the *Bridger Mountain Star*, was five foot nothing and looked harmless enough, which of course she wasn't.

"Never trust a woman who wears a felt fedora," Martha muttered under her breath.

"What was that?"

"One more cinnamon sugar cake," she said.

The tongs reached. "Who's under the knife? That unlucky woman the cat dragged in?"

"In a manner of speaking," Martha said. Not twenty-four hours had passed since she and Sean had taken up the blood trail, but the story had already been on the front page of yesterday's afternoon paper. Which perturbed Martha, but gave her no reason to lie.

"You know, during the hunting season I open at five," McSweeny said. "Died down now with Sunday being closing day, but if you'd been here earlier, the line ran right out the door. Sold more doughnuts than I did all last weekend. You'd think the woods would be empty, but that's where they were headed. Seems like everybody wants to be the one kills that cougar."

"Seems like," Martha agreed. "I'm just hoping they don't kill each other."

McSweeny folded the bag and rang her up.

"I heard somebody shot a dog," he said. "Heard the bullet passed through and hit a house."

Martha nodded. "Sharon Bower's place up Eagle Creek Road. Candy, her chocolate Lab."

"Chocolate Lab doesn't look anything at all like a mountain lion."

"No dog does."

"I heard Buster Garrett's going to run it. Put his hounds on the scent."

"Who told you that?"

"Buster Garrett. He was in earlier."

"It's like Grand Central Station here."

McSweeny handed her the doughnut bag and her change, which she dropped into the mason jar on the counter. The words on the jar read ALMS FOR THE WICKED.

As well as making the best doughnuts in town, McSweeny was the president of the local chapter of the Libertarian party. He also took pride in being a member of a warlock and witches' coven, leading séances every first Thursday of the month. An invitation to a séance was considered a social coup in three counties. Clothes were rumored to come off, shenanigans to ensue, but perhaps that was wishful thinking. Martha didn't care what happened at their séances as long as they were consenting adults and trying to bring the dead to life, rather than the other way around. Still, you couldn't make this stuff up.

She looked Grady up and down, apron hem to cap.

"You look like you're chasing snakes out of Ireland," she said.

MARTHA'S GREETING TO ROBERT Hanson, the county medical examiner, followed a routine. She would hold out the bag of doughnuts between thumb and forefinger, shake it, raise her eyebrows, and follow Hanson into his office for a cup of coffee, where she would run her eyes over the photographs on the wall. The photos, when she'd first met him, had predominantly outdoor themes—the Chinese Wall in the Bob Marshall Wilderness, the White Cliffs of the

Missouri River, the River of No Return in Idaho. They were bucket list destinations. Several were places he'd been to and were rewarding enough that they merited an encore.

But in the past three years the photos on the wall had changed. Before, they'd had no women in them, now several showed Hanson with the handsome, dark-haired woman who had finally made him happy, and the settings were in Italy, mostly, for she was Italian.

"How's Sophia?" Martha asked.

"Still in remission." Hanson rapped his knuckles against the wood top of his desk.

"Where to next?"

"Sicily. She has people there."

"Land of revenge served cold," Martha said.

"And hot," Hanson said. "There was enough blood spilled on that island to go around."

"Speaking of which, I suppose you've heard about Sharon's Lab. We've become our own little island of revenge. A lot of itchy trigger fingers."

Hanson nodded. "I had breakfast at Josie's and the cat was all the talk, but I swear, Martha, I never once heard anyone express any sympathy for the victim. For the dog, yes, but not for the woman. Remember how, before the Emancipation Proclamation, a black person was counted as three fifths of a human being in the Constitution? Our Jane Doe is rumored to have been a prostitute, so that makes her life less valuable. What we're experiencing is human nature at its basest denominator. It's an excuse to run a cleaning patch down a dusty bore and answer a primal call to arms. To slay the dragon that threatens the community. People say 'poor girl,' but that's lip service. The victim is only the excuse for vigilantism. The value of her life has been lost in the shuffle."

"Well, that's why I'm here, Bob. To see if we can't make her a larger fraction of a human being, preferably one with a name. Are you going to be able to help me?"

"I'll just mop the powdered sugar off my mustache while you cover up."

Martha unbuckled her duty belt, emptied the cylinders of her revolver, pocketing the ammo, and donned hospital scrubs. She shuffled into the examining room wearing paper booties.

Hanson drew back the sheet that covered the stainless-steel examining table. Martha thought she was prepared, having seen the remains earlier, but that was on the mountain where death was the grist in the cycle of life and, as such, beautiful in its way. By contrast, in the sterile atmosphere of the morgue, the same tissue and bone looked obscene.

"What am I looking at, Bob?"

Hanson directed her attention with a steel pointer. "In terms of cause of death, this is straightforward," he said. "Although part of the throat is missing, the neck vertebrae, specifically the C-two and C-three, are dislocated and the wounds to either side of the neck are consistent with those that could be made by a cat with large fangs. Here, here, and here."

"Cats have four canines."

"This one apparently doesn't. Where the fourth fang should have penetrated, the right upper"—he pointed—"we have bruising but no penetration. So it is not entirely missing, but broken short. Note also the subconjunctival hemorrhage in the whites of the eyes." He pointed to the blood spotting. "That can be indicative of strangulation. Whether she died from suffocation caused by the grip on her throat, or by the interruption of the spinal cord, that I can't tell you. But one or the other or a combination of the two killed her. You'll

want to see Wilkerson. She's running markers on the victim's DNA
to see if we get a bingo with someone who gave a sample in an arrest.
Gigi also requested the right boot the woman was wearing, complete with foot and a few other specific tissue samples. I'd rather you
get her professional opinion than try to put words in her mouth."

"What about fingerprints? I distinctly recall seeing a hand up
there. If she was a pro, she'll have been arrested, and if she's been
arrested, she'll have been printed."

"There we have an issue. I received no hand parts from recovery."

Martha frowned. "Well, shit, Bob. How do you explain that?"

"I can't."

Martha nodded, though she was cursing herself under her breath.
She had made the decision to leave the remains in the state in which
they were found, for proper cataloging and transport. She and Sean,
and Sam, for that matter, had heaped branches on the bones and
draped their jackets, and Sam had urinated for good measure. But
apparently that had not been enough, and in the two or three hours
between the time they had left the kill site and the WHART team
had arrived on scene, something had removed the hand, and with it,
the easy ID. *One of the eagles? A coyote?* It didn't matter.

"You've got your faraway face on," Hanson said. "You must be
thinking deep thoughts."

"Yeah. 'Deep Thoughts Martha,' that's me."

THE METAL QUONSET HUT that housed the regional crime lab
looked more like a building where you'd judge a dog show or hang
confiscated game animals for public auction—purposes for which it
had previously served—than a structure designed to solve crimes.
But there you were, and Martha was happy to have it, happier yet

that it was run by Dr. Georgeanne Wilkerson, Ouija Board Gigi as she was affectionately known. In addition to being a senior crime scene investigator, Wilkerson was the foremost forensic scientist in the state, and, as captain of her own ship, had the authority to prioritize cases her team was personally involved in, though she was fair-minded, as a rule. One of the people who could get her to bend was Sean Stranahan, and Martha was heartened to see his response to the message she'd texted him after leaving the morgue.

She found Wilkerson at her desk, which was set against the curved inside wall of the hut. She was, as always, surprised-looking, with her goggle eyes magnified by the powerful lenses of her glasses.

Wilkerson rose and they shook hands. "I've invited McGregor for a look-see, as she's the regional biologist and a bit of a cat woman. I was hoping Sean would be with you."

"He's on his way."

Even as Martha spoke, Wilkerson was looking past her, a smile spreading the corners of her mouth. "Speak of the devil," she said.

Martha had known Sean for eight years, and he remained one of those people you can't quite put your finger on, who keep that little bit of mystery about themselves while seducing practically everyone they meet, men and women alike, but particularly women. Some wanted to mother him, to tell him not to take so many chances. Some wanted to do other things with him. Martha suspect that Gigi fell into the latter category.

"What have I missed?" he asked.

"Nothing yet." Martha's tone was businesslike. "Gigi? Doc said you were running a DNA comparison with the database."

"He was jumping the gun. I'll run the test, but it takes time. You'll know when I know."

"Then why am I here?"

"Because we don't need DNA markers for basic tissue identification. We have a spectrometer that can do that in the field. With respect to species, I can tell you right now that saliva from a mountain lion was deposited on what were human remains. Also saliva identified as belonging to a bald eagle."

"Tell me something I don't know."

Wilkerson opened a drawer and placed a transparent reclosable plastic bag on the table. Martha bent over it, studying what looked like a long stiff hair with a banding pattern. "Is that a mountain lion whisker, Gigi?"

"I think so. That's one of the reasons I invited McGregor, who's standing right behind you." She looked past Martha's shoulder and smiled.

The state biologist from region three tipped an imaginary cap as she approached the group, belly first, for she was well along in her pregnancy. She shook Martha's hand, kissed Wilkerson on the cheek, and pressed the palm of Sean's hand against the swelling. "Almost cooked," she said. "Dinger's set to go off in a month. Yep, April sex. What else is there to do in the spring except get stuck in the mud?"

Martha's false smile was the smallest of gestures. She handed the plastic bag to the biologist.

"It's a cat whisker," McGregor said. "I can tell that much. *Puma concolor*, I can't say. That's a cougar or mountain lion to you lay types. But it could also be a lynx whisker. Bobcat, I doubt. Their whiskers are shorter. Where did you find it?"

Wilkerson told her that it had been on the housecoat found with the body. McGregor nodded. "They're brittle. You often find them at kill sites. The whiskers are so sensitive they actually help the lion position its bite. I got a video of a lion killing a bighorn sheep, a ram.

You can slow-motion it way down and actually see the lion's whiskers vibrating against the sheep's throat. Pretty cool."

But, Martha thought, like the saliva identification, the whisker was no more than corroborative evidence that a cat was at the scene. "Anything else, Gigi? We're assembling a task force and I've agreed to give a statement to the media this afternoon."

"Well, I have some irons in the fire, DNA-wise. I'd say a couple days. You're first on the list when I have the results."

"Anything you can tell me now?"

"The victim had breast implants. One was missing; the logical explanation is the cat ate it. The other was excised very neatly, probably with one claw. My guess is it didn't like the taste of the first one—they were silicone implants, not saline—hence the removal of the other."

"A prostitute with breast implants doesn't exactly narrow the field."

"How big were they?" Sean said.

Martha looked hard at him.

Sean shrugged. "I'm trying to put together a picture of the victim. If she chooses small implants, maybe she just wants to enhance her appearance. Wants just enough of a rack to hang her clothes on and figures if God didn't give it to her, a surgeon can. If she chooses big implants, then she wants to attract men, to please them. She could have low self-esteem."

"Aren't we the psychologist this morning?" Martha said.

"I've never seen the attraction of big breasts."

"Good to know," Martha said.

"No, he's right," Wilkerson said. "It's a valid question. They're on the smaller side. I called Gary Robson, the plastic surgeon, about an hour ago. Gave him the dimensions and gram weight. He said an implant of this size would up the bra size by only a cup or cup and a half. A woman who was a thirty-two-A might jump to thirty-four-B. I checked the size on a couple bras the victim had in her luggage and they were thirty-four-B. She was still a petite woman."

"Thirty-six-C, that's what I'm packing," McGregor said. "All natural, too. Nothing like a pregnancy to give you killer boobs. I tell Karl to enjoy them while I got them."

"Let's get back on track," Martha said. "Gigi, is there any chance the implant can be traced? Without fingerprints, we're still looking at a Jane Doe."

"I put that question to Robson. He said all breast implants have a lot and serial number but that the serial numbers aren't always physically stenciled on the implants—they're just in the records. He's going to come by for a look, but my preliminary doesn't show any numbers or labeling. But there is something I can leave you with. May be important, may not be."

"Jesus, Gigi, don't keep us in suspense."

"You know I told you we have a spectrometer to determine tissue origin that doesn't require genetic testing?"

"Yes, it confirmed that a lion ate the remains."

"Well, we don't have the victim's fingers for a print match, but what we do have are two acrylic fingernails. They were buried in the snow near the victim. The color is black, which matches the nail polish found in the trailer. Apparently the nails broke off, possibly in a struggle. The interesting thing is that each nail has a small deposit of tissue adhering to the underside. I ran the tests just before you came over."

"Lion flesh," Martha prompted.

"No. It wasn't lion. The tissue is human."

There was silence as they absorbed this.

"As in she scratched somebody," Martha said. And when there was no reply, added, "Well, what do you know?"

"WHEN'S THE TASK-FORCE MEETING?" Sean asked.

They were walking to their rigs.

"Four. You're invited, of course. But I ought to tell you, Buster Garrett will be there. I know you've had your differences."

"We've had words," Sean said.

"As I recall, the last time you had words, you left him lying on a barroom floor in his own vomit."

"Actually, there weren't many words. He told people that the next time he saw me, he was going to flush my head in a toilet. I decided to end the suspense."

"You cold-cocked a drunk."

"He swung first."

"You say. But it was his hangout, the witnesses were his cronies. If he'd pressed charges, you would have assault on your record and the county wouldn't get near you. We wouldn't be having this discussion."

"Do we always bicker like this?"

"Only on Wednesdays."

"Don't we usually have sex on Wednesday nights, Martha?"

"That's me forgiving you for nothing you did wrong or me trying to get away from myself. A little of each. And it works, sort of. I seem to get brighter right on through to the weekend. But there's a desperate quality that shouldn't be there. We should be celebrating each other, not arguing about things that don't matter."

"What do you want to do about it?"

"I don't know. One difference between men and women is men

look for a solution and women just want someone to listen to the problem. And despite popular opinion, I am a woman. So I guess I just want you to listen."

"I'm listening."

"I know."

"Hey, I've got an idea. We could move sex up a day to Tuesday. Then maybe you could be on an upswing the rest of the week. Pre-empt the blues altogether."

"Are you saying that because today's Tuesday?"

"Is it? I don't keep track."

Martha laughed.

"I guess you can't blame a guy for trying." They were at their cars. "Meeting's in the Trophy Room. Second floor, just down the hall from Judge Brown's court."

"Are you going to bring up the fake nails?"

"No, I don't want to confuse the issue. We have a mountain lion at the scene of a human death. Two and two equals four. As concerns our course of action for right now, anyway."

"You sure you want me in the same room with Garrett?"

"Considering most everyone will be packing heat, I think we can keep the peace."

CHAPTER EIGHT

A Three-Pipe Problem

With four hours and change until the meeting, Sean drove to the T-junction in town without knowing which direction to turn and letting the rig make the decision. He called it "following the wheel," a term he'd made up as a kid when riding his bike and heading nowhere in particular—and after a moment of indecision, he let up on the clutch and followed the wheel up Grand Avenue to the Bridger Mountain Cultural Center. His art studio had previously been in room 221A, but when the adjacent room opened up the previous fall, he traded, not so much because it was better digs, though it did have two more windows, but because 221B had been Sherlock Holmes's address on Baker Street in the stories of Sir Arthur Conan Doyle. The number was etched into the stippled glass door, just above the words BLUE RIBBON WATERCOLORS, and below, in discreet script, PRIVATE INVESTIGATIONS.

Reaching the second floor, he saw a man sitting on a bench across from his door. The man rose as Sean approached—he was two or three inches shorter than Sean and looked a few years older, ballpark mid- to upper forties. Silver wings at the temples framed dark, wavy hair that looked like it could withstand a zephyr before losing its part. He wore a worn corduroy sport coat over a button-down shirt that showed fraying at the cuffs. It was professor attire, right down to the elbow patches on the jacket. The smile that creased the man's cheeks tried for sincerity and faltered, and the hand that Sean shook was clammy.

"Where's your deerstalker cap, Detective?" the man said.

"It's hanging on the hat rack in the studio. You're one of the few people who made the connection."

"And I suppose you have a big drooping old pipe, too?" The voice had initially been chesty, authoritative, someone used to being a presence in a room, but now it was shaky, followed by a dry cough. Sean saw the Adam's apple work as the man swallowed.

"Actually, the drooping pipe is called a calabash," Sean said. "Holmes never smoked one. It was only for the stage. Come inside and I'll show you the ones he did smoke." He smiled encouragingly.

The man followed him into the studio. Sean indicated the chair opposite the desk that served double duty as his fly-tying table, and took the facing chair.

"I don't see a deerstalker hat," the man said, running his eyes around the room and taking in the artwork.

"I might be guilty of a white lie there, but I was telling the truth about the pipes." He opened a drawer in the desk and withdrew three pipes, setting them down, one after the other, on the oak surface.

"In the stories," he said, "Holmes often smoked a briar"—he pointed to a straight-stemmed wood pipe—"or a cherrywood"—he pointed to a larger pipe with a burl bowl and a flat bottom. "He smoked one or the other when he was in the mood to talk, as you are, Mr. Johnson."

"How do you know my name?" The voice was defensive.

Sean did not answer the question directly, but said, "I've been expecting you."

A silence gathered in the room's corners. Sean could hear the man's intakes of breath.

"Aren't you going to ask about the clay pipe?"

No reply.

"Holmes's favorite," Sean said. He picked up the third pipe and turned it in his fingers, then handed it to Johnson. "He saved it for times he was in a reflective mood, when he was trying to get to the bottom of something. If the mystery laid before him required a lot of thought, he called it a three-pipe problem. I don't think we have a three-pipe problem here, two pipes at the most. Why don't you tell me about it?"

Johnson set down the pipe. "Tell me something about myself. Isn't that what Sherlock Holmes would do? Notice a speck of mud on a trouser cuff and deduce a man's livelihood and where he'd been that morning and why?"

"Fair enough." Sean leaned back in his chair and laced his fingers behind his head, a habit he'd picked up from Martha. "First," he said, "the color of your cheeks and the white skin at your temples tells me you've had a shave and a haircut, and the length of your stubble suggests that it was directly after you came out of the mountains. You are trying to change your appearance. That means you weren't just doing a bit of hunting. You were seen there by someone who might recognize you. It must have been under low light conditions.

If he'd seen you in daylight, close up, or was someone you knew, a bit of barbering wouldn't be much disguise. You're wondering how I knew to come to your house and how much I know, and you're afraid because whatever you got tangled up in is a serious business."

Sean brought his hands back to the desk. "Those are the obvious deductions. Besides that, you play the piano and at least one stringed instrument, probably several, but including a violin or viola. My guess is the former. You had a dream once of being a famous musician, but settled for a career a few steps down from the top rung of the ladder. Still, it was a comfortable life until recently, when you suffered a reversal of fortunes that is causing your family a lot of stress."

For a long moment the man sat in a stunned silence that seemed to echo. "My children knew I went into town to get a haircut," he said in a small voice.

"I think that's the least of it, don't you? It's why that matters. I know you want to tell me, and I can promise it will make you feel better afterward."

"You can't promise any such thing."

"You're right, I can't. I gave your daughter one of my cards. Here is another."

Sean penned a number on the back of the card that read USUAL SUSPECT INVESTIGATIONS. He pushed it across the desk. "That's Martha Ettinger's direct line. Do you know who she is?"

Johnson nodded.

"I work for her. You can verify with that number. You'll be expected to make a full statement, probably to one of the sheriff's deputies."

"But . . . I don't know anything. I mean, I'm just a hunter. What do you want from me?"

Sean looked at him, noticing a tremor in the fingers that had picked up the card. He didn't look like a hunter, in his elbow-patch jacket, but that was Montana. Everybody hunted, the grandmother with the purple hair who hustled pool at the Depot, the barista at the Tree Line coffee shop with world-class dreadlocks tucked under a watch cap, the married gay-couple architects who had an office two doors down the hall.

Sean let the silence stretch. He felt a little guilty at the way that he was treating the man as an inferior. Sean prided himself on being a kind person; it was his stock-in-trade as an investigator and opened doors that otherwise might have stayed closed. But something about the man's manner bothered him, and Sean found himself slipping into a part rather than being himself.

Johnson quit fiddling with the card and crossed his arms, his hands cupping his elbows. He feigned indignation at the suggestion that he had anything to do with anything.

"What I want from you, Leonard"—it was the first time Sean had used the man's name and he drew out the word—"is the truth about your relationship with the woman who was living in the trailer. She's dead, but I'm sure you know that. The sheriff will be making a public statement this afternoon. Whether she says the department is talking with a person of interest in the case who is being noncooperative, well, that's up to you."

"But I don't know about a woman in a trailer. Yes, I saw it. You can't help but see it, but there were no lights in the windows, no generator hum, no truck parked there, nothing." His voice trailed away.

"If you had nothing to do with her, then why did you park in back of the trailer, where no one would see your truck?"

"How do you know—I mean, why do you say that? I parked farther up the road."

"No, you parked behind the trailer. We read your license plate."

"What are you talking about?" Again, the indignation, but an effort required. Sean watched as beads of sweat formed on the man's temples.

"When you left Sunday morning, you backed into the snowbank trying to turn around. The raised letters on your plate were stamped against the snow. If you'd stopped the truck one inch short, 'Maestro Five,' you wouldn't be sitting here getting an education about pipes."

"Okay, okay. I was there. But what the hell? It was a place where the snow was beaten down. When I drove in, there were hunting rigs in the other good spots to park. I mean, swear to God. All I was doing was hunting—you got to believe me. I don't know anything about this dead woman."

"So you've said. But why lie about where you parked?"

"I didn't. Okay, I was going to park there, but then I thought, whoever was with the trailer, they were probably out hunting somewhere else, up some other trailhead, and when they drove back, I'd be in their spot. So I turned around and left to park somewhere else. That must have been when the license plate hit the snowbank."

Sean nodded, his expression agreeable, waiting. Give him time enough and he'd fill in the silence.

"I never even saw her. I thought it was hunters, you know, drove off somewhere to hunt."

"Leonard . . ." Sean put disappointment into his voice.

"It's the truth!"

Sean watched the hands clench together on his desktop. He noticed the short fingers that the daughter had mentioned as being her inherited curse.

"Come on. This isn't a murder case. I'm just trying to piece together the last hours of a human being's life. I need her name and I need to know how you knew her and what you know about Saturday night. Nobody has to make a house call and disrupt your personal life."

"My wife doesn't have to know?"

"Good chance, no. Not if you tell me the truth. She certainly will know if you don't cooperate, or I have reason not to believe you're telling the truth."

"But I am telling the truth. I didn't know she was dead. I thought maybe, okay, I don't . . . I didn't know what happened to her." He hung his head and shook it. "Is it true? Did a . . . lion get her?"

Sean didn't answer him.

"Where it dragged her, that's tough country."

"How do you know where it dragged her, if you didn't follow it?"

"I could see a light. It was way up high, up on that ridge that rises behind the trailer. She went out to get wood for the stove. And something, it . . . it just took her. I was going to report it, make an anonymous call, but I . . . it was too late. I mean, she couldn't have survived."

"Did you hear anything?"

"No, nothing. I just got worried when she didn't come back."

"So she left the trailer and when you went to look for her, you saw the light of her flashlight on the mountainside."

"I think it was her. I don't know what else it could be."

"You were sleeping with her." Sean made it a statement. He expected the man to hang his head or at the least not be able to hold his eyes. But here he was surprised.

"I won't apologize for it," he said.

CHAPTER NINE

Love on the Cusp of Nowhere

He'd met her in the Sleeping Bear Lounge, he said. Across the border in Last Chance, Idaho. Sean knew the place, a spacious log cabin with a center fireplace, a pair of Bernese mountain dogs named Mutt and Jeff who slept on a rug by the fire, a bar, and a cook-it-yourself grill. You grilled your hamburger patty, then ate it under the glassy stares of mounted game. There was even a ratty stuffed fox like you'd spot in an English pub. It was one of those optimistic operations that limp along for a few years but aren't close enough to a ski resort to stay afloat during six months of winter. It would burn to the ground sooner rather than later, arson suspected. Collect the insurance and start all over somewhere else. Preferably warmer.

"Go on, Leonard," Sean said. "Start from the beginning."

Johnson said he'd been hunting up Mile Creek that morning and twisted his ankle and quit early. The bar was only a few miles away and there was a woman sitting on a stool. She was the only patron in the joint, had a beer on the counter. He'd stood her another, and she'd told him her name was Cheryl and that she was from Tucson, Arizona, but had grown up in Montana on the Flathead Reservation in St. Ignatius. She said no one in her genealogical tree ever owned up to having Indian blood, but she suspected she had some—people saw it in her cheekbones and the line of her chin. She had been visiting relatives and was on her way back south, trying to beat the first heavy snows because she didn't have snow tires, and her truck had broken down and was being repaired in Ennis. In the meantime she'd been living in a trailer belonging to a friend. It was parked up in the Gravelly Range on national forest land. Did he know the Johnny Gulch Road, south of Ennis?

Johnson said he did, and after another beer he offered to drive her back there. He lived in Ennis. It wasn't that far out of his way.

Sean interrupted the narrative. How did she get from the trailer to the bar if her truck was broken down? It was fifty miles away.

Johnson said she'd been hanging out with a friend in Last Chance, just up the road from the bar. The friend had a family emergency and had dropped her at the bar, didn't know when she'd be coming back, and left her to the "kindness of strangers," as she had put it to Johnson. She'd been hoping someone could give her a ride. He had come along. Her lucky day.

It had just the right touches of detail to be true, but Sean remained skeptical. He urged Johnson to continue.

Johnson shrugged. He'd driven her back to the trailer.

"When was this?" Sean asked.

"About eight p.m.," he said. "Friday night."

When he'd left the bar, or when he'd got to the trailer?

When he got there with her. They'd left the bar about six-thirty.

"So, her lucky day turned out to be your lucky night," Sean said.

The man hung his head, then shook it minutely. "I'm not proud of it," he said, "but you don't understand my situation."

He said Sean had been right about him suffering a reversal of fortune. His wife wouldn't even sleep in the same room with him anymore. She looked at him like he was a stranger.

"I . . . I did something," he stammered. "I mean no, I didn't, but because she said I did, I lost my job. It was in the newspaper. Everybody knows."

"Because who said?" Sean asked. "Your wife?"

"No, not my wife. It was a girl in the orchestra."

Johnson said that he'd been giving the second-chair cellist private lessons at her home. He said he always made sure there was an adult in the house when he gave lessons, but this time her parents had to go somewhere and so they were alone. When the mother and father returned, the daughter told them that Johnson had touched her inappropriately, had reached across her body to demonstrate a bow position and pressed the back of his hand against her breast. The parents had filed a complaint with the principal.

Johnson opened his palms in a what-can-I-do gesture.

"I never so much as shook that girl's hand," he said. "I'm very careful about that kind of stuff."

"Why would she say that if it didn't happen?"

Johnson said it was to get back at him. The accuser had previously been the first-chair cellist. The girl who at the time was second chair had challenged her for her chair, and he had been the judge.

"I thought the second chair was better and jumped her to first," he said. The girl who accused him resented the decision.

"She doesn't know what it's like to have a family that depends on you, how something like this can upend a man's life."

Sean vaguely remembered a newspaper story earlier that fall about the alleged misconduct.

Johnson shook his head when Sean mentioned the piece. The story had been kicked around the state in print and on air, and while it presented the accuser's story, there was not one word about the competition for the chair. That was unfair. If people understood that she had a motive, maybe they would sympathize with him. But no, he was guilty because a girl who had an ax to grind said he was.

As a result, he'd been suspended from his job and become a pariah in the community. "My wife won't look at me," he pleaded to Sean. "Hell, she thinks I did it. Even G-Ma, she looks at me and shakes her head. 'Oh, Lenny, how could you?'"

Sean read the defeat in his eyes.

"They used to call me 'Maestro,'" Johnson said.

Now, he said, nobody would hold his eyes. So hell, yes, he'd taken some comfort when it was offered. His wife hadn't expected him home until Sunday night, wouldn't have cared if he walked off a cliff. Cheryl had told him it was scary to be alone out on the cusp of nowhere.

"That's what she called it up there—'the cusp of nowhere.' We made our own world."

Sean picked up the briar pipe and tapped it on the desk. "You spent Friday night with her. Tell me what happened Saturday."

Johnson said they hadn't done that much. Got up late. Made coffee. She had a book of crossword puzzles, surprised him by how good she was—politics, history, geography—he hadn't expected that. When he'd said something about it, she said, Don't judge a book by its cover. She told him that she'd majored in English at the University of Arizona and that she'd wanted to be a writer. But then she'd got tangled up with people she shouldn't have, and dropped out of college, and the dream died. He had the impression that some of the things she'd done to get by, she'd been ashamed of. But they didn't talk very much about her past. There was a wall there. She let you think you knew her but you didn't, really. He didn't even think that Cheryl was her name.

That afternoon, he told Sean, he helped her out with chores. Shoveled snow, split firewood, like that. They'd had a dinner Saturday evening that she cooked on the woodstove and then made love. Afterward she wanted a smoke, so they'd pulled on their boots and stood outside under the stars and passed a cigarette back and forth. She had on his jacket and looked dwarfed inside it. "Look at me," she'd told him. "I'm almost gone."

They'd turned in early and he'd lain awake a long time after she fell asleep, thinking that her words were prophetic and that when he left the next day, he would never see her again. It made her the perfect affair, heaven while it lasted, then gone without repercussions. Only he didn't see it that way. He saw it as a candle dying, a glimmer of light that would never brighten his world again.

He looked up at Sean, brought his forefinger up in front of his mouth, and blew on it. "Pfft." He shrugged. "Gone like smoke. You don't have to believe me, but you feel what you feel. 'The heart is a hunter whose aim is true.' Somebody said that. I don't know who."

"When did she leave the trailer?" Sean asked.

Johnson guessed about nine p.m. She'd told him she would get up in the night at least a couple of times to go to the bathroom or add wood to the stove, and shook off his offer to stoke the fire. The sheepherder's stove could be tricky, she'd said, and she knew the tricks. So when he felt her shifting weight and awoke to the sound of the trailer door handle turning and the brief cold wind of the night as she stepped outside, Johnson thought nothing of it. He had drowsed, waiting for her to return, and then minutes later, it could have been longer, he came awake feeling the cold where she should be lying. He'd gone to the door and called out her name. It was snowing lightly and he got his flashlight and began to follow the depressions of her tracks. He came to the place where she had apparently fallen and saw a drag mark in the snow. He began to follow it and then, thinking he'd heard a noise, turned around and saw spots of blood that he had kicked up while following the trail. Just a few, but ruby red, nothing else it could be. He'd gone back to his truck and got his rifle and that's when he saw the flicker of a light way up on the ridge. He saw that the light was moving and thought it must be a lost hunter. It couldn't be her, could it? He tried to force his legs forward but couldn't. Whatever had happened, he was too late to help, anyway.

At this point in the telling, he put his head in his hands and began to cry. Sean thought, *He's either told me the truth or he's told the lie so often to himself that it has become the truth.* He waited for the man to compose himself, and after a minute the breathing slowed and Johnson lifted his head.

"I abandoned her," he said. "I was only thinking of myself. I should have followed. I should have gone and got help. I should have done something. Instead, I just tried to get away and I couldn't even do that right." He told Sean about getting his truck stuck in the snowdrift and having to wait for another hunter to drive in and winch him out.

"God help me," he said.

"No," Sean said. "God help her."

"Do you think . . . Was it over quickly?"

"No, Leonard. The woman you call Cheryl was breathing all the way to the top of the ridge. She left the skin of her fingers on branches, that's how hard she clung to life." Sean looked at him, let that sink in.

"You heard her scream, didn't you, Lenny?"

"How did you know? I mean, I heard something, yes. I didn't know what it was. I didn't know if it was human. But how—?"

"You could have at least shot your rifle into the air."

"I didn't think of that. You have to understand—"

"No, I don't," Sean said. "All I know is that you left her up there, and that you're not telling me the truth, not all of it. Why don't you try again, going back to buying her a drink. How much did she say it was going to cost you?"

"She isn't . . . she wasn't." Johnson took a big breath. As he let it out, his eyes swam away somewhere, and when they came back, his voice, when he spoke, was steady.

"You can think about me however you want—it can't be worse than what I think of myself. But it wasn't like that. I mean, sure, she took money sometimes, but it wasn't what you think."

"Then what was it? Pro bono? Or did you trade services, a ride back to the trailer in exchange for a BHB?"

"A what?"

"I think you know."

Sean made a show of switching on his phone and scrolling through the photos that he had taken of the hidden pages in the book.

"The last entry, ah, here it is. 'BHB.' It says so right beside your name." He paused before reading aloud, " 'November twenty-three— nine p.m.—Lenny—BHB.' That's you." He pushed his phone across the desk. "You were the last person to see her alive."

Johnson blinked his eyes as his forefinger swiped the photos. "Where did you find this?" he finally said.

Sean told him.

"I didn't know. I swear I never saw it."

"Leonard, I'm trying to help you out here, but if you want your part in this to remain confidential, you have to tell me everything."

Slowly, he nodded. "She told me about the prices. SP, that was a spike bull. It was shorthand for a hand job. BHB was a brush-head bull, oral sex. SP-Six meant a six-point bull, which was intercourse."

"How about IMP?" Sean said. "What was that? The whole ball of wax?"

"IMP was short for imperial, like an imperial elk rack, a seven-point bull. That was all night, anything you wanted."

"Your entry reads 'BHB.' A blow job is a long way from making love with your soul mate, comparing her to a candle."

"That's just . . . she had to write something down. She had to take some money in case she got checked up on. They weren't going to believe she could have an honest relationship with no transaction. She had to protect herself or they'd think she was flying solo or overcharging and pocketing the difference."

"Protect herself from who? Who are 'they'?"

"The other woman, her friend who left her at the bar—she was in the life. That was the deal. The cost of the rent. If Cheryl stayed in the trailer, she had to turn a few tricks and pay a percentage to the friend, who had her own arrangement with the person who had the trailer."

"Like subletting an apartment?" Sean said.

He shrugged. "I suppose you could look at it like that."

"Did she mention a woman named Jenny? Ginny Gin Jenny?"

"No. Who's that?"

"They call her the Elk Camp Madam. A trailer or a wall tent at the end of an access road, that's her MO."

"I never heard of any Elk Camp Madam. I don't travel in the circles where someone like that would be brought up. Or didn't. Now, my circle has been reduced to anyone who will have a drink with me."

Johnson had gone from righteous indignation to contrition to tears, and now self-pity, all in a few exhaled breaths.

A silence played out in the room. Johnson's eyes roamed the paintings on the walls. When he spoke, his voice was barely a whisper.

"She wrote that on Friday. Just two more days, she told me. The hunting season would be over then and her truck would be fixed and she'd have made enough money to drive back to Arizona. She'd put the life behind her. Or at least try to."

He raised his eyes to Sean.

"She said it was an apt metaphor, hooking, that she felt like a fish on a hook. She would run out the line, and sometimes it was like she could escape to the sea and be away from her problems. But the hook was always in her mouth, and just when she thought she was free, she'd be reeled back to reality. Story of her life."

His shoulders fell and he shook his head.

"You ask me to give you her name . . . but what happened to her, it was fate."

Sean glanced up from Johnson. Though it was midafternoon, long shadows were already darkening the snow on the windowsills of his studio. Soon it would be time to meet Martha at the task-force gathering.

"Do me a favor, Leonard," he said. "Take off your shirt."

"What the—?"

"Just do it. If you don't want what we've talked about to get back to your wife, you have to cooperate. It's either take it off for me or you can follow me to Law and Justice and do it in front of the deputy."

"No. I mean, okay." He shrugged out of his corduroy jacket and removed his shirt. His body was pale and rubbery-looking, the hairs of his chest thin and scraggly.

"There. Are you satisfied?" he said.

"Turn around."

"What is it you're looking for?"

"Just turn around."

He turned around. Sean saw no indication that his body had been raked with fingernails, fake or otherwise. He nodded and told the man to get dressed.

"I don't want anybody to call me at home. Not on the landline."

"I understand. Give me your cell number. If the sheriff wants to talk to you, she'll call it."

"Will she, do you think?"

"That depends on how much of the story she thinks you left out."

"I took off my goddamned shirt. What the hell can I have to hide?"

"You know the answer to that better than I do. Go home now, Lenny. Don't leave the county."

"I won't." He hesitated. "All that stuff you said about me, what I was and how I was in trouble. How did you know?"

I got almost all of it from your daughter, Sean could have said, but didn't. "I can't give away all my secrets of deduction," he said.

"Then tell me one thing. How did you know I played the violin? Everyone knows my children are pianists, they figure I must be, too, that's where it comes from. But violin?"

"I shook your right hand. Your fingertips were smooth. But when you handled the clay pipe, I noticed the calluses on the fingertip pads on your left hand. That told me you played a string instrument, and that the calluses were from pressing the strings against the fingerboard."

"But why not a guitar or mandolin? Why viola or violin?"

"First, they are classical instruments, and you conduct classical music. But the answer is in your face, what you see in the mirror. The right side of your face is developed more than the left. It has a more pronounced musculature. That's because the right side of your face has to partially support the left side, which is supported by the chin rest of the instrument. It's an inequality in workload, and more noticeable in musicians who started playing when they were young and the facial bones had not fully formed."

Johnson looked at Sean incredulously. Then he nodded, the answer obvious. "You must have played the violin," he said.

"Never touched one. But my sister played, and she didn't like that her face was becoming lopsided. Vanity, pure and simple. So she quit and took up the cello."

"But you said I probably played violin. Why not viola? They're bigger, heavier, the asymmetry in the face should be even more pronounced."

"That's easy. You had dreams of becoming a great musician, and the violin is a dreamer's instrument. Nobody begins a musical career with aspirations to be the world's greatest violist."

Johnson started to speak, and stopped. Then shook his head. "And look where dreaming got me," he said.

After he had gathered himself and his footsteps in the hall rang into echoes, Sean picked up the clay pipe. It had been white originally, but the client who gave it to him had bought it used, and red-hot coals had blackened the bowl. Sean hadn't smoked the pipe since the previous summer, while fishing at night above the bungalow belonging to the Madison River Liars and Fly Tiers Club. The dregs of his long cut were in a foil wrapper in his fishing vest, which was back at Martha's.

He brought the pipe stem to his lips and lit wishful tobacco with a conjured coal from an imaginary fireplace. Johnson had painted a picture of stolen love between two broken human beings that was worthy of a Hallmark card. But it was not the whole picture, he was sure of it.

Maybe it was going to be a three-pipe problem, after all.

CHAPTER TEN

Hard Day on a Horse, Soft Night in the Saddle

By the time Sean climbed the steps to the Trophy Room—an inside joke, the only "trophy" on the wall being a jackalope with forked antlers and rabbit ears—the conference was under way. Or rather chairs were taken, coffee poured, doughnuts picked over. Sean knew most present—Carson Taylor, the Fish, Wildlife and Parks biologist who had spearheaded mountain lion studies in both Montana and the Andes Mountains of Patagonia; Calvin Barr, a government trapper who had captured most of the wolves for the species reintroduction into the Rockies twenty-five years ago; Judy McGregor; two deputies representing adjacent counties; and Buster Garrett.

"Buster," Sean said.

Garrett, a lumberjack of a man wearing pegged wool trousers and a flannel shirt with suspenders that read WEYERHAEUSER, inclined his head. "Sean."

Sean could see the C-scar on his left cheek, made, he'd heard, by a broken beer bottle in a barroom brawl. Garrett called it his Budweiser kiss and wore it like a badge of honor.

The houndsman smiled, his eyes crinkling up in an expression of self-amusement. He tapped his chest, pointed at Sean. "You and me." Mouthed the word "after."

Great, Sean thought. *Just what I need.*

"Gentlemen." It was Martha. "I thank you all for coming on such short notice. The purpose of this meeting is to assemble a task force to deal with what looks like a mountain lion in our region that has turned man-eater. I'm talking about the woman who was killed north of Specimen Ridge in the Gravelly Range late Saturday. As most of you have no doubt heard, the scent trail of a lion was picked up near the site of the kill and run by hounds belonging to Ike and Jed Dusan. They reported that the lion was cornered on a cliff face and killed one of the dogs. Its whereabouts are unknown, but until we find another trail for hounds to follow, consider us to be the dog pack, so to speak. So let's get our noses to the trail. Carson, you led the WHART team that recovered the body—what's your take on this?"

Taylor, a compact, muscular man with smiling eyes and a manner of confidence extending to his smallest gestures, scratched the FW&P emblem above his left breast pocket. Like most biologists, he had worn many hats since donning the khakis. Sean had first met him when he was taking a creel census and remembered a mustache, a toothpick, and a smile. The hair and the smile were gone, but the toothpick remained, and he spoke around it.

"I won't bore you with statistics. Suffice it to say that aggressive human encounters attributed to pumas, forgive me for using the scientific nomenclature, have doubled in recent years, although fatalities remain very rare. In the past year we've had two deaths attributed to lion, neither in Montana. One was a bicyclist in rural Washington State, the other a woman hiker in the Mount Hood National Forest in Oregon. In addition, we've had some near misses, including, this summer, an attack at a campground in Glacier Park. Lion took a sleeping girl out of a tent and started to drag her away. Father beat it off with the lid of a Dutch oven. The fatalities are significant in that both bodies were consumed. Now I wouldn't label the recent increases in aggression and instances of man-eating epidemic, but they are concerning. You want my opinion, Martha, I'll give it. But it will cost you that last jelly doughnut."

Taylor placed the doughnut on his paper plate. "Anybody gets a hankering to reach for that is going to have to beat me to the draw." He slapped his right hip where his holstered handgun rested. He smiled, worked the toothpick from one side of his mouth to the other.

"My o-pin-ion"—he stretched out the word—"is that human encroachment on habitat is primarily to blame for the majority of confrontations. Second homes, vacation residences, road building, and to some extent timber harvest. Also, we're pushing into more remote habitat—call it the lion's stronghold—for purely recreational purposes. Used to be this was all Jack London country, silent and brooding nine months of the year. You had your horse riding and your hunting and that was about it. Now you got bicycles, backpackers, ice climbers, skiers, ATV riders, motorcyclists, people collecting shed elk antlers, what have you. It's become a playground. This spike in human activity, combined with habitat loss, pushes the cats into proximity with humans, where their natural fear of us may erode over time. They see us every day, they look at our kids, some no bigger than a fawn deer, their bellies are hungry, and where they used to see danger they see opportunity."

He sat back and pushed his chair an inch away from the table. "I understand this may not help a lot in the present situation."

Martha bit her lip, another in an ever-changing litany of thinking gestures. "If you had to profile this cat, what would you say?"

"Well, as a rule, most lion/human confrontations that occur in semi-developed areas involve immature male cats that have been pushed into fringe habitat by larger toms. Confrontations in the backcountry often involve females. But to carry that poor woman a quarter mile or so up the side of a steep ridge? That's a tremendous feat of strength. I'd have to say an adult tom."

"What's the biggest cat you know of?" Martha asked.

"We've had a couple weighed on meat scales at one seventy-five, one eighty. I've seen photos on the internet of a cat supposed to be two forty, but a wide angle can exaggerate the size of the subject."

"As any fisherman knows," Sean said.

That brought a few smiles.

"How about you, Calvin?"

Heads turned to the salt-and-pepper-haired trapper. Unlike Taylor, who had long ago traded the trail for the desk, Barr looked like he'd spent his life outdoors. He had the lined face from the elements, the thick, crablike hands and knuckly fingers that came from hard work, along with the bowed legs of someone who had sat in a saddle since childhood.

"I've seen a few big-uns. Over two hundred? Maybe one." He scratched at the thinning wool of his hair. "Lion, he'll eat what he kills, where he kills it. Maybe drag it a few yards into cover first, scrape some sticks over it when he's finished his meal. But to carry it up that ridge, all that way? You ask me, you're talking about learned behavior. Cat's shaped by his experience. Maybe he was shot at and wounded the first time he was run by hounds, so he won't tree no more. Or maybe he was driven away from a kill by a wolf pack and learned to carry his kills a ways first, eat in peace. You see more of that now with lobos in the country."

His eyebrows crawled. "Something you might want to consider is sending drones up with cameras. That's new technology to me, but I know that Wildlife Services uses them to locate coyote packs for aerial gunning."

"Sounds like a good idea. I'll take it under advisement. Buster, that leaves you." Martha looked pointedly at the houndsman. "What do you make of this situation?"

Garrett made a show of scratching the stubble on his neck. "All this talk about sex and size is beside the point. Cat's out there. I got dogs that will run it. I mean no offense, mate"—he jutted his chin toward Calvin Barr—"and I respect your opinion, but if we find a track and my dogs will bark 'treed' inside six hours, you can bet your firstborn on it. You can put it on the scales and see if it's got balls after I shoot it out of the tree."

It was common knowledge that Garrett had grown up in Australia, at least among those in hunting circles, and not only because he wore a cap with a Tasmanian Devil on it. Still, Sean was surprised to hear the accent. That hadn't registered before, although, when he thought about it, except for one brief meeting, his only conversation with the man had been exchanged in fists.

Garrett appeared to be reading his thoughts. "I go Down Under to see the folks," he said, "I start chewing words. Aussie English is like a cancer—it keeps coming out of remission. Guaranteed to lower your IQ by fifteen points."

He scratched at the blue-black stubble on his cheeks. The nap of hair looked hard enough to strike a match on.

Martha cleared her throat.

"Before we get any further along, I want to put it out there that the goal is to take this cat, or any other mountain lion that falls within our net, alive. Let forensic evidence identify the guilty party. To this end, Carson has brought along several tranquilizing guns. After the meeting, he'll instruct anyone who needs a refresher course on their use and provide armed darts and antidote. We aren't in the business of killing innocent cats, and we're going to be in the public eye until this is sorted out. In India, when a tiger turns man-eater, my understanding is it has a team of defense lawyers take its case to court to make sure no harm comes to it."

Garrett snorted. "This isn't India."

"No, but we'll be in a media spotlight. If the ID of the killer can be confirmed in the field, then you'll have the go-ahead to shoot to kill. As you were saying, Buster . . ."

"What I was getting to is no track, no cat, so cutting trail's got to be priority one. Last trail's what, two days old? And it's colder than a witch's tit out, no offense to the lady in the room." His smile for Martha was unreturned. He shrugged and went on. "Dogs can work a scent in cold weather, but only to a point. You get into the single digits, the moisture in the air that carries the scent particles freezes. It's like burying the scent in cement. My dogs can work an old trail, but it would be awful slow going. And the cat could be out in front miles by now, be anywhere. But if we can use trails and roads to establish a perimeter and check the line for fresh tracks every day, then when a cat crosses, we'll have a hot trail to work."

Martha nodded. "That's a good idea, Buster. Once you establish your perimeter, I'll call in some search-and-rescue guys with snow machines and skis to help you monitor it. But let's get around the room before we talk specifics. I'm giving a statement to the press and this thing's going to break wide open. We need to be on the same page."

She paused. "Speaking of being on the same page, I forgot to tell you that State Investigative Services has agreed to loan out Harold Little Feather on a part-time basis. Most of you know Harold, if not in person, then by reputation. Our department never had a better field man or tracker. He still has some mobility issues from an injury, so he'll be working the digital trail with Carson to collate and analyze data culled from the mountain lion study Carson headed up. I'm told that in addition to GPS and radio telemetry data, there is hard copy, digital, even some game-trail photos. It's probably too much to ask that the guilty cat is wearing a tracking collar, but if there's a needle in the stack, I trust Harold will find it."

She glanced at her notes. "Let's get down to the brass tacks of this situation with regard to cooperation and jurisdiction. Buster, you and Sean, Calvin, you, too—if you need a bathroom break, want to stretch your legs, go ahead. Be back in, say, twenty minutes. No need to bore you with the politics." Her eyes went to Garrett, went to Sean. "Jail's just around the corner, either of you gentlemen need a place to cool your heels."

"Won't be any need," Garrett said. He left the room and, after a few seconds, Sean followed. If he didn't, what would it say about him?

He found Garrett smoking a cigarette at the foot of the steps by the main entrance. Garrett was speaking with a tall, long-haired man who stood with his arms crossed and who presently broke away and took the stairs in two bounds, trailing an air of self-importance as thick as a vapor as he passed Sean. No nod, just a momentary acknowledgment of his existence with one pale-blue eye. Something about the cheek in profile. A sickly gray taupe color, like putty.

"Who's that?" Sean asked.

"Frederick Blake. Called Drick. He's a cat man, self-proclaimed whisperer. I worked with him on Carson's study." Garrett frowned, seeing Sean's expression of surprise. "What, you think I can't come within sight of a lion without feeding it a bullet? I was the houndsman for a lot of the captures. I'd have introduced you, but he's picking up his sister at the airport and just has time to poke his head in and say hello and offer his services. If they're wanted."

"Why wouldn't they be wanted?"

"He's the kind of bloke who doesn't play well with others. Ego as big as the Outback. Knows his cats, though, I'll give him that." Garrett nodded. "Tell you what. You and me, let's start over." He extended his hand, and Sean, hesitating only a moment, stepped into the circle of the man's powerful aura and shook it.

They were about the same height, six-one, Garrett thicker, mostly where it counted. He had a face that reminded Sean of the heavyweight fighter Jack Dempsey, the Manassa Mauler, a cold face that had taken punishment and dished out even more. Sean had met Garrett while working a case for the county, and circumstances had indicated that Garrett might be involved. He hadn't been, and had held a grudge against Sean for bringing him under scrutiny that, six months later, led to their fight in the Roadkill Saloon. They had not crossed paths in the time since.

"No hard feelings," Garrett said. He fingered a pendant worn on a rawhide lanyard that peeked out from his chest hair.

"The same," Sean said. A few moments of uneasy silence passed. "What's that you're wearing?" he asked.

Garrett tapped the pendant. "Lion's claw. I wear it to remind myself to be a better man." He shook his head. "Look, I was an asshole. Not just to you. A lot of people. Lost my wife. Damned near lost my boys. I've been sober three years, two months, and six days. Do the math and that's about a month after our altercation. Made me take a hard look at myself. I should thank you, though"—he chuckled deep in his chest—"I do think you were a bit of an asshole yourself. Fair fight, but you took advantage of my inebriation. You and me, we have anger issues and hair triggers. I got help for mine. I'd advise you to do the same, if you haven't."

"I had a period there when I just didn't care," Sean said.

Garrett nodded. "I know the feeling. Also caring too much. Edge like a knife blade. I'd fall off one way or the other." He chuckled again. "Said like a man who's been in court-mandated therapy. So why am I seeing you here? Carson, the other honchos, I know why. You, I can't figure."

"I tracked the cat where it dragged the woman away. Found the body, what was left of it anyway. Ettinger asked me to help out with the victim ID."

"That's right, you're a gumshoe. She's a working girl, you ask me. One in Jenny's stable, you can be sure of it. The madam, she's the one can make your ID." He rubbed his fingers together. "Ask Ettinger to front you a couple pineapples."

"Pineapples?"

"Money, mate. Fifties. It's Jenny's first language. And her second."

"Do you know her?"

He fingered the pendant. "In the biblical sense? No. A few of my clients have rewarded themselves after a hard day on a horse with a soft night in the saddle, if you catch my drift."

Garrett scribbled an address and a few lines of map on a sheet of cigarette rolling paper he fished from a shirt pocket. Then, before handing it over, he took a plastic bag from the same pocket and shook a few olive-colored buds into the palm of his hand.

"Medicinal. Make you love your fellow man and screw your fellow woman. Make a human being of you. You have something to put this in? No? Then take the bag. I got more."

He put the marijuana back into the bag and tucked it into Sean's breast pocket. " 'Ave a go, mate." He snapped the pocket over the bag. "I never gave this to you."

CHAPTER ELEVEN

Lions in Ordinary Dress

He's a changed man," Sean said. "Says he's been in therapy. Wants to make amends for past transgressions and become a better person."

They were standing by the steps where Sean had talked to Buster Garrett an hour before.

"That's therapy talk, all right," Martha said. "Let me tell you something, Sean. People don't change. Once an asshole, always an asshole."

"That's a bleak way of looking at the world."

"It's Law Enforcement 101."

"He told me I ought to see the madam, Jenny. Gave me an address in the Jefferson Valley. I was thinking of heading over."

"The only thing that will accomplish is you'll have two people lie to you in one day. It's too late to knock on doors and it's starting to snow, if you haven't noticed. Stay home tonight. We can watch TV and do a puzzle, practice being a married couple. Save the madam for the morning."

"You make it sound so enticing." Sean brought out the plastic bag.

"Is that oregano? Or what I think it is?" Martha said.

"Buster says it will improve our sex life."

". . . not if I arrest you and throw you in a cell."

"It's legal, Martha. That was the vote."

"Not until next year." She held out a hand for Sean to turn over the contraband. She crushed the buds in her fist and they watched the dust blow away in the breeze. Five o'clock and change, and already dark enough to smear the outlines of the cars in the lot.

"Meet you back at the house," Martha said. "Don't worry. Married people can have fun, even without THC."

"Is that a promise?"

She said he'd find out, and after he did and Martha had snuffed out the candles in the deer-antler candelabra on the nightstand, Sean found his mind returning to his conversation with Garrett, and to the man he had referred to as a cat whisperer.

"You awake, Martha?"

She exhaled a sigh. "Trying not to be."

"What do you know about Drick Blake?"

"The biologist?"

"Yeah, he was talking to Garrett earlier. He said Blake was going to offer you his services."

Martha sat up in the bed. "I'm lighting just one candle, and that's for five minutes only."

"I'm listening," Sean said.

"His father was South African, some kind of game ranger, so the son was brought up in the bush. How he traded zebras for elk and wound up here, I don't have any idea. Half of a brother-and-sister act. They live up the Wise River, some nowhere drainage. Beavertail, something like that. He worked on Carson's lion project, strictly independent contractor. Used to be on the FWP payroll, but you know how it is in a bureaucracy: You go off cowboying by yourself, you don't get invited back."

"How do you know him?"

"I don't. I'm telling you what Carson told me. Or warned me."

"What was that?"

"He said not to involve Blake too closely, that he'd try to take over the search and create friction."

"How does he support himself?"

"Donation to donation, grant to grant, according to Carson. His sister makes nature documentaries of his work and promotes them at film festivals. Carson said she had a feature at Sundance, strolled around town with a lynx on a leash. Got a little too chummy once and has claw marks on her face to prove it. Turned people's heads. But her reputation is she has that effect on men, scars or no scars. They solicit money from celebrities, environmental organizations, whoever she can rub up against until the money falls out of the pockets. There's a website where they sell DVDs. Neither married. No children. The two of them out there in the woods all by their lonesome. Teeny bit weird." She held her thumb and middle finger an inch apart.

"Are you saying they're incestuous?"

"Sean, I don't know. I'm just repeating what I was told. 'Weird' was the operative word."

"Did you accept his offer of help?"

"Blake? I told him thank you, we'll contact you, if and when."

"What did he say?"

"Nothing. He left before I called the task force back to order."

"Why didn't I see him go out?"

"Probably he went out a different door." She snuffed out the candle. "Not your circus, Sean, not your monkeys."

Maybe, Sean thought, as he looked past Martha's form to the stars in the window. But they ought to be somebody's monkeys.

AS MONTANA ROAD TRIPS GO, the drive from Bridger to Wise River, including thirty miles of washboard gravel with one undistinguished rise of land called the Unnecessary Hill, is on the stepping-back-in-time side—two ghost towns, another that might as well be, more jackrabbits than cattle, more rattlesnakes than people.

Where the road cut through the canyon of the Big Hole River, Sean turned into a pullout to let Choti go about her business. He'd collected the little sheltie and left before Martha was awake, had scribbled a note and placed it on the five-hundred-year-old Ponderosa pine stump desk. The note hadn't mentioned the Blakes. When he'd got behind the wheel, his intention was to visit the elk-camp madam, then return to the valley. But what he'd heard of the couple intrigued him, and he'd driven as far as the Beartrap Canyon before deciding that, as he was in neighborhood, very broadly speaking—southwest Montana being quite a large neighborhood to anyone except Montanans—he might as well make a detour.

The madam, he rationalized, would be the more nocturnal of the animals he was pursuing, and he'd still have plenty of time to swing by Silver Star, where she hung her petticoat, as Garrett had put it, on the drive back.

Sean punched in Martha's number. No reception. His eyes drank in the mist over the river. To the east a horizon the color of a pearl choker was fastened tightly to the peaks. He thought about making

a few casts—the Big Hole was one of his favorite trout streams—
then thought better of it. You tell yourself you'll make five casts, and
five later, you say five more. Sean had fallen victim to this sort of
tomfoolery as often as anyone.

Reaching Wise River, he finally picked up a bar and left Martha a
message. "I'm practicing to be a married man," he told the dog, who
opened one eye.

When he'd first consulted the map, no tributary named Beavertail
Creek leapt out at him. But a Swallowtail Creek flowed into the
Wise River from the West Pioneer Mountains. That was close
enough, Sean thought.

He found the turnoff, crossed the river on a wing-and-a-prayer
bridge, and locked in the hubs. He followed yellowed tire tracks, a
heavy tread that was smeared by at least one cycle of freezing and
unfreezing. Three miles in third gear brought him to a NO TRES-
PASSING sign riddled with bullet holes. The tread marks continued
beyond a locked gate and up a rise, where a pigtail of smoke curled
through the pines. This was recluse country, where meth cooked on
one burner of the stove, venison stew on another, and the shotgun
was loaded with double-ought buck. Sean parked, skirted the gate,
and began to climb without having formulated a plan, his "no-plan
planning," as Martha called it, the kind, she had told him more than
once and with a raised finger for emphasis, that got a person killed.

A yurt came into sight. Parked in front was a Land Rover, its hood
cold. Sean stepped up onto the plank decking past two south-facing
solar panels. He rapped on a door with a center knob. While he waited,
his eyes searched along a line of Tibetan prayer flags hanging from
the branches of an aspen sapling, their patchy colors winking.

"Around back," a voice called, "but I'd advise you to leash your dog by the door. You'll find one hanging from a nail." A masculine voice that carried. "Tatiana doesn't much care for dogs."

Tatiana?

Sean found the leash. "You heard the man," he said, as the little sheltie began showing signs of unease. It was never a good sign when Choti wagged her tail to the left. Whatever she could smell was nothing she wanted a part of.

The man Sean remembered from the steps of Law and Justice was sitting in a galvanized stock tank with his body concealed by steaming water. Underneath the tank, squatting on cinder blocks on the deck, was a sawn-off steel drum, where a fire had burned down to the embers.

Like many self-absorbed people, Blake had selfish eyes that seemed in no hurry to acknowledge Sean's presence. Sean used the moment to take in the man's appearance. Dark-blond hair fell in loose curls past his shoulders. He was lantern-jawed and had a long, gray, creased face with ruddy patches that had either seen a lot of weather or weathered a lot of liquor, or both. Sean glanced down. A trail of wet footprints—the left foot leaving fainter stains than the right—led from the tub to the back door of the yurt. Someone had gone inside only moments before his arrival. Someone who limped.

Sean introduced himself, mentioning that he was part of the task force Sheriff Ettinger put together to hunt down the mountain lion. "We met," he reminded Blake. "Briefly."

"If you call a nod meeting. But yes, we did. I apologize for not introducing myself, but I had to pick up my sister at the airport and was running late. You're the fellow who took Buster Garrett down a notch."

"It's not something I'm proud of."

"He can be an asshole. He was one of the houndsmen on the mountain lion project. We were in on some of the early captures."

"That's what I wanted to talk to you about."

"Why didn't you contact me through the website? There's a link that includes the landline here. Scarlett and I are not recluses, regardless of what you may hear."

"I like to speak in person when I can."

Blake paused, a word on his lips, then nodded. "So do I. We'll go inside. If you'll just hand me that robe . . ." He indicated a white terry-cloth robe draped on the rail of the deck. Sean picked it up, noting the embroidered lion's head on the lapel and cursive lettering that read EST. 1931, THE IMPERIAL, NEW DELHI.

He heard a sloshing of water as Blake stood in the tub. His physique was hard and angular, with ropy muscles stretching across his frame and whorls of body hair on his pectoral muscles and sprouting across his shoulders. An arrow of dense hair searched downward from his sternum to the forest that cloaked his genitals. The hair on his forearms and legs, thin but very long, was plastered to his skin. Sean recalled Martha's comment about monkeys. He hadn't thought to take it literally.

"It's not polite to stare," Blake said, shrugging into the robe.

Sean thought he saw coins of amusement dancing in his eyes and looked away.

"I like to see people squirm," Blake said. "I've been called hirsute since puberty, mostly behind my back because I had hard fists and used them, but the term is incorrect. Hirsutism is a condition specific to women, symptomatic of an endocrine disorder. I have a genetic condition called hypertrichosis. That means I'm hairy as an ape. The length is due to a longer anagen, or growing phase. If you

want to know a secret, I'm proud of it. I've always admired the Asi-
atic lions. They have beautiful curly hair compared to their African
cousins. When I was studying lions in the Gir Forest, in India, our
guides called me 'Kesin.' It means the 'Long-Haired Lion.' You can
call me Drick. Help me out."

Sean took the offered hand, noting the furry knuckles and the
long length of the fingers, which were shriveled from immersion in
the tub. Blake spoke to the closed door of the yurt.

"Scarlett, would you please make our visitor feel at home? I'll be at
the enclosure and back shortly."

There was no response.

"Should I go in?"

Blake smiled. "Scarlett's hearing is acute. But, like a cat, she doesn't
always answer your call."

"She is your sister?"

"She is my sister. She is my wife. The latter relationship is cultur-
ally unacceptable, so it is not said to my face. We are *inseparables*, if
that is a word. With the other, anything is possible. Without, nothing. We are compatible in every way, including the way of a man and
a woman. We are not conceiving a child, so the problems associated
with consanguinity are not an issue. Let us live our lives as others
do theirs."

Sean knocked and then entered the yurt, which was airy, with a
large living space, a small sleeping quarters, and a tidy kitchenette.
The floorboards were knotty and figured, the peeled-log furniture a
warm blond. A woodstove was set upon a foundation of river stones.
A love seat sported an African-animal motif, and there was a casual
arrangement of hard-back chairs centered around a white birch table, one end of which doubled as an office. Two worn zebra rugs made
a geometry on the diagonally laid floorboards, and running around

the yurt's interior at chin height was a continuous shelf on which squatted an arrangement of bleached skulls, showing cavernous eye sockets and large canine teeth.

All this Sean took in at a glance, but as he entered, his eyes were arrested by the woman sitting on the love seat. She had long strawberry-blond hair that partly shielded her face. She set down the glass she was holding and gently moved the head of the cat that that lay beside her, resting its chin on her lap. She rose and turned to face him. As she did, her hair shifted and Sean saw that the right side of her face was scarred. An angry worm of raised white scar tissue, starting in the hair at her temple and skirting the orbital bone of her right eye socket, ran diagonally across her cheek, ending in a blister near the point of her chin. Another scar, starting an inch from the first and running parallel to it, disappeared under the lapel of a terry-cloth robe identical to the one Sean had handed her brother. She walked to greet him with purposeful strides, her limp all but unnoticeable as she closed the distance. "I am Scarlett. And this"—she turned to the cat, which had not moved from the love seat—"this is Tatiana."

CHAPTER TWELVE

Tatiana

S he is beautiful," Sean said. And the cat was, with her frosted blue-gray coat, flared facial ruff, trapped-in-amber eyes, and tufted ears.

"Tatiana is a Canada lynx and she is more than beautiful," the woman corrected. "She is transcendent. But I must warn you. I raised Tatiana, but she is still a very wild animal and we must keep our voices down and refrain from sudden movements."

"Can she smell my dog?"

"Perhaps. She most certainly can smell your dog on you. That creates tension that shows in her eyes, which are dilated more than you would expect from the brightness of this room. With cats, one must read their expressions like a book, always turning pages quickly because the cat is writing as you are reading, and you must pay attention to what you read. It is when you fall behind and become complacent that you risk being caught off guard."

"Is that what happened to you—you were caught off guard?"

Absently, she traced a forefinger down the longer of the scars. "No, that was not Tatiana." For a moment, she seemed to go somewhere far away.

"How did you obtain her?" Sean asked.

"A bear hunter found the den. It was May, no tracks of a lynx in old snow, so he thought the mother must be dead. He reported the den and FWP consulted with us—we were involved in a lynx study at the time—and the decision was made not to intervene but see if the cubs—Tatiana had two brothers—could survive by catching mice and rabbits. Typically, lynx stay with their mothers for at least a year, learning to hunt, and the cubs looked to be about six months old. A trail camera was placed by the opening of the den, but the males moved away and were not seen again. Tatiana remained close by but grew weaker and became very thin. Four days passed when she did not trigger the motion sensor of the camera. It was assumed she was dead.

"I found her alive, but breathing shallowly. I wrapped her in my coat and carried her back to where we were living. Drick criticized me for not letting nature take its course, but of what scientific value would it have been to let her perish?"

"Your husband said he'd be at the enclosure. Do you keep other cats there?" The word *husband* was out before Sean could reel it in.

"Is that how he called himself? My hus . . . band." Drawing the syllables out. "He *would* say that. It implies possession more than the other word. Brothers and sisters are more easily thought of as equals, don't you believe so? They do not take a vow to honor and obey. But to answer your question, no other cats for several years now. We had an African lion from Botswana. Tuft, we called him. Before we got him, he'd been living behind a fence on a game farm where there were no thorns to tear out his mane, so he would bring better money from a hunter when he shot him. *Hunter* is not the word. *Murderer,* perhaps. But that was long ago. Only his bones are here now."

She turned her head. "There," she said. "I can hear my *brother's* footsteps."

Sean could hear nothing, but turned to see Blake coming through the doorway. "I see you have not offered our guest coffee," he said.

"I thought we might show him the enclosure first. I assume you placed the quarry."

"Yes, we are ready."

They pulled boots on at the door, and Scarlett snapped a leash onto Tatiana's collar. The cat became immediately alert, her eyes burning. Scarlett explained that the lynx knew that when she was led to the enclosure, which was double-walled with cyclone fencing and covered several acres, one of two things would happen. Either the carcass of a deer would be hidden for her to uncover or a rabbit or pheasant would be released for her to chase.

This morning's sacrifice was a winter-phase snowshoe rabbit. The grounds inside the fencing, Sean saw, were grown up with small trees and bushes, with great boulders and rock ledges with overhangs and dark cavities, and even a rivulet that crooked down toward Swallowtail Creek and was dammed to make pools of water.

Drick opened the outside door and then the inside one, and Scarlett entered the enclosure and freed the cat from the leash. The lynx, untethered, bolted forward in a blur, then slowed to a stalk, one forepaw up, poised, then the other, her belly low to the snow. Sean watched, fascinated, as Tatiana passed within twenty feet of the hare, which, sitting on a patch of snow, was all but invisible, only its pebble eyes, cinder nose, and the black outlines of its large ears giving its position away.

Scarlett returned from the enclosure and took Sean's hand in her strong fingers. "Watch now," she said. "It can be over in a blink."

Then the cat saw the rabbit. She crouched in the snow, her long rear legs tucked underneath her, alternately pumping. A heart-in-the-throat moment stretched and Sean could feel Scarlett's fingers squeezing. Then Tatiana seemed shot from a cannon, a gray-blue streak as the hare burst away in a spray of snow. The chase was on. Sean found that he was rooting for the rabbit, which was all but caught several times, but then, with an extra kick or sudden change of direction, escaped. Suddenly there was a blur of white; the hare, jumping, was caught midair by a paw, and, flipping end over end in the air, was caught by the cat's teeth as it fell back to earth. A drawn-out squeal, then a crunch Sean could hear from sixty feet.

The victor lifted her head, the rabbit's neck clamped in her jaws, and carried it into the trees in the farther reaches of the enclosure, the long rabbit legs dragging in the snow. She was gone from sight.

Sean turned to Scarlett, who relinquished her grip on his hand. She turned to him, her face flushed from the excitement. He saw a tremor of thrill in her eyes.

"Isn't death beautiful, though," she said. "It never fails to make my heart race."

"Have you ever thought of trying to return her to the wild?" Sean asked.

It seemed an innocent question, but neither of the Blakes ventured an answer. Sean heard the *shook-shook* call of a Steller's jay. The bird's sharp eyes had seen the blood on the snow.

"Let's go inside," Drick said at length. "We can all do with a spot of tea, as the Brits say. If I am to be of service, then I need to hear every detail of your last few days. They appear to have been eventful."

AS SEAN RECOUNTED THE STEPS that had led to the discovery of the body, Blake listened with rapt attention, leaning forward from his chair with his chin resting on steepled fingers. He occasionally prodded Sean with a question, and several when Sean described the scream that he had heard in the night. But for the most part he simply nodded, while his sister, having resumed her position on the love seat, seemed to have retreated into that other world, as Sean had seen her do in glimpses when they'd met. After Sean finished, Blake asked him to repeat his story about being stalked, and as he listened, Blake sat back and laced his hands over his abdomen. He let the silence settle a little, and a little more, then spoke with the air of a professor who knew his subject, and warmed to it.

"There is a name for what you experienced, when the sudden growl caused you to freeze. It is called crypsis, a defense mechanism that is hardwired into a region of the brain known as the amygdala. If becoming motionless is not effective at removing the threat, and the predator becomes aggressive, your glycogen will break down, and you will experience a surge of energy. Your bladder and colon may evacuate. Your hair will stand on end. Then a decision in the subconscious will be made. Fight or flight? The good news is that if you are attacked, endorphins will kick in and you might feel nothing at all as your bones break. I've heard survivors of lion attacks in Tanzania call it a dream state. On the other hand, others experience great pain indeed. So there is luck involved. But you came here to ask about man-eating, and I will tell you what I know."

Blake nodded to himself. "Understand, Sean, that in seven out of ten cases, the circumstance that has turned a cat into a man-eater is a wound. In the eighth case, it is old age. In the ninth, scarcity of natural prey. There are places in Africa and India where there is simply no more game for the great cats to prey upon, and of necessity they turn to the one animal that is both vulnerable and in plentiful supply. I think we can dismiss prey scarcity in the present scenario."

"You implied there was a tenth case."

"Yes, it is that, contrary to common wisdom, humans are in fact natural prey of the great cats, and have been since their coevolution. The only reason the human death toll is not higher is because the cats have learned that man, or rather his weapons, poses a threat, and so they avoid conflict. This avoidance behavior is passed from mother to daughter and son. But pockets of habitual man-eating persist. The most noted examples are the Ganges River Delta, called the Sundarbans, in India, and in Kruger National Park in South Africa. Each year, young Mozambican men attempt to illegally cross the park to find work on the farms and in the mines of South Africa. It take three days for these men to run the gauntlet of Kruger's three hundred lion prides. Estimates of deaths run into the thousands. Some I have met do not view it so much as a tragedy than as a form of natural border control." Blake shrugged. "My sympathies are with the victims, of course."

"I understand that your father was a game ranger."

"Yes, in Kruger. You have done your homework. I followed in his footsteps and was part of a team assembled to try to find solutions to the problem. That is why I am not sympathetic to the situation faced by your Sheriff Ettinger. She refuses the help of the one person who has hands-on experience with man-killing cats."

"Why did you leave and come here?"

"That is a long story and not pertinent to our shared concern. I became persona non grata, let's leave it at that."

"Do you think this cat will strike again? My understanding is that serial killing by a mountain lion is very rare."

"Unheard of," Blake said. "Most mountain lions that have killed humans in present times—that is, have eaten them—have themselves been killed before they struck again, or disappeared afterward without apparently claiming more victims. Yet that possibility exists. I would urge you to tell your sheriff to not be so preoccupied by the present situation as to neglect the past. There is a possibility that this unfortunate woman was not the cat's first victim, or even its second. If, in fact, that proves to be the case, then you are facing a state of emergency, for the odds that it will claim another life rise dramatically."

He abruptly rose to his feet. "Come, I wish to show you something."

He walked to the shelf with the skulls and picked up one that was enclosed in a plexiglass case. He opened the case and handed the skull to Sean. It was surprisingly heavy and, compared with the others, darker by a shade. Sean saw that the right upper canine tooth was broken and the front teeth were worn to the bone.

"You are looking at the skull of the Chowgarh tigress," Blake said. "She was reported to have killed sixty-four humans in the foothills of the Himalayas. I have inserted a metal hinge so that I can open and close her jaws." He worked the great jaws open and shut. "That is for demonstration purposes when I speak at film festivals. I have had a checkered career, Sean, and in one of those checkers I produced and directed films. Nature documentaries, but movies, too, ones you might categorize as indies."

"Coproduced."

Sean turned to regard Scarlett. She raised her eyes. "It was my camera, after all," she said.

"Yes, thank you for the correction."

Sean looked from one to the other, surprised by the sudden tension between so-called inseparables.

"My point is that one of those indies made me a tidy sum—"

"Us."

"Yes, us. In any case, when I heard that the private party that owned the skull had put it up for auction, I depleted my bank account—*our* bank account—to obtain it. I don't regret a penny."

"I do."

Scarlett smiled briefly. It was the first false note of expression Sean had seen from either of them. "I think I'll go out to the spa," she said. "So you men may speak without my . . . clarification."

Blake frowned into the space she had vacated. He then went on as if there had been no interruption. "What do you see?" he asked.

"The broken teeth, of course." Sean had not mentioned that the wounds on the victim's throat showed that one canine tooth had been broken short. Had it been the right front canine? He couldn't recall, but it would be a strange coincidence if it was. He made a mental note to check with Doc Hanson.

Blake was speaking again. "Yes, the injury is undoubtedly why this cat became a man-eater. Now, I'm going to tell you what you cannot see, and what could not have been known in 1930, the year that she was killed. Until, in fact, much more recent advances in science."

He took the skull from Sean's hands. "I had this examined by a paleobiologist at Montana State University. He was able to identify the isotopes and mineral composition of the teeth to confirm that this animal's diet was largely human. He also used a method called X-ray microtomography that allowed him to see inside the teeth and examine their patterns of growth. These X-rays showed that when the tigress was in the prime of her life, several months passed when she ate next to nothing at all. I think it's safe to conclude that this behavior was precipitated by the wounds to her mouth, most likely the result of gunshot. As the first human kill attributed to the tigress was in December of 1925, we can make an educated guess that the wound occurred prior to that."

Blake replaced the skull inside the cube.

"Think of that, Sean. Despite being on the brink of starvation, this tigress refrained from killing the one large mammal she could overpower. She must have been very near death before finally succumbing to her desperation. Such an animal merits our sympathy, not our hatred. She broke no laws of nature, only of man."

"This is very interesting, but I don't see how it helps us get closer to our lion."

"That is because you didn't permit me to finish speaking. What I'm trying to tell you is that this tigress had to adopt drastic measures in order to complete her function in life. That function is, of course, to pass on her genes to the next generation. To do this, she would have to somehow survive, and this she managed to do by having one of her grown cubs, a female, take over killing for her. The extent to which she depended on her cub became apparent after it was killed, for she was so deteriorated that many of the villagers she attacked subsequently were able to survive the assault, if with horrific wounds."

He looked pointedly at Sean, as if he had said something revelatory and was waiting for the second shoe to drop.

"Are you suggesting this is our situation?" Sean said.

"Not necessarily a mother and cub. The cats could be siblings or mates. Male cats will sometimes provide for the female during the time they are together. As we are discovering, mountain lions are much more social than previously thought. I see you remain unconvinced, but I do have evidence. Your words *are* my evidence."

"I'm not sure I follow you."

Blake opened the laptop computer on the end of the table. He began to click keys. "I want you to hear something," he said. A minute later, a long, drawn-out, very humanlike scream filled the room. It was a somewhat modified rendering of the scream Sean had heard on the mountain the night that he backpacked out the last of Martha's elk meat.

"What you heard is called caterwauling," Blake said in a matter-of-fact voice. "It's the mating call of a female mountain lion, but males and young cats will on occasion caterwaul as well, either because they are agitated or as a means of communication. You told me that the sound you heard came from the ridge where you saw the lights, where this woman was killed. It makes no sense that a lion, having just made a kill, would leave that kill to cross a steep canyon and visit an old elk kill, or whatever it was you smelled. However, if it was providing for another lion in the vicinity, then it is logical that it would call to it. You do see what I'm getting at."

"Yes," Sean said. "There were two lions on the mountain that night."

"And they were both very hungry. You do see that you are lucky to be here, don't you? Yours was not a normal encounter. You were very much on the menu."

"I do."

WHEN BLAKE EXCUSED HIMSELF a few minutes later, saying he needed to check on the lynx, Sean thanked him and left by the front door to unleash Choti. He led her to the side of the yurt, where

Scarlett sat in the tub. She was enshrouded in steam, her presence as much felt as seen.

"Don't worry—I can't see anything," he said to her. "I just wanted to say thank you and good-bye."

"Did Drick flatter you into soliciting his help in the hunt?"

"He said he would participate if asked."

"My brother does enjoy his effect on people. Sometimes, he is flattered right out of his clothing, especially on our fundraising tours. I can hear him being flattered in the room next door. Of course I am only his sister. And he is raising money we need for our nonprofit. What call do I have to object to his indulgences?"

Sean had nothing to say to this. After a brief silence, she said, "Forgive the bitterness of my tone. I see you have your dog. A sheltie, isn't she?"

"Her name is Choti. It means 'small' in Hindi."

"Yes. I don't speak the language, but I do know a few phrases. Drick and I worked in the Gir Forest. Did he tell you how proud he is to be called Kesin, the Long-Haired Lion?"

"Yes."

"Did you notice the skin grafts on his cheeks?"

"I noticed the skin was sort of sunken."

"He had mountain lion whiskers implanted with skin grafts. They didn't take. He also had his nose flattened and made wider to resemble the nose of a cat. He's quite mad, you see."

"Your brother doesn't seem mad."

"You, who know him so well."

A ticking of near silence ensued, made more conspicuous by the whispered bickering of the coals heating the water.

"He had a very interesting theory."

She listened as he told her.

"Yes." She nodded slightly. "My brother always has interesting theories. Some are on the mark. In this case, knowing what you told us, I would tend to agree with him. Would you like to hear my advice?"

"Of course."

"Never turn your back. On *any* predator. Would you please hand me my robe?"

Sean picked it up from the railing. "I'll avert my eyes."

"No, keep them open. I am not modest, and I want you to see the stakes of the game you are playing."

"I wasn't aware I was playing a game," Sean said.

"That would be your mistake."

She stood from the tub, her hands crossed over her chest. She turned her face, so that he could see the scarring on her cheek, and then dropped her hands to her sides. Naked, she turned to face him. Enshrouded by the steam, she looked at him for a few long seconds, her ghostly appearance seeming to shiver, her breasts rising and falling, her chin held high, her expression frank. What Sean saw shocked him. Five parallel scars, starting from her right shoulder, scrolled across Scarlett's chest and stomach. The scars looked as if a large paw had raked the length of her torso with one long, deep swipe. The healed tissue shone white against her skin, ugly, yet in its symmetry oddly beautiful, like the ritual scarring practiced by tribal members in parts of Africa. Showing her body to him, Sean realized, was not exhibitionism. What she was showing him was a message written in blood, long dried now, that carried a warning.

"Good-bye, Sean." She put on the robe and shook his hand with the same strong grip with which she had introduced herself, then rubbed Choti under her chin. She looked up at Sean and smiled, and then the smile was gone, leaving all the sad knowledge of the world in her eyes.

CHAPTER THIRTEEN

The Woman with Coffin Eyes

Number four Castle Lane was off a dead-end gravel road outside Silver Star, a two-blink town on the west bank of the Jefferson River. Sean found a boulder painted with the number and brought his binoculars to bear on the house. It was tall, a gabled two-story mounted by a conical stone-and-mortar turret, hence the name of the road. A chimney belched smoke that caught on the gnarled branches of an aspen stand and gave the place a cemetery feel. Stalling, he looked again at the map that Garrett had drawn on the cigarette paper, then he slowly motored up the drive.

A well-kept Tahoe in front of the house sported a bumper sticker in the shape of a home plate. It read ARIZONA CACTUS LEAGUE. Sean squared his felt Seratelli as a woman opened the door and stepped outside, followed by a shepherd with a sable coat that uttered a growl very deep in its chest.

"State your business," she said.

Sean took a look at the dog and did so, taking in the woman's appearance as she considered his words. She was of medium height, but her posture made her look taller. A woman of angles, with broad shoulders, a tapered waist, and long legs. She wore skin-tight black leather pants tucked into black cowboy boots with red roses, and a black doeskin jacket with a fringe. A gray shawl shifted like an uncertain cloud on her shoulders. A silver belt buckle showed off a turquoise stone. Her hair, jet black, a streak of silver at one temple, was pinned up over a face that was more carved than molded. Like her truck, she was vintage but very well kept. He put her at sixty, give or take.

He told her about the woman staying in the trailer who had met her death, possibly at the teeth and claws of a lion. All the while, he watched her face for a reaction, difficult as that might be to decipher with her eyes hidden behind dark glasses. The expression on her face indicated to Sean that this was news to her.

"A mountain lion, you say to me. Like a cougar? I never heard such a thing." She had an unplaceable accent. "You're sure it wasn't a wolf? We had them in the old country. My grandfather would tell stories. Even today they are around. A hiker was killed last year by wolves when she was investigating some ruins on the coast."

What ruins? What old country?

"They say the woman's thigh bones were cracked wide open, that no dog's jaws would be powerful enough to do that damage. A tragedy."

"The evidence points to a mountain lion," Sean said. "Are you Greek?"

"I am Romanian and Greek. What's it have to do with me, this cat?"

"The trailer was registered to you. You're Virginia Jenny, aren't you?"

"Jenny was my married name. My husband called me Virginia because I smoked Virginia Slims."

"What was your name before you married?"

"Adrianna Koslovovich. Is the trailer currently registered to me?"

Sean admitted it wasn't. The plates dated back thirty years, before Montanans were offered permanent trailer licenses.

"If you're talking about an Airstream, that was stolen from these premises many years ago. Parked right where you're standing. I had my suspicions about who did it. I thought he'd hauled it up to Alaska."

"Did you report it stolen?"

"To American authorities? A person persecuted for her service? Don't be foolish. Where is this trailer? I would like it back."

"It's up the Johnny Gulch Road in the Gravelly Range. That's near Ennis."

"I don't know the place. The town, of course, I know."

"Ms. Jenny, I'm not here to poke into your business. I'm just trying to find out who this woman was. She'll have people who will care. They deserve closure."

"Of course you're trying to poke into my business. You think she's a prostitute. Otherwise, why are you here?"

"I'm just trying to put a name to a few bones."

"What makes you believe that anyone would care about what happened to this person? You speak of closure. All that means is she won't be coming around again, dragging her drug addiction behind her, making a person want to lock the drawers."

"I really don't know if anyone else cares. But I do. Someone once told me that when you investigate a case, you join teams with the dead. You stand for them and you wear their colors."

"You're talking about murder. This isn't murder by a human being."

"Nevertheless," Sean said.

A small movement of her chin. "What are we doing standing on the porch?"

"So your dog won't kill me when I go inside," Sean said.

She smiled then, a smile that, if briefly, made Sean wonder what she would look like with her glasses off.

"What's your dog's name?"

"Cerberus. Do you know Greek mythology? No? Cerberus guards the entrance to the underworld. He has three heads. One can never have too many eyes watching out for one's safety, don't you agree? Be careful not to trip. I'm not a vampire, despite rumors to the contrary. I live in darkness because of an eye condition. It is called photophobia. My irises are sensitive to light. That is why I wear polarized glasses when I go outside. Also why I don't wear silver jewelry in the sun. My eyes could be burned by my own bracelet. Indoors, I can take the glasses off as long as I keep the curtains drawn. I am one with the night, and so this inconvenience is minor. And the dark is lovely, is it not?"

Sean followed her into the twilight zone of the house, with its dark, heavy furniture, dark hallways leading to dark rooms, where dark deeds might have been done. In the living room, the only color was the golden pulsing of embers in a stone fireplace.

"I can offer you apple cider or brandy. The cider has a bit of a kick."

"I've been up since four. I could use a bit of a kick."

She brought back tumblers from the cave of the kitchen. "We'll sit here." Indicating chairs. She took the beaded, upholstered chair opposite him, with a low coffee table between them. They touched glasses.

"*Na pane kato ta farmakia.*" It came out as all one word. "Let the poisons go down."

Sean drank the poison.

The woman removed her glasses and set them on the table.

"What is it that you wish to know?"

"Her name, to start with?"

Wool gathered in the dark corners of the room. It was a comfortable silence, nonetheless.

"I'm not evading your question," she said at length, "but I don't know her name. Twenty years ago I would have, because the girls who worked for me were my daughters, some more than others, but I cared about all of them. But times, they are not the same. What do you know about the world's oldest profession, as they call it?"

Sean shrugged.

"Don't answer with your body language. I cannot see you."

"Very little," Sean admitted.

"You're not one of those boys whose father took him to a freight car at the railroad yard? Paid the yard bull to look the other way while he lost his virginity? It is quite common, though today, I am informed, it is in a house in Livingston. Off Front Street, I am told."

"No," Sean said. "I lost my virginity on the bank of the Battenkill River, in Vermont. There were fireflies under the weeping willows."

"Really?"

"Yes. Bats were eating them."

"How . . . quaint."

Silence again, but not heavy.

"This woman who was killed, was she Indian?"

"The person who saw her last said she was white. But she had grown up on a reservation. The Flathead."

"I ask because if she is Native American, I will not be able to help you. There are thousands of Indian girls prostituting themselves and being prostituted by others. That is human trafficking, an industry built upon a drug culture."

"Meth," Sean said.

"Then you know about this?"

"I know that the Mexican cartels target reservations and that the addiction rate among Indians is the highest of any ethnicity in the nation. I know that users will sell their souls to get high, regardless of their color."

She nodded. Sean felt rather than saw it.

She said, "They will sell not only their own souls, but the bodies of their children."

"Ms. Jenny, anything you tell me, it doesn't have to leave this house. And you have your own protection from authorities, from what I've heard."

"True. When you have in your possession compromising evidence about those who would seek to persecute you, you are granted a level of immunity from their persecution."

"This person is beyond protection now, yours or anyone else's. You risk nothing by telling me her name."

"If you are saying that because you believe it, you do not know the people you work for. They would delight in dragging my name into this unpleasantness." She paused. "You say that you join teams with the dead, Sean. May I call you Sean?" She didn't wait for an answer. "Do you really believe the memory of this person is best served by broadcasting her profession and the circumstances of her death?"

Now the silence was Sean's. It was a strong argument, all the more so in the absence of a traditional crime. He took the last of his drink and set it down on a coaster.

"Ms. Jenny—"

"Call me Virginia."

"Virginia. Why now? Why her? These are two questions I'd like to find answers to."

"You do not think her death, it is coincidence? A lion without his kill is no different than a man without his woman. They both need to be fed, and when you are hungry, one meat is the same as another. Go back to this trailer. You speak of the precautions I have taken in my profession. That means you have heard what they are. Perhaps others have taken similar measures."

"You mean compromising evidence. Can you speak more plainly?"

"I think I have. Now I have told you as much as I'm going to. But when you do find out what has happened, I would like to share a bottle of wine with you over a plate of pasta. Somewhere dark. I find you attractive. Very much so. You will find our age difference is of no consequence."

"I'm engaged."

"That is a pity," she said. Then, unexpectedly, he heard a trilling of laughter, like the spilling of coins.

"If I have learned anything in my time on Earth," she said, "it is that the only words that mean less to a man than 'I am engaged' are 'I am married.' I won't walk you to the door, so as I said before, be careful not to trip."

He didn't, and when he turned to look back at her, she had shaken out her hair so that it made a black waterfall down her back. She held her cider glass up, canting it to catch the glow of the fire's embers. Sean shut the door behind him, leaving her to enjoy what glimmers of light her eyes could stand.

HE WAS SIX MILES down the road when the invisible pipe he was smoking gave him one of the answers he sought. He tapped the contacts button on his phone and scrolled to the bottom of the alphabet. The accusatory voice of Katie Sparrow was slightly tinny. Sparrow was a Yellowstone Park ranger who volunteered as a dog handler for the county's search-and-rescue team.

"Watcha want?" she said. "I got a life, you know." A pause. "Sort of." Another pause. "If you count sleeping with a bunch of dogs." The sliding notes of her life, defiance to pathos in one exhaled breath. Sean had heard it before.

"Hi to you, too, Katie. I'm hoping you can put that life of yours on hold for a couple hours."

"When?"

"Now's good."

"Okay." A brighter note. "But only because I'm still in love with you."

"Ditto," Sean said. Their running flirtation had occasionally led to the bedroom of Katie's one-hundred-year-lease Forest Service cabin, and to neither's regret. He told her where to meet.

She hesitated. "I ain't putting Lothar on any cat track, if that's what you're thinking, thank you very much. I heard what happened to that old hound that run him."

"I'm not asking you to bring Lothar. Just your metal detector. And the usual."

"Now you're talking. How will I recognize you? We haven't listened to no wolf packs for a time now."

"That's because I got engaged."

"When did that ever mean anything to the male of the species?"

Sean laughed.

"How's that funny?"

"It's just that you're the second woman who's told me that today."

"Truth has a way of repeating itself."

CHAPTER FOURTEEN

The Shepherd and the Meadow Maggot

To a bird looking down, and there was one that afternoon, a vulture soaring on thermals that lifted from the valley floor, the ranch looked perfectly drawn, the house set back into a copse of skeletal aspens by a creek that fell in a string of pearls to the Madison River. From the vantage given by the vulture's wings, the waters appeared not to move, the smoke from the chimney not to curl, the only movement the slow, silent snaking of the sun-sparked vehicle climbing the road, carrying its message of death.

Martha checked her phone and found a text from Sean saying that he had talked to Virginia Jenny, got a tip, and would tell her over dinner. A year before it would have never occurred to him to check in. She smiled. Maybe he could learn, after all. Then the smile vanished, because that morning she'd received a tip as well.

She had gone to the office and been pulling case files for missing persons, on the off chance that the woman whose body they'd found wasn't the cat's first victim. She had narrowed the possibilities to three, going back six months. They included a hunter who'd gone missing in the Snowcrest Mountains on opening day of hunting season—he was a smoker and a heart attack waiting it happen, and he might have had fangs meet in his throat but more likely had just keeled over dead; a teenage girl, who lived with her mother in the Crazy Mountains foothills who had run away twice before but this time hadn't come back, leaving no trace but her silverbelly Stetson found on a bench of timber behind the house; and a five-year-old boy who had gone missing on Halloween night while trick-or-treating. Martha was considering the missing girl as the most likely victim when her office phone gave its muted trill. It was Gigi Wilkerson, calling from her lab.

Wilkerson asked Martha if she remembered seeing the victim's foot, which had been sheared off at the ankle by the cat's teeth. Martha remembered. A foot still inside the boot was not something you quickly forgot.

Wilkerson said that the WHART team had brought her a regurgitation sample found some twenty meters from the kill site, which she had just got around to analyzing. Cats, she said, throw up all the time.

"Don't I know it," Martha said.

Wilkerson said that the sample contained bone articulations that she had at first thought were sections of fingers, then had positively identified as toes. The toes, she said, were from a right foot.

A pregnant silence followed.

"But the cat didn't eat her right foot," Martha said. "Her right foot was in her boot."

"Yes, it was," Wilkerson said.

"You're sure?"

"Contrary to my husband's opinion, I know my right foot from my left."

"Are you saying . . . there was a second victim?"

"A second person. Not necessarily a victim," Wilkerson cautioned. "We don't know how this person died. But the toes of a different human being were in the cat's digestive tract when it killed Jane Doe. I can tell you it was probably a child, or a small woman, by the size of the bones."

"Tell me more."

"Well, the toes would have to have been consumed within the past week or they wouldn't have remained in the gut system; that much is for certain." She added that the person who had once stood on those toes could have died up to several weeks earlier than that. It had been a cold fall and cats weren't too picky about eating well-aged meat.

"Wouldn't scavengers have got it?" Martha asked.

"Not necessarily. Cats cover up their kills. It could have still been there under a pile of branches when the cat revisited the kill."

And like that, Martha's three possibilities were reduced to one. The hunter was too old for the size of the toes. The girl had been missing going on three months. That left the boy, and after she finished her conversation with Wilkerson, Martha had called the residence to see if she would be welcome and was, if not with the mother's open arms. Martha knocked on the door and watched the vulture circling.

She could have been any ranchwoman of a certain vintage, in her knee-sprung denims and plaid snap shirt, her crow's-feet and defiant, thin-haired mustache. But her eyes were vacant, and an invisible smoke of despair trailed her as she led Martha to her kitchen, then excused herself to open the back door to call out, "Jules!"

"That man," she told Martha. "Cat got his tongue and won't let go. Let me get you some coffee."

Martha knew that the woman's name was Miriam and that Jules was Jules Jackson, her father, who'd stayed on to help run the place after Miriam's divorce, and that it was a two-person operation with seasonal hands hired during the lambing and shearing, and that there was too much going out in money and hope, and not enough coming in.

Like many Montana ranches that had fallen on hard times, the Ross place had gone boutique, Miriam selling off most of her Angus herd for a small bull-breeding operation, and making space for a herd of Rambouillet sheep that produced merino wool and were low maintenance, summering on public forest lands, where they were protected from predators by a Peruvian sheepherder. Martha knew these details because Miriam Ross provided them, starting as soon as they sat at a battered cherrywood table. She had not allowed Martha to get in a word edgewise because she was clearly afraid of what she might say. If the law hadn't come with new information about her son, who she maintained had been kidnapped by her ex, then why had she come?

"I called Maggie Rawlings, like you asked," she told Martha. "She'll bring Ava Ann, but she wants to be present when you talk to her."

"That's fine," Martha said. Ava Ann Rawlings was the little girl who had been trick-or-treating with Hunter Ross when he disappeared.

Martha extended a tentative upper lip to the surface of the coffee. She had grown up on ranch coffee and knew it to be the thinnest, most scalding drink on the face of the Earth. Her father used to say that he didn't know what he needed a branding tool for: You could press the rim of the coffee cup twice to the side of the calf and you'd have your double-ought brand just as clear as if you were using the iron.

The bird clock on the wall struck the hour with a *chick-a-dee-dee-dee.* The words ran out, and the room fell silent.

"She should be here," Miriam Ross said after an interval. "She's about the only one's come around since the missing. You find out who your friends are."

The missing. That was what she'd called it from the start. It sounded like the title of a horror movie to Martha, and she knew that for Miriam Ross it was. "I'm in no hurry," she said, and wasn't. There was going to be no easy way to broach the subject of the lion. If Miriam's son had been kidnapped by the father, who lived two states away and had also gone AWOL, then there was every chance he was alive. But if he had been taken by a lion, there was no hope whatsoever.

Martha heard a light padding as a heeler dog came into the room and snuffed her hand, then turned around twice on a scrap of rug under the table and lay down and shut its eyes.

"My name," Miriam said. "It means 'Sea of Sorrow.' My mother named me that. Sometimes I wonder if she could see the future."

Martha heard the sound of a truck motor.

"Here she is." Miriam walked to open the door. Then, her stoicism cracking, she embraced the visitor and Martha could hear her sobbing.

"It's going to be all right, Miriam. It's going to be all right."

Martha gave them time and shifted her gaze to the small girl who stood behind her mother, wiping the mud off her boots by dragging them through patches of snow.

Miriam broke away from the embrace. "Where are my manners? You come right on in," she said to the girl. The girl did, and took her boots off as one who doesn't need to be told. She was slight and had lank, dishwater hair framing a face that was the near side of pretty. She smiled at Martha, her eyes going right to the badge.

"Are you the sheriff?"

Martha said she was. "And what is it a sheriff has?" she asked the girl.

The girl looked at the toes of her socks. "I don't know."

"Deputies," Martha said. "Do you know what a deputy is?"

"Johnny Muller's dad is a deputy."

"Yes, he is. And what does he have that I have?"

"A badge?"

Martha smiled. She fingered the button on the breast pocket of her khaki shirt and handed the girl a tarnished pewter badge in the shape of a star. It read DEPUTY SHERIFF, JEFFERSON COUNTY, OHIO. Martha had a collection of old badges, picking them up at flea markets and wherever, just for this purpose.

"It's yours," she said, and helped the girl pin it to her shirt. "But wearing it means you have to tell the truth."

"Look, Mommy," the girl said. *She's the only real life in this room,* Martha thought, *not excluding the heeler.*

Miriam Ross placed a glass of milk before the girl. Ava Ann took a drink that left a mustache and slumped in her chair, so that she could reach a hand to knead the heeler's mottled coat.

"Sit up straight," her mother told her. "Sheriff Ettinger would like to ask you a few questions."

"You're not in any trouble," Martha said. "I just want you to tell me what happened on Halloween."

"We went trick-or-treating the house," the girl said. "Me and Hunter."

"Hunter and I," Maggie Rawlings said.

Miriam looked at Martha. "She means that they went around the outside of the house with a flashlight, knocking on each door and getting candy. They did the same at Maggie's house earlier, and I was going to drive them to the Martin place up Bear Creek next."

Martha understood. It was a common practice in ranch country, where the nearest neighbor could be miles away. You could make a night of it with only a few houses, if you hit all the doors several times.

Martha told Ava Ann to go on. What happened after they had trick-or-treated the house the first time around?

"We went into the barn to change our costumes," the girl said. "We usually make like three circles."

"Okay, what happened then?"

"We walked back to the house, only Hunter, he was behind me, and when I turned around, I couldn't see him. I didn't leave him. They kept asking me, but I didn't."

"Nobody says you did, Ava. I just want to know what you remember. Was there a sound?"

The girl fingered the pewter badge. She shook her head from side to side.

"Nothing?" Martha asked. "Are you sure you didn't see anything? Even a shadow, maybe?"

Again the girl shook her head.

Martha heard Miriam Ross sigh. "It's my fault," she said. "I shouldn't have let them go to the barn, not after it was dark out."

"You didn't know they had, Miriam," Maggie Rawlins said. And to Martha, "It was the children's idea to change their costumes."

Martha nodded. "Do you think you could show me where this happened?"

They pulled on boots and walked around the house. The door to the barn was open. It was a horse barn, with divided stalls. Miriam pointed out that there was only one horse, a chocolate quarter-horse mare with white stockings and a lot of years under the saddle.

The horse was being brushed down by a man Martha took to be Jules Jackson. The man awkwardly extended his hand. His Adam's apple rippled as he swallowed. "Ma'am."

Like his daughter, he was a type—overalls, canvas jacket, a string bean with crab hands and a gaunt, fissured face. His prominent ears were so red with cold you could see through them.

"Going to be a corker rolling in tonight." His eyes searched past Martha. He took a felt hat from a nail in the wall. He was one of those men who were given stature by a hat, and he tipped it.

"Miriam said you were with her in the house when the children trick-or-treated," Martha said.

"That's right." He swallowed again.

"So you didn't know they were coming here to the barn."

"No, ma'am."

Martha looked at Ava Ann, who had started to tremble. "I'm sorry," the girl said, barely able to get the words out. She was enveloped in the steam of her breath.

"You didn't do anything wrong," Martha said. "Come on, look at me." She squatted down so they could be at eye level. "You wear a badge now, don't you?"

The girl nodded.

"And you promised to tell the truth."

"Yes."

"Okay. What were you dressed up as?"

"A fairy princess. Same as I was last Halloween. Same as I am in forever."

"You liked being a fairy princess," Maggie said.

"I did when I was in first grade. I'm almost eight years old."

Martha took her hand. "It's okay, Ava. I never wanted to be a princess, either. I was a tomboy myself."

"What's a tomboy?"

Martha realized it was an old-fashioned term. "A girl who climbs trees and catches frogs and plays like a boy," she said.

"I shoot gophers. Does that make me a tomboy?"

"Card-carrying," Martha said. "What was Hunter dressed as?"

"A hunter."

"You mean like with a gun?"

"A BB gun. He had an orange hat and a vest. How original." She rolled her eyes.

Martha knew this from the report, just as she'd known the girl was a princess. In fact, the boy's description as a hunter was in the APB bulletin put out that night, after he'd been reported missing. Which was a mistake, if in fact the children had changed costumes. It begged Martha's next question, which she'd held off on asking until now, when they were in the barn.

"What was the costume you changed into?"

"A shepherd," the girl said. "I had a crook."

"A crook?"

"Like you catch runaway sheep with. Cesar taught me."

"He's the sheepherder," Miriam said.

"From Peru," the girl said.

"The crook she's talking about was an antique, a wood one with a curved grain. I found it at an estate sale and bought it for Cesar."

"But he doesn't use it," the girl said. "Shepherds use fiberglass crooks now. They have, like, locks so the sheep can't twist out of them."

"Where was this crook?" Martha said.

Jules Jackson spoke up. "It was hanging from this ten-penny nail." He pointed. "I found it outside where she dropped it, 'bout halfway to the house."

Martha nodded absently. There had been no mention of a shepherd's crook in the paperwork, nor of any change of costume for either child.

She turned back to the girl. "You dropped it when you realized Hunter wasn't with you?" she asked.

"I guess. I don't remember."

"Okay. You were a shepherd. What did Hunter change into?"

"A meadow maggot."

"A meadow maggot?"

"A sheep," Miriam clarified. "He put on a sheepskin. White rice on green grass."

"Let me get this straight," Martha said. "He put on a sheepskin? Where would he get it?"

"It was hanging from the rail." The girl pointed to a rail that fenced off a space like a crib.

"That would be a ewe we muttoned out last month," Jackson said.

"So the skin was green?"

He swallowed. "I wouldn't say that. It would have dried some."

Some, Martha thought. *But not all the way. It would still carry the scent.*

And felt her heart sink. She could picture it, the lion lying out of sight, perhaps taking cover behind a hay bale—there was one just around the corner from the door—the children walking out into the darkness, the flashlight beam pointed toward the house, the shepherd leading her sheep. And then the silent creeping forward, front paws pulsing, and the pounce, the great jaws locking onto the throat so there was no sound, no blood trail, just the muted padding as the cat carried him away, the shepherd none the wiser. Yes, it was possible.

"Where was the dog when this happened?" Martha said.

"Patches? I think she was with the children," Miriam said.

Martha's eyes turned to Jackson.

"I don't recall, rightly. You got a dog, it's invisible after a while. Like you have a frame picture—it's right there on the wall, but you don't see it."

"Did she bark?"

"Nope, I don't believe she did."

"Was she with you?" Martha asked Ava Ann. "Did Patches go to the barn with you?"

The girl shrugged. "It was dark. She wasn't, like, underfoot, like she always is."

So the dog was either inside or outside and had never made a sound. Wouldn't a dog react to the scent if a lion was around? But then, maybe not. Martha's own Aussie shepherd, Goldie, had cowered at Martha's leg once, when they were out for a hike and had stumbled into a black bear. She'd never made a peep.

"You've all been a big help," Martha said.

She had driven to the ranch to broach the possibility to Miriam Ross that her son could have been taken by a lion, and that they would need a DNA sample from her to match against human tissue, in the form of toes, that had been coughed up by a lion. She had the swab kit in the Cherokee. There was no soft way to introduce the subject, and she knew that it had been negligent of her not to mention the reason behind her visit at the outset.

She would wait now until Maggie and Ava Ann left, wait until they were alone under the vulture's soaring wings, then take a deep breath and say the words that confirmed the nightmare, like the knock on a door in times of war.

CHAPTER FIFTEEN

A Blessing from Heaven

With the mercury in the bowl of the thermometer and a north wind a harbinger of worse weather to come, the Madison at McAtee Bridge isn't the best stretch of the river or the best conditions under which to fish it. Nonetheless, Sean strung the rod, having learned long ago that the key to catching trout was grasping opportunity. Katie Sparrow was to meet him at the bridge, and with time to kill, it was either practice being a Westerner and lean against the hood and work a stem of grass in his teeth, or cast.

Spotting a few *Baetis* mayflies being bandied about on the surface, Sean added a tippet of 5X monofilament to his leader and knotted on a size-eighteen parachute Adams. An early hour for a cold-water hatch, but there they were, sailing down the river with their upright wings keeled over like the head sail of a sloop. Now all Sean needed was a trout rising. There wasn't one, par for the course this late in the season, but points, he told himself, for trying.

A bald eagle had taken a perch on the limb of a tree downriver and Sean kept an eye on it as he changed reel spools to a sinking shooting head. He was muttering to himself, fishing a streamer fly called a zoo cougar that brought a smile of irony to his lips, but not much faith to his fishing, when the rod tip dipped sharply. A trout walloped the surface with its tail, silvering the river, then swung out and downstream in an arc as Sean stumbled after it, trying not to slip on the rocks. The fish wasn't as active as it would have been in warmer water, but it was heavy and gave ground grudgingly. Sean coaxed it in, minutes passing, the sliver of bamboo dipping like a divining rod, and was easing it to hand when he saw Katie Sparrow walking along the bank. He had been so absorbed with the trout that he'd neither heard nor seen her truck crossing the bridge. Had he paused to think, he would have realized that those lost moments were the oblivion he fished for, a forgetting of the world and a glimpse through water's window into his past. As Sean looked down at the trout finning by his boots, the child he'd been, before he'd donned the layers of manners that adults wear like second and third skins, stared back at him in a wavering image.

He glanced away from the mirror—Katie was still some distance away, the eagle still on its branch—then slipped his hand under the trout's belly and removed the hook. The big brown rested, its gills pulsing in crimson slashes as its ventral fins dusted the cobblestone bottom. Spots the size of fingernails blinked inside yellow and aqua haloes. It was there. It was gone.

As a fisherman, Sean had been asked many times to name his favorite river and tell the stories of his most memorable fish. His answer to the first question was generally the Madison, though it was getting too crowded of late, and, as to memorable fish, there were too many to choose from, including this one. But were you to ask him about his most memorable moment while fishing, the answer never varied.

He'd been fishing that day on the Gallatin River near its junction with Portal Creek, a tumbling race of champagne riffles that had never been kind to him, nor was it that evening. He had just made a cast when he looked up and saw a bald eagle flying over his head, a trout in its talons. Sean saw eagles almost every day he was on the water and he saw many catch fish. But none that flew so low he could feel the air stirred by the wing beats or that looked so big and powerfully formed. As the bird passed over him, two downy feathers fell from its undersides and wafted like thistledown in a breeze. One disappeared into the branches of a pine tree on the bank, but the other drifted straight down to Sean, who, after transferring the rod to his left hand, caught the feather as it kissed his palm. As he folded the fingers of his right hand over it, he felt a tug on his line. It was the first strike he'd had since starting to fish. The trout was small and off quickly, but Sean couldn't help but feel that the feather was a gift given from one fisherman to another, and that of all the anglers the eagle had seen that day, he was the one chosen to receive its blessing.

When he got home, he took the feather from the pocket of his fishing shirt and sealed it in a Mason jar. It was so tiny and ethereal, a few filaments of pure white fluff, that there really wasn't anything to see. Like the translucent snakeskins that he had collected in his childhood, this memento of the wild did not maintain its luster behind a piece of glass, and, understanding what he needed to do, he transferred the feather to one of the small spring-lidded compartments in his Wheatley fly box. He'd been carrying it there for six years, waiting for the right moment, and as the eagle on the cottonwood limb flew from its perch and plunged into the riffles to come up with a small fish shining in its talons, Sean realized that the moment had arrived. He shook the feather from the compartment in the fly box and watched it waft away into the sky.

"Whatcha doing? Saying a prayer? Selling your soul to the devil?" Katie Sparrow blew at an errant strand of hair that escaped from her watch cap.

"Offering a gift to a bird of heaven," he said. He snapped the fly box shut and zipped it into a pocket in his vest.

"Which was bigger, that trout I saw you catching or the one that eagle just flew away with?"

"Mine was bigger."

"I'll bet you say that to all the girls."

Sean smiled. "Katie, Katie, Katie."

"Sean, Sean, Sean. You know you like me, admit it. Maybe it's like a whatchamacallit."

"What is?"

"The eagle. Like a harbinger. It will bring us luck."

"Maybe. You got your detector?"

"I got a new one, an AT MAX. The county ponied up for everything but the add-ons. I can find you a filling in a tooth under a foot of granite with this baby."

"Good. Let me change out of these waders and we'll caravan in. Might want to lock in your hubs."

"Ahead of you. Locked and loaded."

"You got the doughnuts?" The doughnuts were the "usual" Sean had asked Katie to pick up.

"Day-old, but you betcha," she said.

CHAPTER SIXTEEN

The Spy in the Woodpile

S o you think it's a camera, huh? Like a game-trail camera that's triggered by movement?"

Sean and Katie were drinking coffee and eating the doughnuts, warming their hands on the hood of her truck. Strung from trees, tatters of crime scene tape flapped listlessly in the breeze.

"I think it's likely," Sean said. "A kind of get-out-of-jail-free card. If a working woman possesses incriminating video of some of the town fathers who can't keep their hands out of the cookie jar, that might cool the heels of an assistant DA who was thinking about prosecuting a case."

"The madam, she could be gaming you—you think of that?"

"Yep. But I don't think she was."

"So she's your hooker with a heart of gold? I always pictured her as a witch."

"Heart of nickel silver," Sean said. "I think she genuinely cares, or cared, for the women who worked for her. But you're right. She might be pulling my leg about there being a camera. It was more like implied."

"You know what I think?" Katie said. "I think she was pulling another part of your anatomy. That's what I think."

By the end of the next hour, Katie had swept all the paths in the vicinity of the trailhead and trailer, as well as the outhouse with its cut-out quarter moon, from ground level to as high as she could reach with a broomstick extender, without once triggering the needle of the readout. Katie rummaged in her pack for a couple of sticks of jerky.

"We caught this one poacher in the park," she said, chewing the tough venison and speaking out of the side of her mouth. "We'd set the camera up at a trail crossing and the motion detector caught him dropping his pants for a number two. The case went to court, and the defense lawyer, he tries to get the video ruled out on the grounds that it's prejudicial. But the judge said it was obtained legally and it put the accused in proximity to an illegally killed bull elk. So they showed the video of this guy squatting down to the jury. I mean, his junk was pixilated out, but still. I was a witness for the prosecution 'cause I'm the one set up the camera, and I was digging my nails into my wrists trying not to laugh. Or I woulda been if I had any nails."

She swallowed the last of the jerky and smiled for Sean. "Good for the jaw muscles," she said.

They went back to work and found what they were looking for. The camera was in the woodpile, ten yards from the trailer door. Sean had seen Katie sweep the coil over the stacked splits and quarter-rounds. And pause. Then she swept it again, back and forth, partially overlapping each sweep with the next.

She looked at Sean with a grin. She pointed to the needle on the control box's readout. "Got the bitch!" she said.

The camera had been artfully concealed in a cavity in a Ponderosa pine round section. The round had been sawn in half lengthwise, then each half routed out to make room for the camera. A small hole in the bark was just large enough to accommodate the lens, and two powerful magnets had been inserted flush into each half of the round, so that with the camera in place, the halves of the round would clamp back together. From three feet away it looked like any other round in the stack.

Katie had tripped the sensor when handling the camera and shut it off. She extracted the SD card and tucked it into a breast pocket. "I got my laptop in the truck," she said.

Ten minutes later they were sitting side by side on the bench seat at the fold-down table inside the trailer. Katie slipped the memory card into her computer and waited for the videos to load. There was something on the order of a hundred, ranging from one to forty-six seconds long, with most lasting around seven seconds.

"They're dated," Katie said. "Lucky us."

"Isn't that standard?"

"Yeah. But you have the option of turning the function off. Same with audio. Infrared, too—that's your thermal detection. And you can set it to ignore the little critters, birds and squirrels and stuff. Maximize your battery life."

She clicked on the first thumbnail. The image enlarged to show the date, time, and GPS coordinates marking the location. The date was October 26 at 3:13 p.m.

"That's the day before elk season opened," Sean said.

Katie hit the play button. Boots, then legs, then the back of a person who was walking into the expanding cone of vision toward the

Airstream. But the trees lining the path were different. Leaf-scoured aspens with gnarly branches instead of tamarack and pine. It was the same trailer, but parked in a different location.

She began to scan the rest of the thumbnails. Five consecutive hunting weekends. Five different GPS locations. But always the Airstream in the background. Not really a surprise. Service the weekend warriors in one location, then change to another before too many hunters told their buddies and one decided to be a Boy Scout.

"Sort of like Christmas morning," Katie said. "Bunch of stockings all in a row, look to see who's been naughty. And guess what? They're all getting coal."

In each of the locations, the camera's lens was directed toward the trailer so that people approaching the door would have their backs to the lens, while those leaving the trailer would reveal their faces. With no exceptions, the visitors who tripped the sensor were clearly hunters, some still wearing their four hundred square inches of hunter orange as required by law. Or a light gray that Sean took for orange, for all videos shot after 5:00 p.m. or so, when it became dark, were cast in an eerie black and white.

"Some of these guys must smell like a bull elk pissing on himself in the rut," Katie said.

In the first four weeks of video, the lens caught fourteen different men coming and going from the trailer, a few more than once. There was only one woman. She had a fringe of dark hair escaping a watch cap with a tassel, but her face was covered with a scarf whenever she came within range of the camera's sensor.

"She knows about the setup," Katie said. Then: "Here we go."

She queued up the first in the series of videos taken from their present location. It was immediately apparent that the woman stepping outside the trailer door was not the same one who'd been in the first four locations. Whereas the latter appeared to be of medium build, this woman was slim and considerably shorter. She wore boots with ruffs of fur at the collars—the first woman had worn knee-high Muck boots—and no hat, revealing shoulder-length hair. Notably, she made no attempt to hide her face, indicating to Sean that she hadn't known she was being filmed. Hers was a face, he thought, that was more plain than pretty, though he knew that in person his impression might have been different. In the videos, everybody looked to have a little zombie in their DNA. Mid-thirties, he thought, maybe older. He was looking at a dead woman.

"I never thought I'd say this," Katie said, "but she looks like a nice person. Not your typical swamp angel looking to get fixed."

It was true. There was something innocent in the woman's face. And her posture, the way she stood, kicking her feet, her arms crossed, hands holding her shoulders. Not a person used to the cold. Someone you wanted to wrap a blanket around, who would smile up at you when you did. She was smiling now, in the frame of the lens, as a man approached her with his back to the camera, walking from the direction of the woodpile. He was carrying a small cooler and set it down. Then he wrapped her in his arms and they stood facing each other for a long minute, her face plainly visible, though the man showed only the back of his head. The size disparity revealed him as a big man, thick through the shoulders and chest, with a mane of ringlets that fell down his back. The couple disengaged and the man fished into his coat pocket for a pack of cigarettes, lit two, and passed one to her. His face came into profile, revealing a full beard.

Katie froze the video at the forty-four-second mark. "Grizzly Adams there looks familiar," she said.

Sean gave a noncommittal nod. He felt a prickling sensation at the back of his neck. "What's the date on this video?"

"The twenty-second. Thanksgiving Day. Two-thirty p.m. When you look at the two of them, I mean, it doesn't seem like he's pitching and she's catching. More like he's being protective."

Katie tapped the arrow. The man and woman unfroze and stubbed out their cigarettes. The man followed her inside the trailer, carrying the cooler. An hour and ten minutes later, the man reemerged and lumbered past the camera's position with heavy footfalls. He was carrying the cooler.

"Whatcha thinking? He was bringing her a turkey dinner?"

"I don't know," Sean said. "Let's move ahead to Lenny Two J. See how much of what he told me was truth." Katie gave him a quizzical look and Sean clued her in about the orchestra conductor who was likely the last person to see the victim alive.

Katie ran through the thumbnails and found the appropriate videos, starting with one of the woman leaving the trailer on the twenty-third, the Friday afternoon when the maestro said he'd met her. She was wearing tight-fitting jeans tucked into the boots with fur collars she'd worn in earlier videos, a puffy zip-up jacket, and what looked like a Cossack's fur hat.

"Night on the town," Katie said. "Where's her ride?"

"Her friend probably parked where we did. The camera wouldn't pick that up."

They watched the videos in silence, Lenny Two J arriving at the trailer in her company several hours later, the pair taking cigarette breaks and walking to and from the outhouse or woodpile over the course of the next day. Pretty mundane stuff. Lenny shoveling snow, the woman dragging smoke into her lungs and letting it out, looking far away, keeping herself to herself. Once, she tilted her chin up to catch snowflakes on her tongue, then kissed Lenny playfully on the cheek. The affection they showed each other and the times stamped on the videos supported the maestro's version of events.

"True love," Katie said at one point. "I don't know how much of it I can stand. You want some more coffee? It's in the truck."

Sean got the thermos from the Ford. When he came back, Katie was looking at an image on the screen. "You better sit down for this," she said.

Sean sat down.

"Time is, uh, a little past nine p.m. on Saturday night. It's the last video before you and Martha tripped the recorder about six a.m. Sunday. And your buddy. What's his name?"

"Sam Meslik."

"Okay," she said, "I backed it up to the start. Tell me what you see."

What Sean saw was the black-and-white image of the woman emerging from the trailer. She was wearing what looked like a fluffy bathrobe and paused on the step to fish a cigarette from a pocket and bent her head to light it. She blew out a plume of smoke and then shook her head as if to say, "What have I got myself into?" She tapped the cigarette out against the siding of the trailer and placed it in a pocket of the robe and switched on a headlamp. Then she began to shuffle toward the camera's position, her boots creaking in the shin-deep snow. The lens caught her lower legs as they came within view of the camera, the furry ruffs of the collars, then, abruptly, there was a flurry of movement, accompanied by a thudding sound and a gasp like the intake of a breath.

A few heartbeats of silence, then a momentary glimpse of the woman's face, her eyes seeming to bulge and roam wildly, and a few garbled words, one of which sounded like a question with the word "water."

Then her face was gone and there was the sound of something being dragged. And one more word before the camera's sensor switched off, or maybe just an exhalation of breath. Then nothing. The woman had been dragged far enough away that the camera could no longer register her movement.

Sean brought the coffee to his lips, stilling the tremor in his fingers. He took a sip. "Back it up, Katie."

They watched the video again.

"Did we just see her being taken by the cat?" Katie said.

"I think so."

"Jesus."

"Yeah."

Katie shook her head. "No, I mean that last word. 'Jesus.' She was calling out to God."

CHAPTER SEVENTEEN

Clean Living

S ean found Sam in his barn, which he warmed with a stone fireplace built as a first step into converting the structure into a
house. Until that day arrived, Sam, Molly, and their two-year-old
daughter lived upstairs over the fly shop, while the barn sheltered
drift boats with Meslik's RAINBOW SAM insignia and pink breast-
cancer ribbons painted on the bows.

"Kemosabe," Sam said. He was wearing paint-spattered Crocs,
cargo shorts, and a T-shirt that read THE TROUT ALSO RISES, the
letters stretched across his plate-size pectorals. On his left cheek
was a flesh-colored Band-Aid above the line of his beard.

"I'm glad you showed up," Sam said. He gestured toward a battered
drift boat resting upside down on extra-wide sawhorses. "Picked it
up at the Green Table," he said.

The Green Table was a hole-in-the-wall cabin in Virginia City, the
ghost town that had been the state capital in the gold rush days, and

remained the Hyalite County seat. Once a month, it was the setting for a poker game for an eclectic group, including lawyers, western reenactors wearing gun belts and sleeve garters, playhouse actresses in prostitute attire, and fishing guides like Sam, who provided illegal Cuban cigars smoked between sips of illegal moonshine while playing a friendly game of five-card just up the lane from the county courthouse.

"You won this playing poker?"

"Shh. I told Molly I picked it up at auction."

"Where is she?"

"She's in town, but she's like a mule deer. Her ears can hear you from the next county over."

"Looks like firewood to me," Sean said.

"Yeah, I hear you. But it came with a pair of Sawyer oars—they're worth more than the boat. Anyway, I always wanted a wood drift boat and was just getting ready to reinforce the bottom. But you have like a nanosecond after you mix the epoxy before it sets up, so it helps if you got two guys working at once to coat the hull."

"Why are you dressed like you're going to a Jimmy Buffett concert?"

"Because, one, I'm a Parrothead from way back, and, two, you get this goo on your clothes you might as well toss them in the fire. You in or you out?"

Sean was in and stripped off his shirt. An hour later, he was sitting down on a lawn chair before the fireplace, accepting a beer Sam tossed him from a cooler. He pressed the can against his sweating forehead, waited a minute before popping the tab, caught the foam bubbling out, and took a long swallow.

"So what brings you here?" Sam said. "Seems like you were getting around to asking me something and didn't."

"Actually, when I was driving over, I was thinking about some advice you gave me last summer."

"What was that?"

"You told me not to drive back to Katie Sparrow's house on the pretext of business, that the first time I might escape with a peck on the cheek but if I did it again, my shoes were going to be at the foot of her bed and I'd be cheating on Martha. You said I should stay faithful and get bored like all the rest of us, meaning you and Molly."

"Yeah, so? I stand by it. It's healthier than dipping your nib into two bottles of ink and dealing with stains that ain't never coming out."

"You're speaking from the position of monogamy yourself?"

Sam crushed his beer can in his fist. "What the fuck are you trying to say?"

"I'm saying Katie and I went back up to the trailer with a metal detector. We found something everybody else missed."

"What's that have to do with me?"

Sean waited.

"If you're asking me to guess, I won't play that game."

"Then I'll tell you. We found a motion detector camera hidden in a block of firewood that was tripped every time someone went into or came out of the trailer."

"Hunters looking for nooky."

"You said it."

"I suppose you're going to say I'm one of them. Of course I am. I found where she got jumped by the cat. You ought to be looking for the guy I pulled out of the snow. He's the last one seen her—alive, anyway."

"I found him," Sean said.

"What did the bastard say?"

"That's a different story. What I want to know is what happened before that guy came onto the scene. What you were doing there on Thanksgiving Day. Why you didn't tell me about it when Martha and I met you up there."

Sam shook his head. "Not what you think, buddy."

"Then what? You met her outside the trailer. You followed her inside. You were there for a while. Seventy minutes, to be exact."

"I was having a cup of coffee."

"How much did you pay her for it? And why did she do this to you?" Sean reached across the space that separated them. With one deft movement, he tore the Band-Aid off the big man's cheek, revealing two deep gouges that hadn't yet healed. "You left your DNA underneath her fingernails, Sam."

"The body didn't have fingers. Cat ate them. You told me that yourself."

"There were two fake fingernails found at the site, painted black, just like the polish found in the trailer."

Sam put his hand to his cheek. "You ripped the fucking scabs off," he said. He shook his head again. "This isn't your business."

"The hell it isn't. You can't just sit on something like this and think it isn't going to come out. Who was the woman who raked your face?"

"Molly would kill me."

"You should have thought of that before you got filmed going into a hooker's trailer."

Sam shook his head once more, then closed his eyes. He breathed in and exhaled, his breath stirring strands of hair that had fallen across his face. He wiped the sweat from his forehead. "Let's get out of this oven," he said.

Sean followed him out into the chill air. Below the bluff, the

Madison River slept in sluggish coils, the drawn-down gravel bars clotted with patches of old snow. Sean watched the steam expand from Sam's body, making his visage ghostly.

"I was trying to do the right thing," he said.

"Sam, it's me. I'm your best friend. You hooking up with someone like that, it isn't the end of the world. My job is to identify the victim, not tell everyone who she was seeing."

Sam nodded, as if coming to a decision.

"Want to show you something," he said.

Sam's fly tying nook in his fly shack was a cubicle a little larger than a phone booth. It was built back into a wall under the steps that climbed to the second floor. The corkboard behind the tying bench was studded with photos held in position with pushpins. They were fishing pictures, clients or Sam cradling trout, holding them so that their gills were still underwater. Sam didn't allow hero shots, where the clients held a trout clear of the surface, stressing the breathing apparatus. The one clear violation of policy was a fading photo showing Sam not long after his army discharge following the first Gulf War.

Sean had never seen Sam with short hair, though he still managed to look disreputable in a skull-and-crossbones T-shirt. He was holding one end of a stringer of crappies that reached at least six feet to the far end, where a girl wearing bib overalls struggled with both hands to hold her end of the stringer clear of the ground. Behind them spread a vast body of water washed of its color.

"Tongue River Reservoir," Sam said. "You count 'em up, there's fifty crappy on that stringer and another fifty in the cooler already filleted."

Sean focused on the girl, who looked to be nine or ten and had fair hair done in braids.

"That's my mom's kid sister's kid. My aunt was forty when she had her, blamed it on Elvis. A guy in a bar was playing guitar and singing 'Only Fools Rush In,' and next thing she was laying on a blanket on the bank of the Flathead with her heels in the air. She goes home, mosquito bites on top of mosquito bites, and, as she tells it, one of the bumps continued to grow. Bit of a situation 'cause, you know, she was married at the time."

"Are you saying this is—?"

"Yeah. The woman who got ate was my cousin. Clarice Kincaid. She's the bump."

Sam took the photo from Sean's hand and pinned it back into place. "Like I said, it's not what you think."

"What the hell was she doing hooking out of that trailer?"

"I'll tell you, but first you gotta know that she really wasn't hooking so much, not to hear her side of it. She'd been one of Ginny Gin Jenny's girls back in the day, and she still had connections, but she wasn't a lifer. She just picked up money the old-fashioned way when times got tough."

"You believe that?"

"Doesn't really matter. She was blood. The way she told it to me, she'd got clean at a rehab facility and wanted to make amends with the family, drove all the way up from Arizona, emptied her pockets just for the gas. Didn't turn out to be the reception she hoped for. She had a history of rifling medicine cabinets and lifting twenties from purses and some of the folks weren't too keen to see her."

"You're talking about your family in Polson?"

Sam nodded. "Her folks live on the rez. They aren't Salish but then most of the people who live there have about as much Indian blood as a mosquito in a Swedish bathhouse. Anyway, to hear her tell it, she bummed some money and was heading back to Tucson when her truck broke down on the Norris Hill. She wasn't planning on seeing me, but she knows I'm a fishing guide on the Madison, so the next thing I get a phone call and end up towing her into town. The tranny's grinding and you know as well as I do that's a death sentence, but I tell her I'll ante up for a rebuild, like a couple thou. Tell her she can stay with us and pay me back when she's got it. Molly, let's just say she was against the idea. That's putting it mildly because, you know, it's two grand we're saying adios to and she knows the stories."

"When did this happen?"

"Week ago Tuesday. In she comes, dragging a suitcase, and first night she nearly burns the shop down smoking a cigarette and falling asleep. Molly's furious, boots her out into the snow in no uncertain terms. Rightfully so, too. She takes it out on me." He tapped the wound. "I give her some money for a couple nights in a motel until the truck's fixed, tell her to keep her legs closed and stay out of trouble. Two nights later I'm in the Silver Dollar and hear a guy talking about getting his ashes hauled in a trailer up Johnny Gulch. I do the math and drive up there Thursday, and sure enough. That's the seventy minutes you were talking about. Clarice tells me she knows the girl who was hooking out of the trailer, who said she needed a couple days off for a family emergency and handed her the key to crash. Old friends in the trade. I reminded her the truck would be ready in just a couple days and she doesn't have to put out because I'll stake her the expenses for her trip. She says her friend will be back on the weekend and will bring her into town to my place. I say, 'I'll pick you up,' but she's sticking to her guns. This is Thanksgiving Day, and I brought her some yard bird, some stuffing and gravy. Weekend comes and I don't hear from her, figure she's just lying low like she promised me or her friend is late showing up. Finally I drive up to hunt the last day, and that's when I find the blood in the snow and call you. I'm thinking it's her friend, you know, that she's the victim. Wishful thinking, I know."

"When did you realize it was her?"

"Not till I saw the body. I remembered the bathrobe. She had it at my place."

"Why the hell didn't you tell me?"

"I was going to. But her having no face to speak of, no hands, I thought maybe she wouldn't be identified and nobody had to be the wiser. I was trying to protect her. She was a good kid, good in her heart, just weak and got herself with the wrong people. I didn't want her name out there as a hooker, or her just remembered as a meal for a mountain lion."

"Did you call her parents?"

"No, man. I didn't have the cojones. Will you do that for me?"

"I'll make sure it's done."

"You won't ask anyone to ID the body, will you? I mean, I wouldn't want her folks to go through that nightmare."

"They'll take a DNA sample from someone in the family and match it up." Sean remembered his visit to the crime lab. "Did your cousin have breast implants, Sam?"

"Why?"

"The victim did. The cat removed one and set it aside when it was eating the body."

Sam nodded, then looked away. "She hugged you, it was like pressing your chest to a pair of traffic cones."

Sean had one more question, but hesitated before speaking. Finally he said, "Why didn't you follow the drag? Don't get me wrong. Calling us was the right thing to do. But I know you."

"Are you asking was I afraid?"

"The reason I'm asking is because I know that fear wouldn't have held you back. It had to be something else."

Sam nodded. "That something else weighs twenty-six pounds, and I want to stick around to see her grow up. Used to be I went from the river to the bar to a night in the saddle with anyone who'd have me. Wake up God knows where. Lucky to be alive and no one to care that I was. But my days of following blood in the snow, they're over, at least if it's human blood."

"I hear you," Sean said.

MARTHA WAS IN THE BARN, checking Petal's shoes, when she heard the Land Cruiser come up the drive.

"You can cut me a check in the morning," Sean said.

"You ID'd her?" She turned down her mouth, arched her eyebrows. "I'm listening."

Sean told her everything, including his opinion that there had been two cats present near the kill that night.

At the mention of Sam's name—"Why am I not surprised?"

CHAPTER EIGHTEEN

Chasing the Echo

One week into the New Year, with the skeletons of Christmas trees littering the alleys of the valley and with the cat suspected of killing Clarice Kincaid still at large, an elk hunter who had drawn a shoulder-season tag in the foothills of the Madison Range found a ewe bighorn sheep that had been killed by a mountain lion.

Like everyone else who had read the stories in the *Bridger Mountain Star*, the hunter knew that the lion suspected of killing the hooker had a broken canine tooth. Where that fourth tooth should have penetrated, the throat of the ewe was only bruised, and in the instant that the hunter registered the significance of that, he became the hunted. Or so he felt. Walking as fast as he could, he retraced his steps to the ranch headquarters, where he had parked his truck, and arrived sweating through his wool coat and out of breath.

The property was owned by a film actor named Joshua Byrne, a decorated marine pilot who had served in the Afghan War and who volunteered his services, and those of his custom-fitted Bell 407 helicopter, for search-and-rescue operations in Hyalite and the surrounding counties. Martha had met him when he'd lived in Cody, Wyoming—the Madison ranch reflected his rise at the box office— and it was Byrne himself who called to inform her of the discovery and to offer his help.

By then it was four-thirty, practically twilight that far north and too late to see anything but gloom from a vantage afforded by a rotor. Martha thanked Byrne and said she'd call the next morning if the cat wasn't accounted for by then. Buster Garrett had assured her at the task-force meeting that his hounds would run any cat any day, anywhere, and, taking him at his word, she called and found him home, and game. He said he could be at the ranch in an hour and a half and had one request, that she provide him with a good man who could keep up and wouldn't get in the way. It was hard enough by day for one houndsman to follow his dogs in rough country. After dark it was a nightmare. Sean was sitting beside Martha at the farmhouse, and as she had the call on speakerphone, he heard the request and pointed to his chest.

He was at the ranch by the allotted time, and Byrne had no sooner shoved a mug of coffee in his hand than Garrett arrived, bringing the scent of his hounds in with him, and with no time for pleasantries. He waved off Byrne's offer to accompany them, and Sean, in an attempt to mollify what could have been taken as an insult, told the actor that he could help them better by getting a few hours of rest, in case he was needed to pilot his helicopter in the morning.

By the time they backtracked the hunter to the dead ewe, it was closing on seven p.m. While Sean shone his headlamp to confirm that there were only three wounds in the throat, Garrett turned the tracking over to the pack consisting of three Walker/Plott crosses he'd introduced to Sean as Boon, Sam, and General Compson, the latter wearing a GPS collar so they could locate him if the pack ran out of hearing. The fourth dog was a big Rhodesian ridgeback with scars on his face and his right ear a stub. Garrett called him Bear and said he was his kill dog. The names rang faint bells in Sean's head as the dogs worried the snow with their muzzles. Garrett explained that because the cat's odor dissipated slowly, the dogs could initially be confused, as likely to work a fresh trail backward as forward. They stood out of the way as the dogs corrected their mistakes and made more, two of the Walkers snuffing the snow, the other running his nose up under the pine boughs to search for scent particles trapped by the canopy.

General Compson struck first, but the bawl ended on a note of inquiry. He wasn't quite sure. But another minute later he was, and soon all the dogs were giving tongue. Garrett gave Sean a Lucifer grin. His battle-scarred Marlin lever-action, wrapped in camouflage tape, was slung from his shoulder.

The scent trail led the hounds behind a heavily timbered knob, where their voices became fainter, and a half hour after their striking the trail, the hounds were out of song. A few minutes passed and the song came back. Garrett fiddled with the GPS receiver.

"I can hear them," Sean said. "They're back on our side of the knob."

Garrett shook his head. "No. You're chasing the echo. It's a rookie mistake. Listen. Hear that, the ringing? That's bouncing off the canyon wall. They're still on up ahead of us." He showed Sean the readout on the receiver, which indicated the hound's position on a Google Earth map.

"How long you figure before they tree?"

"Cat has something to say about that. He gets up in the crags, dogs could lose him. But before we catch up, I want something understood. That crap Ettinger talked about at the task force, tranquilizing the cat until it can be proven guilty, we're past that now. It's just that I saw you stuffing a tranq gun into your backpack. This tom we're on, he's got the broken fang, he's the one, all right. If we try to dart him, then that means I have to pull the dogs away and you'll have to hold them back while I take the shot. Isn't as easy as it sounds, and without the dogs to hold him, he's like to sail off and it might be miles before he trees again or we lose him altogether. Then he kills another person, it's on our heads. So he comes out of the tree with a 420-grain flat-point through the heart, no two ways about it. Are we on the same page with this?"

Sean nodded.

"Okay then, let's get this over with so the valley can sleep tonight."

But it wasn't over, not in the next hour, nor the four that followed. The hunt seemed to unfold in a trance. Twice, they came close enough to hear the hounds change from openmouthed bawling to chop barking, the harsh staccato barks meaning the cat had treed. But each time the cat jumped out of the tree before they caught up, and the chase continued.

They were by now eight miles from where the dogs had first struck and were following the icon on the GPS receiver exclusively, even the echoes too distant to hear. They stopped often, putting their hands on their knees, blowing, the night raw enough to show the steam of their breath.

"Tell me if this ain't more fun than eating apple pie," Garrett said between his stentorian breaths.

"You ever think of pulling the hounds, pick the track back up in the morning?"

"Hell, no. I couldn't pull them off if I wanted to."

"Why are their names familiar?"

"Those are the characters in 'The Bear,' William Faulkner's story. That done it for me. I was working in Staunton, Virginia, at the insane asylum; shut that book cover and bought myself a bred bluetick the next day. I named her Lilly after me mum, nose as cold as a well digger's balls. Said my good-byes to the loonies. Headed west and didn't stop till I found something to run that was bigger than a coon. What? You didn't take me for a reader, did you? I'm a fuggin' Aussie. We like a yarn." He cupped a hand to his ear. "Listen. That's no echo, boy. They've turned our way. We're getting close."

It wasn't an echo, and a few minutes later the hounds were barking treed, and stumbling after Garrett down the far side of a ridge, Sean saw them for the first time in five hours. They were jumping up and rebounding off the trunk of a big pine tree, snapping shapes in a moonlit darkness. There was a sudden snarl from the lion as Garrett ran the beam of his big flashlight up the trunk of the tree. Sean followed Garrett's flashlight beam and saw the cat. It was about thirty feet up, crouched on a branch, its teeth bared and its tail hanging down, long and thick.

Garrett handed Sean his rifle and, one by one, he leashed the dogs, all but Bear, pulling them a short distance from the tree and tying them off to saplings. He told Sean to stay with them and keep hold of the leash on Bear. He couldn't tie him to the tree or he'd hang himself trying to get at the cat.

"Give me the gun."

Garrett started fitting a long-barreled flashlight onto a mounting system on the Marlin. "He comes down, whatever you do, don't let go that leash. Even if Bear takes your hand off, don't you let loose. I can't have a dog on a cat before he's dead. I've had a dead mountain lion rip a dog apart."

He sighted down the rifle, the light swirling up the tree trunk. The cat was gone. "What the . . ." Sean heard Garrett say.

Then a shadow seemed to fall from the night sky, and the shadow of the cat met the shadow of the man, and Sean heard a sharp whelping sound and saw Garrett down on the snow. The lion, only its tail visible, was leaping away in great bounds into the ink of the night. The dogs were going crazy.

Sean felt a hard yank as Bear broke free of his grasp and disappeared into the same blackness as the cat.

"What the fuck? I tole you not to let go."

"Are you okay?" Sean shone his light. Garrett's hat had come off and blood was streaming down his face and the back of his head. Sean helped him to his feet.

"Fucking tom got me good. Loose them hounds. I'm gonna catch that bastard it's the last thing I do."

"We've got to get that stitched up," Sean said.

"Do as I say. It's a scratch. Cat was just trying to get away and got a claw caught."

And so the chase resumed. But this time, instead of unfolding in a trancelike way, there was a hard-edged reality to the hunt, the hounds baying and the two men's labored breathing, and the night cold and the snow frozen hard enough on top that they had to post-hole through it. When they stopped to bend over and catch their breath, Sean could see the blood, black in the night, dripping heavily into the snow from the gash in Garrett's head.

"This is crazy, Buster, we gotta get you fixed up."

"What are you, a broken record? Fuck fixed up. It's not like I'm pretty. Not like I don't already have scars on this mug. Come on, now, he's tired, he ain't going up anymore, and he's gonna tree, I can feel it."

And the cat did—it couldn't have been more than a half hour later. This time it had chosen an isolated Ponderosa pine, the trunk as big as a culvert pipe, and Sean tied the hounds back, including Bear, and put his fingers in his ears, waiting for the thunder of the shot. He waited, seeing the shadow of the big houndsman shifting, Garrett angling for his vantage, the gun coming up, and still no shot. He saw Garrett vigorously rub at his face with his arm, and then he was walking to Sean, holding the rifle out. "You gotta take the shot, mate. I can't see for the goddamned blood. Center of chest. Wait till you're sure."

"I've never shot anything in my life."

"Then it's baptism by fire. Take the fucking shot."

Sean found the cat in the circle of light and aligned the sights. His finger found the trigger.

Ka-wham! The butt of the rifle pounded his shoulder. Sean brought the rifle down out of recoil and saw the cat pitch forward, then its claws were scraping at the bark and, turning upside down, it fell a few feet. Then Sean heard a branch crack loudly and the cat was on the ground. The heavy thud as it hit the earth was as final as the closing of a coffin lid.

He ran the beam of his headlamp over the huddled shape under the tree. As the light swarmed up and down, the cat's body became painted with colors—tan, white, the red of blood. Sean jacked another round—a metallic *shuck-shuck*—but the mountain lion was motionless.

"Count to a hundred slow," Garrett said. "You want to make sure."

Sean counted. Then he touched the lion's right eye with the rifle barrel, as he'd seen Martha do after she shot the elk. He crouched and thumbed back the lion's lips.

"It's him, right?"

Sean barely registered the sound of Garrett's voice. "Yeah, it's him," he said.

In the eye of his headlamp beam, Sean could see that the right upper canine was broken short, hardly more than a stub, and was a sickly yellow-brown hue, like the nicotine-stained teeth of a smoker. The other three canines shone white in the moonlight. He also noticed partially healed wounds in several places on the cat's body. *Fights with other tom lions?*

"You don't sound like you're too goddamned happy about it," Garrett said. "Shit, mate, you just saved a life. Hell, maybe a couple. This cat wasn't going to find God. He was going to keep killing. You and me, we're going to be fugging heroes."

Garrett had freed the hounds. "I always like to let the dogs worry a cat once he can't bite back. They earned it."

Sean averted his eyes as the hounds swarmed over the shape of the dead lion, growling, digging into the thick fur with their teeth. He turned his back to the sight. Now that the adrenaline was flushing out of his system, he found that he was moved by the cougar's death, man-eater or not, and he felt hollow and curiously sad.

Garrett slapped him on the back. "Cheer up, chappie—better than sex on a Sunday morning, what say?"

CHAPTER NINETEEN

The Bright Carpet

The headline on the front page of the Tuesday afternoon edition of the *Bridger Mountain Star* was top of the fold.

KILLER CAT KILLED IN CHASE

County Breathes Sigh of Relief

Sean, sitting opposite Martha at her kitchen table, read the lede out loud:

> A mountain lion believed to have killed and partially eaten a woman in the Gravelly Range last November was trailed by hounds Sunday and shot dead. Hyalite County Sheriff Martha Ettinger confirmed that the same animal may also have claimed the lives of one or more

other Montana residents in nearby mountain ranges within the past several months.

Clarice Kincaid, 38, of Mesa, Arizona, and formerly of St. Ignatius, Montana, was killed the night of November 24. Her death caused alarm and some panic among Hyalite County citizens, sparking increased sales of firearms and vigilance over children and pets.

"I'm just happy we got him before someone else lost their life," Ettinger said at a press conference this morning. "We put a lot of man-hours in on this hunt, and for a while there I was afraid the cat had more than nine lives."

The lion was killed after a six-hour chase on Sunday by Buster Garrett, 46, whose four hounds treed the lion in the Wolf Creek drainage of the Madison Range on a ranch owned by well-known Hollywood actor Joshua Byrne. Garrett was accompanied on the trail by private detective Sean Stranahan, 40, a member of the sheriff's task force. The adult male lion weighed 176 pounds and appeared to be in good physical condition, with the exception of a broken canine tooth.

Ettinger said the tooth linked the cat to Kincaid. Her body showed a bite pattern consistent with the injury to the cat's teeth. A DNA analysis will be conducted to verify that the lion is the same one that killed Kincaid.

Ettinger, who spearheaded the task force's hunt, refused to release the names of other possible victims, pending genetic confirmation and notification of next of kin.

"Let's all get a good night's sleep tonight," Ettinger said. "The long nightmare is over."

The story jumped and Sean turned the page to see that he had a photo credit. It was a picture he'd taken with Garrett's cell phone. The photo showed the big man holding up the dead mountain lion in a bear hug, the cat in the foreground in the wide-angle image, which stretched its size, the congealed blood making a horror of Garrett's face. The photo had been taken with a flash and the cat's eyes glowed an eerie green-white.

"I wonder what causes that." Sean's voice was casual. He didn't really expect a reply.

Martha took the paper.

"It's called the *tapetum lucidum*," she said. "It's a layer of cells behind the retina of the eye. The English translation is 'bright carpet.' It helps night vision by bouncing back the image to the retina. The eyes of golden-eyed cats like mountain lions glow green, the eyes of blue-eyed cats, like Siamese, glow red. I came into the house when we had a power outage and there were my two cats looking at me in the beam of the flashlight, Sharmala's eyes green as jade, Sheba's like rubies. I thought I'd stepped into a Stephen King novel."

"But this cat was dead when I took the picture."

"All but its eyes," Martha said. "It watches us even in death."

"This is a morbid conversation."

"What would you rather talk about? The party?"

With three failed marriages between them, they'd agreed upon a simple civil ceremony in June—"fewer people to demand their gifts back," as Martha put it—though she'd acquiesced when Patrick Willoughby, the Madison River Liars and Fly Tiers Club president, offered to host a party for the newlyweds on the clubhouse grounds after the ceremony. A casual affair with fly rods welcome, waders acceptable attire, what with the caddis and *Baetis* mayfly hatches coming into full swing.

Sean smiled. "Anything for you, darling."

"Now you're mocking me."

"No, I'm just having fun with the love of my life."

She looked at him a little askance. "There are times I just don't know what to make of you."

"Am I really forty?" Sean said.

CHAPTER TWENTY

Confessions in a Virgin Mary

Of Montana's four recognizable seasons—mud, fishing, hunting, and skiing—it is mud season, roughly that interval between early March and late May, that moves most slowly and has the least to recommend it. Many weeks had passed after the lion's demise when Georgeanne Wilkerson received the genetic test results performed on the toes found in the mountain lion's regurgitation. It was not the news she might have hoped for.

In a phone call with Martha Ettinger, Wilkerson explained that digestion of genetic material begins in the stomach, not in the small intestine, as was previously believed. The DNA found in the human toes had been degraded by pepsin, a stomach enzyme, to the point where it was no longer useful for comparative purposes.

"I'm sorry," she said. "I know that's not what you wanted to hear."

"What will I tell her?" Martha asked aloud, after she'd switched off the phone. The question was rhetorical. She'd tell Miriam Ross the truth, that forensic science could neither confirm nor deny that a lion had eaten the flesh of her son. And so the closure the woman desired would remain elusive.

But Miriam Ross's personal nightmare was not the mood of the valley. It emerged from the winter darkness as a bear emerges from winter's sleep, gradually, with blurred eyes and a cautiously snuffing nose—a bit of muck-up around the barn at an hour when none would dare be so bold only weeks before, a long-dormant snowmobile clearing its throat for one last hurrah, a fly rod assembled for the first time in months to catch whitefish for the smoker.

The boys who played night hockey on the frozen tennis court in Bridger, and who had been forced indoors by the threat of the lion, cleared the snow off the last of the good ice and chose sides for the first time since the rink had frozen, with nothing but bent sticks and testosterone to protect them.

And so, as the slipstream of routine chased the past into perspective, into a story, the transformation between dark and light, between winter's dread and spring's promise, was complete. Perhaps memories would have been longer had the victim been more significant. But who was she, really—only a hooker mourned by no one. If anything, it was the mountain lion's stature that rose in the weeks following his death. He had given people who led comfortable lives a taste of primal fear, a thrilling glimpse into a time when the land was ruled by tooth and claw and man rolled boulders against the cave mouth and cowered within. And then he had conveniently made his departure, and just in time to pacify the Chamber of Commerce, where the phones were no longer ringing off the hook.

Life had returned to normal.

For all, that is, except Buster Garrett, whom Sean bumped into one day at the Ace Hardware. Garrett, with Sean's blessing, had taken the larger share of the credit for treeing and killing the cat, becoming a minor celebrity in the valley. He'd even been the focus of an online feature in *Field & Stream* titled "Hunt for a Man-Eater." Garrett told Sean that he couldn't stick his head into any bar in southwest Montana without someone standing him a drink. Too bad, he said, that all he drank these days were O'Doul's near beer and nonalcoholic cocktails. He'd offered to buy Sean one at the bar off the lobby in the Bridger Mountain Cultural Center. Told Sean that Robin, who owned the joint, made the best Virgin Marys in the valley. They each had one. Garrett dabbed at his lips with a napkin.

"Remember how I told you that our fight made me take a long look at myself, that I started going to AA just a few weeks later?"

"I remember."

"That's only part of why I turned around. Something happened around that time—I couldn't forgive myself for it. Changed my life." He took another drink. "Seven hundred seventy-seven days ago."

"You know the exact number?"

He nodded and stared into his glass. "Seven, seven, seven," he said. "My wife tells me it's an angel number. It means I'm going down the right path now. I had been going down the wrong path and this was a low point. Or some mumbo-jumbo. She believes in angels, crystals, all that kind of stuff."

"I thought you two had split up."

"We did, we didn't. Ties that bind, you know. We still have a few."

"What happened seven hundred seventy-seven days ago?"

"What happened?" Repeated the words quietly to himself. "What happened is that I created a monster."

"No, you slayed the monster. We did."

He shook his head. "Do you know *Beowulf*?"

"Only that it's a legend or something."

"It's an epic poem, the oldest written story in English literature. Man versus nature. Beowulf is a hero from a mythical land called in to slay a monster. Monster's name is Grendel. He kills him, then finds that his job isn't finished, that in killing one monster he has raised another from its slumber."

"What are you talking about? I thought you Aussies were straight shooters."

"I'm sorry for being cryptic. Blame it on sobriety. If there was some Stoli in these Marys, I'd be confessing with tears in my eyes. But the end of the story hasn't been written yet. I'll tell you when I write it. If I'm the one who does. Maybe it won't be me. Maybe it will be you." He shrugged. "You must be thinking I'm a crazy bugger. Maybe when we get to know each other better. Hey," he said, "here's to being a mate."

They touched glasses. Sean said, "And here's to the lion. May he rest in cougar heaven."

"Said like a goddamned pacifist," Garrett said. "But you know"—his voice became reflective—"I admire them, the buggers, it's their mountains more than mine, and it's getting harder to hunt them in good conscience. I used to think that cherry-picking the older males was good wildlife management. But it just throws a wrench into the natural order and leaves a void. Sometimes that void gets filled by something it shouldn't. Give me another year and I'll be eating granola like all the rest of the ecos. I'm already drinking the Kool-Aid." He laughed and drained the drink.

It was strange enough. Sean had once hit the houndsman so hard that he'd broken the fifth metacarpal bone on the middle finger of his right hand. It was still misshapen, still throbbed in rainy weather, and yet in the echo of the shot that had bound them together, the men had become the most improbable of friends. Well, that was life, Sean thought. You couldn't script it with a cleaver.

"Stand you another," Garrett said.

CHAPTER TWENTY-ONE

Death in the Afternoon

The Saturday before Mother's Day, Sean accompanied Sam Meslik on the five-hour drive to the Flathead Reservation for a belated memorial for Clarice Kincaid. The late date, more than five months after the cremation in early December, had been chosen so that her father could attend. At the time of his daughter's death, he had been in the county lockup for possession with intent and resisting arrest, which had been knocked down to possession and disturbing the peace, and he had been released with time served and a stint of rehab. So turned the revolving door of jurisprudence for Montana's addicted.

The ceremony was held in the St. Ignatius Mission under the soaring peaks of the Mission Mountains, still mantled with snow. It was a somber affair in a gorgeous edifice, the interior of the mission highlighted with more than fifty murals, a poor man's Sistine Chapel.

Whites and Indians alike parked their muddy boots at the door and chose different sides of the aisle. Sean counted thirty heads, not much in the way of expression on the faces. All had witnessed far too many deaths associated with drug use. After the ceremony, Sam introduced Sean to Clarice's parents, the father narrow-faced with a balding head, wearing a Western snap shirt with frayed cuffs and a bolo tie. "My getting out of the clink" attire, he said, a joke that fell flat and no one laughed at but him.

The mother was dark-haired with silver roots over an oval face, a once-attractive woman. But the lifeblood had drained out of her long ago, and her mouth pinched up in vertical wrinkles—a smoker's mouth that had forgotten how to do much more than draw one down and then the next.

Sean walked over to a table arranged with photos of the family during happier times, saw Clarice peering shyly from behind her mother's skirts outside a freshly painted one-story rancher, saw her playing volleyball for Ronan High School, digging one out down on her knees, an Indian headdress sprouting from an orange R on her team jersey. In another photo, she wore a lavender dress as she posed with her prom date. Pretty then, a slip of a thing, with an unforced smile for the camera.

You join teams with the dead, Martha had said. *You wear their colors.* Now Sean knew the colors.

One person seemed to have stepped into the mission from a bygone era. He was thin to the point of being gaunt and was dressed in a Western shirt with piping and diamond snaps, a paisley silk scarf, and a tweed vest. He wore a pocket watch on a fob, the chain hanging just so. When he took off his black flat-brimmed Stetson, you could see where the band had rested on his forehead. Under his nostrils was a mustache that looked like two mice kissing, their long tails curled and waxed. A man who lived and breathed the old West, the one that never was.

Sean thought to talk to him, no reason but curiosity, but the man quickly left the church after the ceremony, buttoning up a waxed cotton duster and squaring his hat. The last Sean saw of him, he was in a white pickup driving away. Arizona plates. Sean asked Clarice's mother about him—he'd seen the two talking earlier.

"Wyatt Bryce," she told him. An old boyfriend of Clarice's, before the only love interest she knew came with a syringe. She'd met him in Tombstone at a reenactment of the Gunfight at the O.K. Corral. He was playing the part of Billy Clanton, who died in a hail of gunfire in a shootout with the Earp brothers. Wyatt had picked Clarice up after the morning show, asking her to lunch and telling her not to worry—if she didn't like him, well, he'd be catching a bullet in the heart at two o'clock and die once more at four. Death in the afternoon. Easy come, easy go.

That's what Clarice had liked about him, Mrs. Kincaid told Sean. He had that sense of humor. And the manners, just courteous as he could be. He was a catch, that's what he was.

"He gave me these."

Mrs. Kincaid opened her purse and extracted three letters that had her name on them, but no stamps or address. Wyatt had told her that Clarice wrote letters almost every day in the eighteen months they'd been together, but to his knowledge she had never sent any to anyone. He'd thought she might like to read excerpts from them at the memorial, but when the time came, she'd lost her nerve. She said that Wyatt had driven all day and night and then some, Tucson to Polson, Montana, and had given her the letters only a couple of hours ago.

"It gives me some comfort," she said. "It does. She said some nice things in these letters, and I'll cherish them. But you tell me, why did she have to get on that stuff? Why couldn't she have stayed with him and made babies, have a life? You tell me that? Why couldn't she have stayed with him? He'd have married her, too, he even asked her. Why couldn't she?" She clutched the letters tight to her chest. "Why?"

Sean had no answer. He pressed her hand and walked out into the bright sunshine, where Sam was polishing off a paper plate of cold ham, potato salad, and deviled eggs. He heard Sean out, wiped at his mouth, shrugged.

"Blast from the past, Kemosabe. Back when cooking was something you did to make food. Come on, get yourself some ham and let's vamoose this joint. It's depressing."

On the drive back, they stopped at the Blue River Station in Seeley Lake, an old-fashioned soda fountain, so that Sam could get a malt and play the half-broken, coin-operated tabletop baseball game. While he struck out and swore, Sean saw that he had a message on his phone from Martha, and stepped outside to punch the call back.

"How far out are you?"

"Ah . . . four hours," Sean said. "What's up, Martha?"

"A sheepherder seems to have lost his sheep."

Waiting for her to elaborate, Sean heard a muffled whoop behind the shop's heavy door—Sam, presumably, smacking one out of the park.

Martha elaborated. A part-time Madison Valley resident who co-owned a house on the upper Madison River had heard shots in the night, thought little enough of it, this being Montana. Then, a few days later, he opened the door to find forty sheep in the yard. The man put the sheep together with the shots and called the county dispatch.

"And this adds up to foul play somehow? When did it happen?"

"The shots? Let me look at the printout. Ah, last Tuesday. Four days ago. The sheep showed up on the property yesterday. I got in touch with the managers of both ranches that the herder works for. Was told it was nothing to worry about, that the combined flock ran to seven hundred, including a hundred and twenty Rambouillets that had a tendency to stray."

"We got the right cat, Martha, if that's what you're thinking. Broken fang and all."

"Not saying you didn't. Not saying this has anything to do with cats. But I thought you might want to check it out, seeing that the call came from your pals' clubhouse. One of your cronies."

"Why didn't you tell me that in the first place?"

"Because I'm telling you now."

"Which crony?"

"Max Gallagher."

Gallagher was a crime novelist who sometimes used the Madison River Liars and Fly Tiers clubhouse as a writing retreat, usually in the "R" months.

"Another thing," Martha said. "One of the ranches this guy tended for is owned by Miriam Ross. The mother of the boy who went AWOL last fall. You know how I feel about coincidence."

"Then I'll check it out."

"You want me to give him a heads-up?"

"Gallagher? No, I'll call from the road."

He told Martha he'd swing by the clubhouse after dropping Sam in Ennis, said good-bye, and put his head back inside the store.

Sam gave him a pointy-toothed grin. "I got my swing back, Kemosabe. Top of the seventh and I'm up by two."

"Game's over," Sean said.

Over, he thought, *or starting again?*

CHAPTER TWENTY-TWO

Night of the Nagual

With his bloodshot eyes and Colgate smile, his shirt unbuttoned to show a cowlick of chest hair as black as a hitter's heart, Max Gallagher looked like Clark Gable halfway into a bottle of tequila, or Satan gone to seed.

He waved from the porch as Sean's Land Cruiser growled up in second gear.

"Painter man, fishing guide, gumshoe, thief," Gallagher said by way of greeting. His voice was thick.

"Guilty on three counts," Sean said. "Not sure what I stole, though."

"Neither am I, but I'm a scribbler and 'thief' fits the meter. Come on in. If you'd got here this morning, you'd have had to straddle sheep to get to the door, but they went back up into the hills. You shouldn't have much trouble finding them. But those shots were like four days ago. If they meant anything else except old Cesar scaring away some coyotes that got too chummy, then he's beyond succor now. Forgive the archaic word. I'm writing—my vocabulary tends to expand."

They went inside and Gallagher poured coffee. "You want it black or with a happy ending, I forget."

"Black. Tell me about this herder. How did you meet him?"

"Last summer I got into the habit of taking a hike in the afternoon to clear my head. He had his sheep up Bobcat Creek and was living out of a wagon like you'd have seen on the Oregon Trail. Hitch it up with a horse and pull it to new pasture every couple weeks or so."

"Does he speak English? Martha said he was from Peru."

"Not so much. But I used to write pilots in Español and do some series work for Mexican TV, still my fallback. Cesar, the old man's alone with his dogs about eight months of the year, only moves the herd back to the low country dead of winter. Once the ewes are sheared and the lambing's done, it's back to the hills."

"Does he have a family?"

"Wife and three kids. Sends all his money home. Makes twelve hundred a month on a three-year visa. Said in Peru he'd be lucky to make a hundred a month for the same work. He wants to become a dentist, of all things, and him with like six teeth missing. I call him an old man but he's not more than forty, I would think. The life he leads ages you quick."

"Tell me about it, his life."

"Well, the work's twenty-four/seven. He spends days with the herd, keeping the sheep together, he sleeps nights in a wall tent, grabs the gun when the dogs growl, drives away anything with teeth."

"I thought you said he lived in a wagon."

"A wagon after the mud dries out. Somebody from the ranch brought the tent up on a four-wheeler."

"Does he have a horse?"

"No horse. He's on foot."

"What else should I know?"

"The dogs are the main thing. He's got four border collies—they work the sheep and spend the night by the tent. They might give you a little lip, but that's all. But he's got two akbash guard dogs that are with the herd round the clock. They wear spiked collars to protect them from wolves and they'll take your hand off if you try to pet one, or, God forbid, touch one of the sheep. Major league gringo deterrent."

He nodded to himself.

"One more thing about the sheep, they're all white except for six. Those six are black. They're the markers. You count all six, then the herd is together. You see that one or two are missing, that means the herd is broken and it's time to round them up. That's another thing worries me. There was one black sheep in the yard. Cesar was vigilant. He took his job seriously. He would have seen one was missing and gone looking for the strays."

"Did he say anything about seeing a lion?"

"Thought you'd ask that, and no. But he had an interesting take on them. His family's from Lake Titicaca—that's in the Andes. But he has an uncle who grew up on the Amazon River who would visit and talk about naguals, you know, shape-shifters. Everybody had an animal they could change into, which one depending on the day of their birth. Cesar was born on the day of the puma, so, growing up, he identified with them. He even had the head of a puma tattooed on his chest. He never really tried to become one because you have to make a pact with the devil to change form. The irony was that as a sheepherder he was at war with the cats. His heart was conflicted."

"You know a lot about him."

"Guy like Cesar, five thousand miles from home, he finds someone speaks his language, he's got a lot to say. Cesar is very spiritual. We talked some deep shit. He refused to believe his spirit animal could threaten his life, so he wasn't worried, even though he knew about the woman being killed. But he had his dogs to protect him, and he put a lot of store in them. Between the dogs and Jesus, he had his ass covered. I'm thinking about putting him in my next book. Hey, you know, I'll go up there with you if you want me to. I know the country and I won't get in the way."

He has the look of a man who wants to be talked out of it, Sean thought.

Sean smiled. "Best if I go alone. I can get up there and back by dark if I hurry. Just give me a starting point. If I come across any lions, I'll ask if they speak Spanish."

"You joke, but that shape-shifting shit, Cesar took it for real."

FORTY MINUTES AFTER PARKING the rig at a Forest Service trailhead a quarter mile from the clubhouse, Sean found the greater part of the herd. They were in rolling, semi-open country beyond the national forest boundary, three black sheep in a sea of white, but no dogs, which gave him his first inkling that something could be wrong. He walked into the herd, the sheep parting for him. As they moved, the ground underneath was obscured by a spreading carpet of wool. Ahead, Sean could see where the sheep stopped and the land picked up again. He found himself backtracking on a funneling trail, where thin snow cover and mud had been chewed up by thousands of hooves. Sean followed a beaten arrow of earth over a low ridge and across a swale. The wall tent was pitched in a stand of aspens, the leaves long gone to ground, the gray trunks scarred where elk had eaten the bark.

Sean moved cautiously forward, speaking in a low voice so as not to alarm the dogs, if in fact they were within hearing. The tent flap had a series of ties, untied, and was like a door to an empty room. You knew nobody was home before you reached for the knob. Not much furnishing—a cot, a table, a sheepherder's stove, cold to the touch. A gas lantern, a Jesus in a picture frame. A short-wave radio. A Bible. The bones of a meager existence.

All the snow at this elevation had melted. Plenty of tracks—dog, man, sheep—all a muddy mess. He began to walk in circles around the tent, each larger than the last, and had made four circles when he came upon a deeply worn trail. Turning onto the trail, he came to a latrine that consisted of a folding shovel and a roll of toilet paper on a branch stub. A few yards away was a muddy depression threaded by a six-inch creek. Sean followed it a few yards and found what he was looking for and at the same time dreading to see. Pugmarks. Not a bobcat's. They were too big. They were lion tracks, not as large as the tracks of the big tom that had killed Kincaid, but lion tracks all the same. Nearby on the ground was a scoped rifle. Sean turned it in his hands. It was a .270 Weatherby Vanguard with a four-round magazine. The magazine was full, with a live round in the chamber. The safety was in the "on" position.

Gallagher had told Sean that he'd heard five shots spaced irregularly over the course of a minute or so. It was about an hour after dark and he'd been free-associating at the typewriter, drinking a Cognac and hoping for lightning to strike, literarily speaking. Sean had asked him what he'd done after hearing the shots and Gallagher said he'd shut the window and poured another brandy.

Assuming the rifle was fully loaded when he took it to the latrine, the sheepherder had apparently fired all the rounds, then had time to reload before the cat was upon him. This struck Sean as odd. If you empty your rifle and the teeth keep coming, you jam one cartridge into the chamber and shoot. You don't take the time to reload the magazine. And you certainly don't put the safety back on. He looked around for empties but didn't find any. Also odd.

Don't draw conclusions, he told himself. Follow the evidence at hand.

The evidence at hand consisted of a dozen or so lion tracks. Sean tried to follow them, but they were indistinct and days old, and the trail petered out where the tracks left the creek bottom and crossed open ground, where they had been degraded by the elements. Unable to follow them for more than a few yards, Sean returned to the latrine. Lots of boot prints here, but only one line of human tracks continued on toward the forest wall. Sean had taken no more than a few steps on this trail before he heard a low growl. He froze. He heard the growl again, this time picked up by a chorus. Colors flashed between tree trunks, then the collies were on him, three false-charging, their lips pulled back, their teeth exposed, while the fourth, staying back, worried a mound of tan material.

The closer Sean approached, the more agitated the dogs became, so he sat down on a log to reduce his height and, hopefully, his threat. The dogs would bound toward him, then veer around, circling, darting forward to nip at his boots, then pulling back. Sean was good with dogs, even better when he had venison jerky in his pocket. After more feints and circling and a couple bits of jerky apiece, two of the three collies that had been nipping at him joined the other dog by the tan material. A jacket?

A dip in the terrain partly obscured the dogs and, as Sean watched, a human arm rose from the tan mound and a hand waved, seeming to beckon to him. The arm and hand were bare. The arm seemed to shiver, then it flopped to the ground, out of sight.

Sean's mind registered three conclusions in rapid succession. One, whoever the arm belonged to was dead. Two, the limp limb was an indication either that rigor mortis had not yet occurred, and that the person had been dead for only a few hours, or that the rigor had passed and the stiff muscles had relaxed. He would have put money on the latter, based on the forty sheep that had strayed so far afield, and guessing that the herder had probably died the night that Max Gallagher heard the shots. Sean's third thought was that his initial assessment of the situation, that the dogs were protecting the body of their master, was wrong. The dogs had blood on their muzzles. They weren't protecting the body. They were eating it.

PART TWO

THE BANGTAIL GHOST

CHAPTER TWENTY-THREE

Sinew and Bone

As it watched the plume of exhaust exhaled by the metallic bird that passed between the dawn clouds, the cat drew back its lips in quest of scent. For a moment, a fire danced in its eyes, and the long tail that made a question mark flicked from one side to the other.

Dropping its head, the cat returned its attention to the house nestled into a fold in the foothills. In the half-light, for the Earth below the sky still slept, the one color the cat's eyes registered was yellow. As it watched, one of the yellow squares that marked the windows of the house went dark, only to reappear in another location. The cat had anticipated this, having watched the routine of the lights for five mornings as it had grown both steadily bolder and incrementally weaker.

The next light to appear would be the dome light of the truck squatting in the drive. The cat heard the motor cough to life, and as the orbs of the headlights searched down the graveled drive toward the ranch gate, the cat shrank back from where it had taken cover behind the root ball of a fallen tree. It lay motionless but for the last six inches of its tail, which flicked against the ground.

Then the bright eyes of the truck swept past the cat's position, the truck a blocky silhouette, and the motor idled down and stopped, and the smaller rear eyes blinked shut. The cat waited for the human to step out of the truck. On some mornings this wait was short and on others longer. This was one of the longer times, as the cat, watching the shadow in the driver's seat, saw the outline of a head move up and down and heard snatches of submerged music that was not the song of birds, the only music besides the running of rivers that it had ever known. It heard the music now, the notes faint and foreign to its ears, and saw the head moving to the rhythm, and waited for the music to stop and the door to open and the human to step outside.

If the routine had not altered, the human would bend down for a long few moments on the far side of the vehicle and be out of sight. Then the truck door would shut and the human would come into view over the hood as it walked a few steps to a gate that consisted of weathered posts strung with barbed wire.

Reaching the gate, the human would use the cheater lever that squeaked as it drew the post far enough back to create the slack needed to slip the wire loop over the top of the post. Then, with practiced movements, the human would step through the V opening created by the slack and replace the wire loop over the post top. It would go to stand at the side of the oiled road and shift its weight from one foot to the other as its head was enveloped by the clouds of its breath and the morning gradually painted the night away into lighter shades.

Five minutes, then ten, the landscape yawning, no sound any-where. Then a faint rumbling as the bus came up, first heard and then seen coming over a rise, the bus seeming to grow as it slowed to a stop, the hinged stop sign levered out, the diesel engine idling, the fuel smell and the ratchet of the folding door and the human would climb the two steps into the dark interior and the bus would grind away into the progress of the day.

All this time, beginning when she was a shadow moving her head to the beat of the music on the radio and ending only after the bus door shut and she went to sit with her best friend, Jess, fourteen-year-old Marci Mirecourt did not know she had been stalked by a cat. Nor did she know it was starving, its right foreleg withered, its lithe, powerful body reduced to sinew and pain and bone, or that in failing to follow through with its intent to satisfy its hunger on this day, it would of a certainty try again the next.

She did not know that an angel of death had descended from the mountains, and that with the cessation of one fear, another had be-gun, haunting the land like a dark wind. And that this time, the terror had a name—the "Bangtail Ghost."

CHAPTER TWENTY-FOUR

The Good Shepherd

Martha Ettinger slapped the afternoon edition of the *Bridger Mountain Star* on the kitchen table in front of Sean's cup of coffee. The stories that prompted this reaction were second-day news—yesterday's paper had reported only the known facts, that a sheepherder had been killed in the Gravelly Range, apparently by a predator, and that mountain lion tracks had been found in the vicinity. Martha had been quoted as saying that valley residents should take precautions, but that the identity of the predator was not confirmed. The new stories included details that had not been released by authorities, specifically that the victim had been eaten by his own dogs, and also stepped over the official line by giving the suspected killer a name.

The big tomcat that had killed Clarice Kincaid had gone by several names. The list included the "Madison Valley Mauler," the "Specimen Ridge Man-eater," "Old Broken Tooth," and the "Silicone Canyon

Man-eater"—someone having leaked that the cat had excised one of its victim's breast implants with its claws. None of the names had been acceptable to Martha, who hated trigger words, especially those that triggered panic.

Sean had suggested that this time she preempt matters by naming the new cat herself. She'd come up with the "Bangtail Ghost." The Bangtails were an isolated mountain range in the north of Hyalite County. Closer to home, a trickle of water known by locals as Bangtail Sally Creek tinkled out of the Tobacco Root Mountains. Then, too, in eighteenth-century England, a "bangtail" was a prostitute, and the creek had been named for one of the more notorious madams who serviced gold miners in the 1860s. Clarice Kincaid being in the trade, the name made sense.

"Sounds good to me," Sean said. He'd added yet another caveat. A "bangtail" was the name for a horse whose tail was cut straight across, as was Martha's Appaloosa mare.

So it was settled. Martha had introduced the name at the emergency meeting of the task force the day before. Less than twenty-four hours later, Gail Stocker, the *Star*'s reporter, had put it in print, attributing it to a source close to the hunt for the cat.

What grated on Martha was not so much that Stocker had appropriated the name, her name, but that someone in the task force had to have leaked it.

"It's like she can read your mind," Sean said, a teasing note in his voice.

Martha said, "Yeah. That and she's screwing someone on the task force. I wonder who it could be. Wait a second. Anyone. They're all men but me."

"So I'm a suspect, too?"

"You're top of the list."

"You got to admit, Martha, she looks good in her Wranglers."

"I don't *got* to admit anything. She's a munchkin. Take off the hat and she's so short you have to pick her up so she can drink out of a fountain. Yeah, yeah, I know, not PC. So sue me."

But it wasn't the release of the name that really upset her. It was one of the three sidebar stories. The first was a biography of the victim as far as it was known, and noted the financial and emotional plight of Peruvian herders in general. The second was an interview with a survival expert who talked about dogs eating their own- ers. Apparently, a canid reacted to starvation no differently than a hominid from the Donner party. It was the third story that Martha deemed inflammatory, in that it focused on naguals and the victim's kinship with pumas. The reporter had even been privy to the infor- mation that the herder had a puma tattooed on his chest.

"Just what I need," Martha told Sean, "a bunch of shape-shifters growing claws and howling when the moon comes up."

Sean knew the source of this last story, and wondered if Gail Stocker had somehow known to contact Max Gallagher, or, more likely, if it had been the other way around. But he kept his mouth shut. No need to add fuel to the flame of Martha's already consider- able ire.

Instead, he finished his coffee, kissed her on the top of her head as she bent over the paper—"I love you, anyway"—and took his day pack from the nail in the mudroom. Buster Garrett had been a no- show at the task-force meeting, but Drick Blake was a surprise at- tendee, and he had offered to hike up to the scene of the attack to see if he could spot anything that the WHART team had overlooked. Martha had grudgingly given consent, on the condition that Sean accompany him.

A little less than two hours after Sean left Martha's farmhouse, the olive Rover Sean had seen parked outside Blake's yurt grumbled to a stop before a locked Forest Service gate where the two had arranged to meet. Sean hadn't seen Blake for months, and he had grown a beard that partially shrouded the puttylike appearance of his cheeks. With his pelt of body hair hidden behind clothes, he was, Sean had to admit, a good-looking man. Even the broadened nose, which his sister had said was the result of cosmetic surgery to make the face more catlike, merged seamlessly with the accentuated bone structure of his face. Blake might not be able to complete a transformation into a spirit animal, but he had a good start on it.

With little in the way of greeting, they began to hike toward the open park where Sean had backtracked the sheep herd. Except for a few chips of bright color that were male bluebirds squabbling over nesting sites, and a pair of vultures circling idly above a treeless knob in the distance, the basin seemed devoid of life. Apparently, another herder employed by one of the ranches had moved the sheep to a different pasture. But it was the absence of the two guard dogs, which no one had seen over the past several days, that piqued Sean's interest. Where had they gone? For that matter, where had they been when he discovered the body?

Reaching the wall tent, Sean pointed out the few possessions that served only to emphasize the emptiness.

"A lonely existence," Blake offered. He picked up the Bible and turned to a passage marked by a silk ribbon.

"Juan Dies," he said. And speaking in Spanish, "I say unto thee, he who does not enter the sheepfold by the door, but climbs up some other way is a thief and a robber. But he who enters by the door is the shepherd of the sheep."

He smiled at the question in Sean's eyes.

"I was part of a jaguar study in Belize. The Cockscomb Basin

Wildlife Sanctuary. Either learn the language or scream with the howler monkeys."

Back outside, Sean led the way to the latrine. "I don't know what you're thinking we'll find," he told Blake. "Buster Garrett told me that four days is about the limit for the hounds to trail. We're past that."

Blake nodded. "As far as that goes. But if I can find a physical track, then I can identify the cat a week from now, or a year. You said you saw pugmarks. Where exactly?"

Sean showed him the muddy depression where he'd seen the lion tracks, but they had been obliterated by rain, as he suspected they would be.

"What happened to Buster, anyway?" Blake said.

"The sheriff has tried to reach him at least a couple times. Apparently he's off the grid."

"You might try his ex. He still lives at the house part of the time. Or did. I haven't seen him since that day at Law and Justice. Hazel sanded the rough edges to make him presentable, and give her all the credit, but Buster is an alcoholic, and he has a mean streak. He's a guy you tiptoe around for your own good. Hell of a houndsman, I'll give him that."

Sean nodded. "Come on," he said, "I'll show you the kill site. It's just over the rise. But the WHART guys will have picked it clean, I'm afraid."

He was right. All the bits and pieces of the body that the dogs hadn't eaten had been carted away and rain had washed the ground clean.

They decided to split up and search farther afield. Sean headed toward the knob where he'd seen the vultures circling earlier, while Blake hiked downhill toward the closest heavy cover, the natural line of retreat if the cat had been driven away from the kill site by the dogs.

The buzzards were no longer in sight, but as Sean reached the top of the knob, the country beyond came into view and he saw them, bald-headed, heavy-bodied, ungainly, as they rose with a great fanfare of flapping, then, steadied, sailed away on their spread wings. The smell would have given him the answer if his eyes hadn't. It was a dog, or had been, much of it having been devoured by scavengers. Its coat was the color of the camel-hair coat Sean's mom used to wear to church. He could see the spikes in the dog's collar glinting in the sunlight. Another pile of blood and bone was farther down the hill, and for a few hopeful moments Sean thought it could be a lion. The color was right, but the furry extremity Sean took for a tail turned out, on closer inspection, to be a branch covered in dried moss. It was the other akbash.

The bodies of both animals had been scavenged so completely that Sean knew it would be difficult to determine cause of death. He saw no apparent fang marks on the throats, or on the dogs' muzzles, as there would be if a lion clamped down on the nose to suffocate them. For that matter, he doubted that the lion would have taken on the dogs. One, perhaps, but the two together?

He heard footsteps as Blake came down from the knob behind him.

"What do we have here?" he said. It was not a question that required an answer and Sean gave none. Blake knelt down and passed his hands over the flanks of the nearer dog. If the odor bothered him, he didn't let it show.

"What do you think?"

"If I had to guess?" Blake said. "Poison. Poison or a bullet. I don't see any marks to suggest a lion did this."

"How old?"

He shrugged. "My eyes tell me a week. My nose tells me more. Why don't you have a look at this one while I check out the other."

He went down the hill, and once more Sean thought back to his talk with Max Gallagher. The writer recalled hearing five shots. Sean had assumed that the shots were fired by the herder while he was trying to protect himself from an attack by a lion. It had bothered him that the rifle he found nearby was fully loaded. That meant the herder had fired all the rounds that Gallagher had heard, and then had reloaded, but had not had the opportunity to shoot again before the lion killed him. It made more sense that the herder had never had time to fire even once before the animal was on top of him, and that all the shots Max Gallagher had heard were fired by someone else trying to protect himself from the guard dogs.

Sean knelt beside the dead akbash. He knew that bullets often expended their energy inside the body and came to rest under the skin on the off side from the entrance wound, not retaining enough oomph to exit. He began to pass his hands over the dog and felt what Blake had missed, a small lump under the skin of one of the hindquarters. He prised the skin apart with his knife. It was a bullet, all right, mushroomed and misshapen. The intact part of the slug was approximately as big around as Sean's ring finger between the two joints. It had been fired from either a large-caliber handgun, such as a .44, or a similarly bored rifle.

Sean showed the slug to Blake when he came back up the hill.

"Maybe a horn hunter shot the dogs," Blake said, "somebody scouring the winter range for shed elk antlers." He rubbed his fingers together to indicate cash. Freshly shed antlers were worth good money, and in the spring the lower elevations crawled with young men looking for a windfall.

Sean nodded. It was a reasonable assumption, but he remained unconvinced. Most shed hunters carried bear spray, but relatively few burdened themselves with weapons. More likely, he thought, that it was a bear hunter. Spring bear season was open until the end of the month and a bear hunter would be adequately armed to deal with angry dogs.

Sean pocketed the slug. Returning to the site where the herder had been killed, they decided to give it one more hour, which turned into two, and were finally ready to head back to the rigs when Sean noticed what looked like a tan shoelace. It was partly hidden under damp leaf litter midway between the primitive latrine and the kill site. Sean had searched the ground in between when they'd first arrived, and didn't see how he could have missed it. But miss it he had, and, stooping to pick it up, he saw that what appeared to be a shoelace was actually a loop of rawhide. The rawhide had been threaded through a hole in the cartilage sheath that attached to a curved claw. It was a good luck talisman. It wasn't the first time he'd seen it. The first time it had been around Buster Garrett's neck.

He glanced up. Blake was twenty yards away, his back turned, his eyes on the ground. Sean almost called out, then caught himself. It was not so much that he didn't want to share the find. Rather, he wanted time to process it without the distraction of another opinion. He could always tell Blake that he'd come back by himself the following day. He folded his hand around the pendant and put it away as Blake walked over. They called it a day, and Sean hiked out through the evening gloom with more questions than answers, the biggest one scratching at his chest under his breast pocket.

CHAPTER TWENTY-FIVE

A Man's Brain, a Horse's Hoof, and a Dog's Nose

On the third morning after the discovery of the remains of Cesar Rodriguez, Martha was sitting in her office chair, a half dozen paper airplanes on her desk folded from one-dollar bills, a grim set to her face, her hands laced behind her head.

The past two days had been unproductive, as far as discovering the whereabouts of the cat deemed responsible. That a mountain lion was the guilty party was now a certainty. Saliva samples taken from the body were DNA-matched to the species, and precise measurements of the puncture wounds in the man's throat and the back of the head showed the lion to be considerably smaller than the big tom Garrett and Sean had dispatched. A female, perhaps, or a younger male.

Garrett had still not returned her phone calls, which bothered her, especially with Sean having found his pendant at the site of the herder's death. *What the hell has he been up to?*

Martha had contacted the Dusan brothers, who were of limited help, assuring her of what she already knew, that a trail a week or more old wasn't worth following. Ike, the older brother, added that in the northern Rockies, cats were located by driving roads after a snowfall or coursing snow-packed trails by four-wheeler or snow machine, and only loosing the hounds when a fresh trail was cut. By mid-May, what you really needed were cold-nosed hounds that could trail over rock and rubble. He gave her a number with a Pecos, New Mexico, area code. Cecil Flowers, he assured her, had the best hounds in the Southwest. She'd called the number and left a message, which Flowers had returned that very morning.

Hell, yes, his hounds could track over bare ground. Why, shit, he could train a Pekingese to tree a lion in two feet of snow. His voice had a rasp.

Would he help?

He named a figure.

"We're a small Montana county," Martha countered, and suggested cutting the figure in half.

"Hope your cat doesn't kill anybody else," he said, and hung up.

She said "Fuck you" to the room and called him back. He had her over a barrel.

He said he'd hit the road the next morning, and that it would take him three days. "I don't put the pedal to the metal the way I done when I was eighty."

Eighty?

He added that she needed to buy a bottle of perfume, Calvin Klein's Obsession—none other would do. He said it was like catnip to a lion.

"Great," Martha said, after they disconnected. She wondered if the Dusan brothers were just getting back at her for their dog being killed the previous winter.

MARTHA WAS ROLLING a dart in her fingers when the door opened. No knock, which meant it was Walter Hess, her undersheriff, who acted as if he owned the place.

"Hold it right there." Martha's arm shot forward. The dart quivered. "Gotcha, you dirtbag."

The dart had pierced the eye of a bank robber whom optimistic parents had named Archibald Sterling III; he squinted at her from one of the wanted posters pinned to her office wall.

"Jesus, Marth, you want to be careful with those things," Hess said. "You could put an eye out." He was bony and thin, with an Adam's apple as nervous as a gopher in a badger dream.

"Marth, I got a woman here says she won't talk to anyone but you."

"Well, shoo her in, Walt. Shoo her in."

The woman who came through the door wore a Carhartt jacket frayed at the seams and jeans tucked into mud boots. She was an ash blonde with split ends and a center part, with comma-creased cheeks under wiry eyebrows and a thin nose. One of those windswept women who confront the world with arms crossed under a small bosom while looking out across the prairie. Everything about her dry and dusty but the sparkle of her eyes.

Martha felt the hard clasp of calloused fingers.

"Nice to meet you, Ms.—"

"Just Hazel is fine."

"Hazel, how can I be of service?"

"My husband's missing."

"I know." A beat of silence. "Ms. Garrett—Hazel—I've been trying to reach you for three days. Also your ex-husband."

"I know. I got your calls. I just figured he'd come back and then he'd be mad I called and said he was missing. That's Buster—he's his own man. Going out for days at a time, never saying where, no word till I hear the truck coming up. You learn to live with it. You have to."

"I thought you were divorced. He's still in the house?"

"We never signed the papers, easier all around. He's turned the corner on a lot of things, Buster has. Keeps wanting to move back in. Says we can be friends without benefits till I decide. He's been hanging round a couple months now, sober as a church mouse. But I don't know, I just don't know. He's still thinking about some other woman—you can see his mind goes to her, wistful-like. Could be worse things. Used to be worse. I don't know and I don't ask."

"Ms. Garrett—"

"Hazel."

"Hazel. What's happened?"

"He woke me up. It was the middle of the night and I thought it must be news about my mom—she's going to pass any day."

"He called you?"

"No, he drove up from that place where Arnie Arnold's been pasturing his horses. Let himself in the door. He's really close with my sister—we grate against each other, my sis and me. Nancy's likely as not to call him than me if there was bad news."

Martha made a stab at following the thread of that logic and gave up.

"Anyway," the woman continued, "I got crossways with him, said he shouldn't do such a thing. Why I could of shot him for an intruder. He said it was an emergency, that he knew about the cat. I said, You shot the cat. He says he did, but it was the other one, that there was another and he had to stop it before it killed somebody else. He knew where it was, how to track it down. He come to the house because of Boon—he's my dog when he isn't hollering on the mountain. Got a little redbone in him, give him that even temperament. Not as much hound as some, but that's a good thing. The rest of the pack, he keeps out at Arnie's."

"So he came from this Arnie's place with his horse and his hounds, all but this Boon. Is that right?"

"No, just the horse. Boon was the only hound he was taking. Buster, long as it was daylight out, he liked running cats with only one dog. You got to stay closer to the dog, but there's less confusion. Trade-off is the risk."

"What night was this, Hazel?"

"It was a week Sunday, about midnight."

Martha trapped her lower lip with teeth, her mind doing the arithmetic. Sunday was two days prior to Max Gallagher hearing the shots. She, like Sean, had originally assumed that the shots were fired by the herder, to drive away or kill his attacker. The window for his death was fixed within a couple days by forensic science, as well as by the gunshots.

But if the shots had not been fired by the herder, but instead by someone defending himself from the guard dogs, then the date was more uncertain. It was possible that Garrett had been in the vicinity of the herder's camp while the herder was still alive, or up to a few days after his death. The pendant all but confirmed that he was there at some point. Why, though? That was the catch.

She asked Hazel to describe Garrett's trailer and his truck and jotted the information on a sticky note.

"All right, then what happened?"

"He took old Boon and left. Wasn't in the house but fifteen

minutes. But that's always been his way. 'Bustering around' is what I call it."

"Hazel, I really do wish that you had reported this earlier."

"I know. I shoulda. But you don't know him like I do. I call him in missing, and he isn't really missing, then he takes it out on me. Or used to. He's better about things like that than he used to be."

"Did he have a satellite phone or a cell phone, maybe a locator beacon? A way to get in touch if he got into trouble?"

"Just his phone. He says people use technology like a crutch. Makes you think you can go where you can't. 'A man's brain, a horse's hoof, and a dog's nose, you got that you're good to go.' Something he liked to say."

"Hazel, I want you to listen to me. I'm going to show you something and I'll tell you right up front that it wasn't found on his body, and I'm not saying that he's come to any harm. But it concerns me, and I'm hoping you might be able to shed a little light we can use to find him."

Martha opened a desk drawer and withdrew the lion claw pendant that Sean had found. She felt, rather than heard, the intake of Hazel Garrett's breath.

"Where did you get that? It's his . . . I guess you could call it a good luck charm. He's been wearing it, I don't know, a few years, since around the time of the change."

"What do you mean by that, 'the change'?"

"Since he become more bearable. They say a man can't change, but I seen it in him, like a ray of light, it is."

"An investigator found it near where the sheepherder was killed by the lion. Do you have any idea how it could have got there? Did Buster know the sheepherder?"

She shook her head. "He knew lots of people—running hounds

you get to—but he never said anything about knowing a sheep-herder."

Martha nodded. "Okay, what kind of horse does Buster ride?"

"Roan quarter-horse mare. Calls her Freckles 'cause of her spots."

"Where did he say he was going?"

"He didn't. I asked him and all he says is it's about the lion and don't worry, and then he says do I know where his will is. I say it's under the copper liner on the dry sink where he put it, and he says, I just wanted to make sure you know. Like this was good-bye. I can read between the lines, you got to if you marry a man who spends more words on his dogs than he does on you. Anyway, it made me worry. That's why I came here."

"You did the right thing, Hazel."

Martha caught Walt's eye. "Get Karl Radcliffe." She mouthed the words. Radcliffe was the pilot who worked most closely with the department, and it was his Piper Cub that was on call for search and rescue. Walt nodded and left the room, and Martha turned back to her visitor.

"Does Buster have an office?"

Hazel Garrett said yes, he had a room in the house that he'd kept even during the worst of their time together.

Martha told her to go home and wait, that either she or one of her deputies would drop by to have a gander at the room, and please don't change anything in the meantime.

The hairs at the edge of her sparse mustache shifted as Hazel seemed to search for words.

Finally: "He's dead, isn't he?"

Martha shook her head. "We don't know that."

"You feel the silence different when somebody goes." Hazel gathered herself and stood, and Martha felt the pressure of the calloused hand and then she left. A minute later Walt stuck his head in the door. Karl's airplane was being serviced. It wouldn't be available until tomorrow.

Martha said "Fiddle-de-dee" and punched in the cell number Joshua Byrne had given her. While it rang, she sent a second airplane past Walt's ear and out into the hall.

Byrne picked up. Without preamble Martha asked if his offer to help stood. He said yes and she asked how long it would take to file a flight plan. Byrne asked what was up and she gave him the bones. No, he said, a flight plan wasn't required, not unless he planned to fly under instrument rules. That wouldn't happen unless there was dense cloud cover, which wasn't predicted.

She told him to pick her up at the helicopter pad that law enforcement shared with the hospital. And that there would be a second spotter, Sean Stranahan.

CHAPTER TWENTY-SIX

Eyes in the Sky

The Bell 407 was custom-fitted with searchlights and infrared detection, with its rear seating area configured to accept a stretcher when three of the passenger seats were removed. Sean and Martha sat side by side on forward-facing seats to scan the country to the right and left, Martha wearing a headset to communicate with Byrne in the cockpit. If she wanted to talk to Sean, they'd use hand signals. The plan was to grid-search the slopes of the southern Gravellys first, starting at the wall tent, which should be easily visible.

If the grid search didn't strike pay dirt in the form of a man with a hound, dead or alive, they'd start combing the mid-elevation access roads where Garrett might have parked. Byrne said they had fuel for three hours. If they didn't find Garrett's rig, a three-quarter-ton Dodge Ram with a two-toned silver and white two-horse trailer, then they'd have to refuel at the Big Sky Airport outside Ennis.

"My damned bird," as he'd called it while hoisting their gear into the cargo hold. "She costs six hundred dollars an hour to fly." A not-so-subtle reminder of his largess.

"Oh, I'll bet you make that much just drawing a smile," Martha said.

Byrne drew his smile.

What had seemed like a plan from ground level was put into perspective as the helicopter climbed and flew west along the toes of the Gallatin and Madison ranges, then veered south over the Madison Valley. It was just so much more country from the air than it was from the highway, with an extensive road-and-trail system that was confusing, even though both Martha and Sean could refer to a topo map on a monitor suspended from the cockpit ceiling for orientation. They found the wall tent, and Byrne began flying the grid they'd mapped in advance. Big, open slopes here, the new grasses overlaid with puzzle pieces of old snow. Martha felt giddy in spite of the seriousness of the mission. Below her spread an American Serengeti, a vast, undulating landscape with groups of deer and antelope and scattered elk herds. A grizzly sow reacted to the helicopter's whir by rearing on her hind legs and swatting at the air with a massive paw. She ambled away into the trees, followed by her three cubs. A person could live a lifetime here, Martha thought, and never see his own backyard. You needed wings to appreciate the gift nature had given you.

Three miles south of the tent, Martha spotted the sheep. She remembered Ava Ann Rawlings describing the Halloween costume worn by Hunter Ross on the night of his disappearance. "A meadow maggot," she'd called him. Rice on green grass. Here there were hundreds of them. Martha pointed out the obvious and Sean nodded.

An hour later and Martha's headset crackled.

"You want to heli on up to Ennis?"

"At least as far as Johnny Gulch Road, farther north if we're still good on fuel."

"Plenty in the tank."

"Find me a roan quarter horse with spots and I'll give you a kiss you can feel in your back pocket."

The muted roar of the rotors, then, from the cockpit: "That's a tall order, Sheriff. I get kissed by beautiful women for a living."

"Not by one who packs a Ruger Blackhawk on her hip."

Another pause, then the crackle: "In that case, buckle your safety strap."

Martha caught Sean looking at her.

"I'm going to kiss a movie star and there's nothing you can do about it," she said.

Sean tapped his right ear. "I can't hear you," he shouted.

Martha just smiled.

SEAN SPOTTED THE GLINT FIRST, the sun reflecting off the aluminum coachwork of the Airstream. He gestured to Martha and she spoke briefly into her headset. Byrne canted the helicopter so that she could see out her side. She was mildly surprised that the Forest Service hadn't hauled the trailer away yet, as it was squatting on their land. But then, it had been girdled with crime scene tape, which sort of made it the county's business, too, and so easy enough to pass the buck. Anyway, at the end of the access road was a truck and trailer outfit that fit the description. And standing beside it was a horse. A gray-blue horse.

"Can you set us down?"

A brief crackle and "Will do." And he did, though it took a few passes for Byrne to find an opening in the trees big enough to touch down the skids.

After the rotors stilled, they hauled the day packs out and buckled them on.

"How about that kiss?" Byrne said.

"Not until we verify the horse."

"What kiss?" Sean said.

"The one I'm going to plant on Joshua when I see freckles on that roan."

It took fifteen minutes to hike from the landing site up to the trailhead where they'd seen the horse. It was Garrett's roan, all right, and the wet smack Martha laid on Byrne's mouth lasted a few beats longer than she'd anticipated. Her cheeks flushed, she looked at Sean and shrugged.

"Deal with it," she said.

The roan nickered at their approach, then came forward with her ears up. She was saddled, reins dangling, rifle scabbard empty, a braided lead rope snapped to her halter and dragging on the ground. Apparently, Garrett had been leading the horse when whatever happened, happened. And then, riderless, the horse did what horses do, went back to where she had come from. Martha peered into the stalls in the trailer. A couple of hay bales, a feed bag, a wheelbarrow with a plastic bladder half full of water and a bucket to bleed it into.

"Where is he, Freckles?" Martha said to the mare.

Aware that the horse could be skittish if she faced her head on, where her eyes couldn't focus to see her clearly, Martha stayed to the left side of the mare's head, saw her own reflection in the liquid amber eye, and led her to a pine tree. She took a full wrap around the trunk and used a bowline to secure the rope.

"One of you fellas, how about getting some hay from the trailer and putting water into the bucket. This critter's starved and parched both."

BACKTRACKING THE HORSE was easier than Sean had anticipated, given the elapsed time. It followed nearly step by step the game trail that Sean, Martha, and Sam Meslik had followed when tracking the cat to Clarice Kincaid's body. No trace of that tragedy now, just a dank odor you couldn't place and probably was imagined, and a wind that bit at you and made your hands cold. Sean lost the thread a few times where the ground had dried out, would have to guess and circle upward to cut the track again.

The crest of the ridge was too hard to show horse tracks as more than intermittent U's, but on the north slope the earth was softer and patches of old snow clung in the lees. Here Sean first saw the prints of the hound, where, probably casting for scent, it had strayed from the ridge. He used a stick to point the track out to Martha and she nodded. A few moments later they spotted the beast, first in stripes of color between the tree trunks, then clearly as he came to the edge of a clearing. He approached on unsteady legs, his ears back, teeth bared. But the belligerence was just show, and when Martha called to him, he came up slinking, a brindle pattern showing through the dark patches on his back, his red ears down, tail drooping. Just a cold, hungry, lonely dog smelling to high heaven, all the hound beaten out of him.

"Good boy," Martha said. "Where's Buster?"

After snuffing her hand, his nose wet and his body shivering under Martha's touch, the dog cantered ahead up the ridge, and the next time they saw him, he was standing over a patch of blue that, on closer inspection, turned out to be house paint dried on a frayed jacket. Garrett was lying faceup, his open eyes skinned over and shrunk into their sockets, the beer-bottle scar white against the dark of his stubbled cheek. The body was lying at the center of what looked to have been a violent struggle. The earth was torn up and blood was splattered over a large radius, some as if sprayed by a hose. The blood had rusted to a dull bronze color, but was so copious that the stains on the grass were impossible to miss.

Sean, turning his head from the carnage, spotted the rifle tilted against a tree trunk. It was the battered Marlin lever-action that Garrett had carried on the night that Sean had accompanied him on the trail of the tom. Sean ejected the round in the chamber and measured the exposed bullet against the circumference of his ring finger.

"What are you doing?" Martha asked.

"Checking the size. It's about the same diameter of the slug that I found in the body of the guard dog. At the time I guessed it to be .45-caliber. This is a .45/70 slug. Same diameter. I'm going to guess if we pass them by ballistics they'll come back as both being fired from this rifle."

"So you're saying he killed the dogs? I don't know the man as well as you do, but does that sound like something he'd do?"

"No. Not unless it was self-defense. Or if he was protecting his own dog."

"So he shoots the guard dogs and then, what, stumbles over the dead body of the herder?"

"The collies could have pointed out its location."

"How does he lose the thingy he wears around his neck, the cord with the claw?"

"I don't know."

Martha had taken her jacket off and now rolled up her sleeves. She took her time pulling on blue latex hospital gloves.

"Here's my question," she said. "If Garrett came across the herder, and he was dead, why didn't he call us? You're the one saying how he's become a Samaritan now, making amends. Why didn't he call it in?"

"He was just 'Bustering around,'" Sean said. "Isn't that what his ex told you? He's a cowboy. He'd get around to it when he got around to it. Maybe he was on the cat's trail. You know as well as me it's a dead zone there to here. He couldn't have called if he wanted to."

"Humpff." Martha knelt beside the body. She tugged at the maroon silk scarf wrapped twice around Garrett's neck and knotted at the front, cowboy-style. The tag ends were saturated with blood. She pulled the scarf down and dabbed at the congealed blood on the throat with a blue finger.

"Lion?" Byrne said.

Martha had almost forgotten he was there.

"Looks like a cat, all right. I can see the puncture wounds."

"How many?" Sean said.

"At least seven. It might have changed the position of the bite once or twice." She started unbuttoning Garrett's coat. A few minutes later she sat back on her heels.

"Well?" Sean said.

"His shirt's shredded and there're deep lacerations across his chest and belly. But no sign any of him was eaten."

"Maybe the dog drove it away."

"Maybe. Fly's unbuttoned."

"That could explain how he was attacked."

"How so?" Martha looked at him.

"He dismounted to take a whiz. Most men, even if nobody's

around, they turn their back and pee into a tree well or against a tree trunk. Like marking territory. It's a vulnerable position. If the cat was following him, sees him get off the horse, walk a few yards away, turn his back, that would be the time to pounce. And the lead rope dragging like we found it. That's could be a sign he got off the horse, too."

Martha grunted her skepticism. "I wish Harold was here. He might be able to make sense of this puzzle. I don't think we're fitting the pieces together, or we're missing something." She turned to Sean. "No offense."

"None taken."

Silence.

"I have a thought," Sean said.

CHAPTER TWENTY-SEVEN

The Magic Wand

After the helicopter had silvered off into the sky, Martha fished the lunch she'd brought for them and they sat down upwind of the body. Sean's idea had been to reach out to Harold Little Feather on Martha's satellite phone. If he took the call and said his leg was okay to hike, which he did, then Byrne would chopper up the twenty miles to Harold's sister's place in Pony and collect him. They could be back inside of an hour and set down at a wide spot in the ridge.

"Things are going to go pear-shaped on us," Martha said. She wiped crumbs from the corners of her mouth. "Like the herder wasn't enough. Now we have two deaths in a week. It will be open carry on the streets. The press will be circling like those vultures that led you to the guard dogs. Guess who they'll have for break-fast?" She tapped her breastbone.

Sean shook his head.

"What, Sean? You think this is going to go away? It isn't going to go away."

"No. I'm not thinking about the fallout. I'm thinking about Buster."

"How he turned his life around? You ask me, he was just talking a good game."

"No. Something he said."

Sean looked up. He could hear and then feel the *thump thump thump* of the rotors before he saw the helicopter cresting the ridge. It hovered down, the nearby trees flattening in the wind. Sean and Martha put their hands on their hats.

No smile, no handshakes, Harold being Harold, a little more of him than before, with weight having settled around his middle.

"You're looking well, Harold," Martha said. And knew as she said it that it was the wrong thing to say.

"Bullshit. I look gone to seed. My son, he says give me a few more months and he'll have a BFI for a dad. Big Fucking Indian."

"The ankle still bothering you?"

"Part of the problem. Hard to stay in shape if you can't walk without a stick." He tapped his stick against the ground. "Most of it's the job, now that I've run out my string as an undercover. First time in my life I rode a desk. Going to be the last."

"You're quitting?"

"Thinking about it. Let's see what we got."

Martha was familiar with Harold's methods and made sure they followed in single file and stayed twenty feet back. Harold dipped out of sight after cresting the ridge and Martha held up a hand. A couple of minutes and she heard Harold's birdlike whistle, beckoning them forward. He was bent over the body.

"I see you unbuttoned him," Harold said.

"I pulled some layers aside to see his throat and chest," Martha said. "His fly was undone. Sean thinks the cat attacked him while he was taking a whiz."

Harold nodded. "Most wouldn't think of it, but a man's member is subject to rigor mortis no different than a finger or a thumb. Couple hours after death, he's got himself a hard-on a porn queen couldn't shake the starch out of."

"Too much information," Martha said.

"Tell me how you got here."

Martha did, starting with the conversation with Garrett's ex-wife and her decision to get some eyes in the sky.

"So finding him, the truck, I mean, you're saying it was luck, no solid reason to search this particular drainage?"

"Luck and Joshua offering his services. It was a blanket search. We were checking out all the gated roads and access points, starting on this side of the range."

"This is where the tom with the broken tooth claimed the life of that hooker."

"That's right. The kill site's another quarter mile west along the ridge."

"So to be clear. Two lions, two victims, same place, six months apart. Then, separately or related, you have the herder, apparently also killed by a lion. You see what I'm getting at?"

"I know," Martha said. "It's a lot of coincidence."

"It's a lot of lions," Harold said. "Too many by one." He threaded his braid through the back of a discolored ball cap that read TROUT TAILS BAR AND GRILL.

"Okay, then. I'm going to backtrack to where the horse came out onto the ridge and take it where it goes. I'd appreciate it if you walked back down to the helicopter and waited there."

He was gone, his stick tapping in front of him.

"How long do you think he'll be?" Byrne asked.

"Harold's Harold," Martha said. "He was tracking this guy back when I was a boot, a hunter who shot his partner 'cause he suspected an affair with the wife. Anyway, you could only get to the place where it went down by boat. He says, 'I'll be a few minutes.' I had time to catch a trout, build a fire, and eat it before he came back."

Harold was back when Martha was on her fourth story about him.

"Two horses, two riders," Harold said. And glanced at Sean, who shouldn't have missed something that obvious, despite poor tracking conditions.

"Damn," Sean said.

"It happens," Harold said. "You're looking for a bent blade of grass and miss the moose track."

"Are you saying he came up here with someone, or someone followed him up here?" Martha said.

"Together."

"You're sure about that."

"There are places where one horse track stepped onto the track of the other, and other places where it's opposite. That tells me they were here at the same time."

"The only truck trailer at the trailhead is Garrett's. Do you think they drove in together—it's a two-staller—or the other rider came and went in his own rig?"

"I didn't have time to go back. Or the leg for it." He tapped the stick.

"We'll check on the way out," Sean said. "What's that sticking out of your pack?"

"Something my dad would have called a what-is-it. You grow up on the rez, you find a lot of what-is-its." He drew a metal contraption out of his day pack. It consisted of four aluminum crossbars that vaguely resembled the skeleton of a kite. There was an extendable antenna attached to an electronic instrument panel the size of a cellphone. Harold said he'd found it on the ground along the trail that the second horse had taken when it was returning to the trail- head. His guess was that it had been tied onto a pannier and fallen off or been scraped off the horse's back by a tree limb. He recognized that it was a radio receiver, one designed to pick up VHF signals sent from a transmitting collar. Two of the aluminum bars were bent and the metal surface carried brown stains that Harold brought his nose to and identified as blood.

"I guess we know what he was looking for with that," Martha said.

Harold had removed his jacket and scratched at the tattoos of wol- verine tracks that encircled the lower biceps of his left arm. "Thing is," he said, "transmitting collars—I'm talking about VHF, not GPS— only have a range of two or three miles. Garrett would still have to have known where to start looking."

"Maybe it was the second rider who knew," Martha said. "Buster's ex said he was excited, that he took off in the middle of the night. What would cause him to do that? I'm thinking that he got a call from the other guy who was up here. They met at the trailhead. Then the shit hit the fan and the lion killed Garrett. The other guy flees the scene, trailers his horse, takes off down the road. He was never here. Except that he was. Harold, how far did you get with the data I told Carson Taylor to give you? The lion study stuff. That would have collaring information, right? This cat could have been in the study."

"It would be a long shot. But no, I didn't get very far. Once the big tomcat was killed, all that was back-burnered. I've been sitting on it for the last three months. I only started opening the boxes when I heard about the sheepherder. We're talking a lot of information. If you want, you could give me a hand. See if there's a needle in the haystack."

"All right," Martha said. "I'm up for a needle hunt. You want us to come to your sister's?"

He did. They set the date for the next morning, and after zipping the unpleasant cargo inside a plastic bag and loading it into the belly of the Bell, Harold climbed aboard. Byrne would drop him off back in Pony before turning east toward Bridger and the county morgue. That left Sean and Martha alone on the mountain. The plan was to drive Garrett's rig back to his widow's place, then have a deputy drive them home after they had had a talk with Hazel, as their vehicles were at Martha's. The snag, that Garrett's truck was locked, was a loss of a minute. Sean found the key where half the hunters in Montana placed it, under the right front tire. The other half placed it under the left rear tire. He also found the tire treads made by a second vehicle, one also hauling a horse trailer, so that mystery was solved. Martha took photos of the tread should they be able to match it to a truck and trailer rig later on. It shouldn't be hard. The tires on the trailer were mismatched.

"Who's going to tell her?" Sean asked. "Maybe it should be me. I'm the one knew him."

"It won't make any difference," Martha said. "She'll know soon as she sees the critters."

MARTHA WAS RIGHT. Hazel Garrett opened the door wearing a housecoat with Shetland ponies on it, her face a stone wall that broke into pieces as her eyes went from Martha to the hound on the porch and the horse trailer beyond. She bent down and wrapped up the dog in her arms, speaking through tears.

"I knew he was never coming back. You just get a feeling. How come when you get a bad feeling it's always true, but when you get a good feeling something comes along that lets the air right out of you? How come God lets that happen?"

She seemed to be speaking to the dog, but he had no better answer to the question than Sean or Martha, and while Martha comforted the woman as best she could in her living room, Sean rifled cupboards in the kitchen to make tea.

"To go like that," she said after she had composed herself. "You're sure it was a cat?"

"It looks like it," Martha said.

"Are they going to want me to identify the body?"

"If you will. We'll have the scar and his dental and DNA, so it isn't absolutely necessary."

"I will. You live with animals like I have, you see a lot of death. Is his face . . . ?" Her voice trailed away.

"It's recognizable. I won't kid you. There were wounds."

"Did it . . . like the others. Eat him?"

"It doesn't look like it."

"We wasn't under the same roof sometimes, but I loved him. He ended up the sweet man I first met."

She'd begun to cry again and wiped at her eyes with the back of a hand. "But to go like that," she said.

"Mrs. Garrett?" Sean said.

It took her a few moments to find his eyes. He handed her a cup of tea. She stared at it like it held a secret.

"What kind of system did Buster have for documenting his hunts?" Martha asked. "Computer files? Maybe an appointment book?"

"He's got his phone, is all. He's got the Gmail on it, but he don't hardly check it. But he has his journals. They got all his tax stuff in them."

"May we see them?"

"They're in his place. I suppose there's no harm."

HIS PLACE WAS DOWN the hall, first door on the left. It was a man cave, dark with shuttered windows, heavy on the Y chromosome. Sean took in an oval rug, a heavy plush chair decorated with upholstery tacks, an oak desk with a desk chair on rollers. On the unpolished surface of the desk was a cast-bronze ashtray in the shape of a cougar's paw print. There were two steel file drawers that Martha rifled through and revealed nothing of interest. There was a caved-in napping couch that had seen a lot of napping.

On the walls hung cobwebbed skull and antler mounts of mule deer and elk that stared with empty eye sockets. Hanging behind the desk was a tinted photo of a younger Garrett and his hounds, and there were other photos on a corkboard, Garrett hefting up dead lions and bobcats with various clients. There was the smell of stale cigar and matted dog hair on all surfaces.

The journals, a baker's dozen, were sandwiched between spaniel-head bookends on a mantel over a fireplace that opened into both the office and the living room. Sean leafed through the journals— they were as mismatched as the furniture, some bound, others spiral-ring, entries in pencil and ink. They were the records of the makes and misses of a houndsman's life, outings that never turned up a scent, others where the scent was lost or the trail led where dogs couldn't follow, as well as those hunts that resulted in treed cats. Each entry included a date and location, the weather, a mileage log, paper-clipped gas and restaurant receipts, dog food receipts, snapshots, and a short account of the chase and outcome. The journals went back a full decade. The latest entry had been only two weeks before.

Martha had stayed with Hazel in the living room and Sean heard steps as Hazel came into the study. "Would you trust me to borrow these?" Sean asked her.

"I suppose it's okay. I got to have them to do the income tax next year."

"I can get them back to you in a few days. Do you mind if I ask you a personal question? How did you and Buster end up together?" He made his interest sound casual, just passing the time, when what he was really doing, and not particularly liking himself for it, was ingratiating himself to peel back that last inner skin that might cover something untold, the outer skins of reticence already having dissolved with the shock of the death.

"His real name is Jack. Was Jack. It was his dad called him Buster. He grew up on a cattle station in New South Wales. I was on holiday and the tour bus broke down, and he came by on a horse and fixed us up. I had a fella back home, but who can resist a man on a horse? Oh, he was a charmer. I got my bag and rode to the station with him on the back of the horse. He introduced me to his mom and dad and told them he was going to marry me. A month later we were married."

There was a flicker of a smile as she thought back. "That whole time," she said, "he never tried to do anything more than kiss me. A gentleman, he was. We were going to take over the station, but he got into an argument with his brother, who wanted the place, too, and his wife was a witch about it, and finally Buster sold out his half to them and decided to try his luck here. He got a job in a loony bin in Virginia, but then my mom died and left me this place, so we come out here. Buster, he had a thing for the dogs far back as I knew him, liked to hunt those wild pig in the Outback. I knew I'd always run second to the pack when it came to his heart. But I signed up for it. I don't have any regrets. You get past him being Buster, he was just Jack. He was my person."

Sean was thoughtful. "Hazel, the thing that puzzles me is how he knew where the cat would be. He didn't say anything that could be a clue? Maybe got a phone call from someone?"

"No, but ever since that harlot come to her end, he was out there driving the roads. Always had a hound with him, always had his wand. Even after he killed the bad one. It was like he thought he'd got the wrong lion or there was another out there just as bad. It was an obsession. I told him, I said, 'Buster, why are you taking this so personal. These people the cat's got, it's not like you know them.' All he'd say was that as long as the county was reimbursing him for his gas, he was going to keep hunting. It haunted him. It was like he thought it was his fault for what happened."

"His wand?"

"His radio receiver. Called it his magic wand. That's how he thought he might find the cat. Keep driving the roads and tuning in for a signal. Got to get lucky sooner or later."

Sean asked the obvious next question. "What made Buster think that the cat was radio-collared?"

"I don't know. Maybe it was him put it on it. He collared a lot of lion going back a stretch. Part of that study they had."

Sean tried to dig deeper into the subject of the collars, but she didn't know and he wasn't learning anything of note. He handed her one of his cards, the one with the fly on it. "If you think of anything that might help us know why he was up there, that particular place . . . ?"

She nodded. "I will, but he played his cards close to his chest. His dogs knew him better than I did."

WHEN THEY WENT BACK to the living room, the hound rose from the couch where he had been lying and went up to Hazel, the question mark of his tail wagging. She bent down to stroke him.

"They say you can't make a house dog of a hound, but they haven't met old Boon, no, they haven't." She sat down on the floor and tucked her legs underneath her, the dog resting his head on her lap. She was sitting that way when they left a few minutes later, her housecoat with the Shetland ponies making a puddle on the floor. She looked up at Martha, who had heard people in shock say all sorts of things, and added a new one to the list.

"Look at me," she said. "I'm melting."

CHAPTER TWENTY-EIGHT

The War Room

Y ou're certain he said seven hundred seventy-seven days ago?"

"Yes, he made a point of it being an angel number."

Martha grunted. "Then why aren't we seeing anything worth changing your life over?"

They were sitting at her home desk, the day just long enough in the tooth that Martha had turned on the track lighting. Buster Garrett's journals were spread out on the polished surface of the stump. Sean had recalled to her Garrett's confession that something had happened that changed his life. "I created a monster," he'd told Sean, one that stood between him and heaven. When Sean had pressed him further, he'd declined to elaborate.

Sean counted back to the date. He found the corresponding page in one of the journals, or rather where the arithmetic said it should have been. However, Garrett had made no entry for that date. Nor had he for the dates immediately before and after it.

"Well, hell," Sean said. "If something happened then, it didn't make his book. And everything made his book."

Martha, leaning over his shoulder, kissed him on the top of his head. She muttered, "What would you do without me?"

"What?"

"You counted back from today's date, not the date when he told you the number."

"Oh."

"When was it you two drank your Virgin Marys?"

"Back in February, I think. It's too long ago to remember." He paused. "No, I do remember. I sold a painting that morning, the Kispiox River with the Telkwa Range on the horizon. It was titled *River of Lesser Gods*. We toasted the sale."

"You and Garrett?"

"Yeah."

"Do you have a record of the sale in your phone? I know you never erase anything."

Sean found the date of the sale.

"Count backwards from there."

Sean picked up a pencil.

"It's December tenth," Martha said. "Two years ago, plus a few weeks."

Sean looked at her.

She shrugged. "I've got a head for figures. You know that."

He nodded and found the journal entry.

> **Client:** *Jeremy Walker, Macon, Georgia*
>
> **License:** *Mountain lion hound-training season, photos only.*

Location: Black Butte east slope, Gravelly Range. Lower Fox Meadow.

Conditions: Crust snow cover, depth six inches in timber. Drifts in parks. Road passable to mile 7. 34°F, wind negligible.

Hunt: Crossed track Lower Fox Meadow. Struck 10 a.m., Mary Jane, Boon, General Compson. Treed tomcat in forty minutes two drainages south. I told client photos only. Perfectly clear in contract. He took the rifle from my scabbard and shot at lion while I was engaged with dogs. Maintained it was going to jump out of the tree and was afraid it would attack him. Lion bailed out and ran, leaving intermittent blood trail. Blood pattern showed it had been shot in right paw or leg. I found one of the toes along the track. Pulled the dogs from further chase and read client the riot act.

A note was written at the bottom of the page in pencil.

I cut the track of this same lion later that winter (see entry Feb. 26). The right front paw print showed a space where the toe would have been. The track was near an elk kill that showed evidence the lion had broken canine on upper right side. I concluded wound to the toe and to the tooth occurred at same time from same bullet. Decided not to run the cat. Client upset as it was the only track we cut. But as I took responsibility for the wounds this animal suffered, I took satisfaction seeing that the cat was still alive after several months and had apparently recovered

enough to catch prey. Bad luck cat, I wished him luck
and good hunting.

The entry included a snapshot of a lion track in snow, showing the
space between the toes.

Sean felt a temperature change in the room. He said, "Buster knew
as soon as we killed the cat and looked at its paw that it was the same
one his client had wounded. He probably already suspected from the
tooth marks on Clarice Kincaid's neck. Something happened between the time he cut its track and when it took her life that turned
it from a lion suffering an old wound into a man-eater. That's why it
was so personal. He took responsibility for a human death."

"But you shot that cat and Buster was still hunting, going out every
week or so, according to these journals. The cat that killed him, he
was waving his magic wand trying to find it. The obsession was still
there. There has to be a thread that connects the two, that connects
all of it."

"I'm with you, Martha." But what that thread was remained one of
those problems he tried to solve with imaginary tobacco, and he was
no closer to connecting the dots when they pulled into the muddy
ruts of Harold's drive the next morning.

Martha turned to Sean after her knock. They could hear Harold's
stick tapping. "Five gets you ten," Martha said, "that stick will be
nowhere in sight when he opens the door. 'Never show your weakness.' The code he lives by."

Harold opened the door and Sean caught Martha's half smile. No
sign of the stick.

"Martha, Sean. Janice is out of town, so you'll excuse the mess."
Janice was Harold's sister.

"Meaning you can't pick up after yourself?" Martha said. "You'll have to do better if you want a woman to stick around for a month of Sundays."

"I suppose so." He pointed to the geriatric golden retriever sleeping on a dog bed on the one couch. "I blame Imitaa." Using the Blackfeet word for "dog." Her remark had stung, Martha thought, and felt ashamed of herself. But if Harold took note, he didn't let it show, any more than he'd shown the stick.

Martha remembered the woman Harold had been cohabitating with since the winter. They had been living in the converted barn up the hill. She was a lanky blonde with a gap-toothed smile and a tinkling quality in her voice. "How's Carol Anne?" she said, hoping she'd got the name right.

"She's back in Missouri. Got a daughter there."

Harold's tone said there was no certainty she'd return.

He smiled. "Either I'm too much Indian or not Indian enough. Just can't figure."

"I'm guessing it's because you're just too much Harold," Martha said. Her own relationship with him, which had simmered for years, had cooled to the degree that she had learned the true nature of a man who confronted the world with cheekbones, armband tattoos of animal tracks, and few words. At least too few words for most women.

There were few of them now. A moment of silence stretched, elongating like a water drop at the tip of an icicle.

"I see you put up a hoop on the barn," Martha said, trying for small talk.

"My physical therapist says shooting a basketball exercises the Achilles and promotes healing. Been ten months. Hasn't seemed to make much difference." Another drop of water elongated.

Finally: "I heard you two are getting married. Congratulations. I should have said something yesterday. You get on a track, you know how it is. You don't think about much else."

"How's Marcus?" Martha asked. Marcus was the son that Harold had not known he'd had until the previous June, and who'd suffered the same injury as his father. It was a long story, one that was written in blood and bound them together, Sean and Martha included.

"You wouldn't know it ever happened," Harold said. "Kids, they recover. He's home this weekend. Took the truck into Ennis."

"It would be good to see him," Martha said. She thought to preempt another water drop succumbing to its mortality. "Harold, you invited us over for this powwow. What do you got? Right now all I got is a ninety-year-old houndsman from Arizona who promises his dogs can track a lion over hard rock, if he doesn't die before reaching Montana. That and a fifty-dollar bottle of perfume guaranteed to be catnip. So I'm hoping you got something."

Harold smiled. "Well, like I said, I've started looking at the lion study data." He gestured, indicating a worm-holed desk that looked like maple. On it rested a desk computer, a printer, an elk antler lamp, and several stacks of photocopied maps pinned down by chunks of petrified wood.

"Janice calls this my war room," he said.

Behind the desk, three identical topographic maps were taped to a metal plate that was bolted onto the wall. The maps had been pieced together from digital USGS downloads, and each was covered with a thin sheet of clear plastic. The Madison River ran south to north roughly through the middle of each map. The left-hand map was studded with circular magnets in several colors, each about the circumference of a shirt button. There was also a sprinkling of miniature magnets shaped like crosses. The other two maps had been drawn upon with dry-erase markers in patterns consisting of red dots linked by blue lines.

Martha set her hands on her hips. She blew at an errant strand of hair. "This one looks like something you'd see in MoMA," she said. And when Harold didn't respond, "That's—"

"I know what MoMA is," Harold said.

"I didn't say you didn't. Most men have about as much interest in modern art as foreplay. It wasn't a racist comment."

Harold stone-faced her. "Like your saying 'powwow,'" he said. Then smiled as her face reddened. "I'm just fooling with you."

Martha muttered under her breath.

"What's that?"

"Amusement," she said. "That's what I've become. People's source of amusement."

"We love you anyway," Sean said. "You, too, right, Harold?"

"Oh, sure."

"Shut up, the both of you. What exactly am I looking at?"

Harold tapped the left-hand map with a pencil eraser. "The red magnets mark mountain lion encounters of a threatening nature. Ear-flattening, hissing, following, crouching with paws pumping, so on, but short of physical contact. Take off the magnets"—he took one off—"and you'll see I've marked each location with a date of occurrence and a number. Also, the GPS waypoint, which is not written out because it's too long, but the coordinates are logged in my computer. The data goes back three years. You go back any further, there's just too many encounters to keep track of. As it is, we have thirty-seven reds.

"The encounters I've graded by threat, one-to-ten scale. For example, this here"—he tapped a magnet—"man was cutting firewood and a lion advanced on him even though he was revving up his chain saw to deter it. Broad daylight, the cat as close as ten feet, follows him all the way back to his truck. Solid ten. Whereas this guy"—he pointed to another magnet—"cat growls at him after nightfall and then follows him for a few hundred feet, but not all the way to the trailhead, where he'd left his vehicle."

"Like what happened to me," Sean said.

"Similar. Five points."

Martha nodded. "And the black magnets? I count seven."

"Actual physical contact. As in contact with hand or arm, ski pole, stick, whatever the victim tried to protect himself with. Four of the victims were hospitalized with lacerations. Only one, a mountain biker up Hyalite Canyon who was chased down, had life-threatening injuries."

"I remember that one," Sean said. "Didn't he lose an eye?"

"It was an ear," Harold said. "He was a wildlife artist. People started calling him van Gogh." He pointed to another magnet. "This one's my favorite. Guy fishing Elk Lake, lion attacks, only weapon at hand is his spinning rod. Called an Ugly Stik. He manages to beat the cat away. Company that makes the Ugly Stik catches wind, hires him to do television commercials hyping the durability of their product."

"And the silver sparkly ones?" Martha said. "What did you do, Harold, paint theses magnets with fingernail polish?"

"As a matter of fact, I did. The red is CoverGirl Frosted Cherry. The dark is called To the Moon and Black. The sparkly polish is Starry Night. Carol Anne left some girl stuff behind. You look surprised."

"I just have a hard time envisioning you with a woman who paints her nails. Did she wear lipstick, too?"

"Lip gloss. You ever wear lip gloss, Martha?"

He turned back to the maps as Martha blushed. She'd put on flavored lip gloss on nights they'd made love. Raspberry Sorbet.

"To answer your question," Harold said, "the so-called sparkly magnets mark places where people went missing and proximate lion activity makes a cat a reasonable suspect." He tapped one. "Cross-country runner, training run, Johnson Coulee, Tobacco Roots. This other"— he tapped another magnet—"boy hiking in the Spanish Peaks, part of an organized outing, lagged behind, never seen again. And this one, a young woman on a horse rides out from that Rocking R guest ranch in the Paradise Valley. Mare came back, she didn't. Fresh cat sign found along the trail. One trait most of the missing shared was short stature—right in a lion's wheelhouse."

"'Short people got no business to live.'"

"Say what, Martha?"

"Nothing. Old song lyrics. Go on. This is interesting."

"Okay, the crosses are self-explanatory. They're the known fatalities—Clarice Kincaid, Cesar Rodriguez, and, as of yesterday, Buster Garrett. I debated whether to award a cross to the Ross boy. I held off and gave him a sparkly magnet instead, but in my book he's a probably. Wearing a sheepskin, might as well have advertised himself as a lamb chop. You with me?"

"As long as you're going to get around to the VHS receiver we found on the mountain yesterday."

"About to. How much do you know about radiotelemetry and GPS tracking?"

"Give me the 101."

Harold scratched at his tattoos, this time the wolf tracks encircling his right upper arm.

"Okay," he said. His voice assumed a professional tone. "A VHS collar emits a radio pulse. You have to be within two or three miles for your receiver to detect the signal. Unless you're in a plane. Then you can pick up the signal from quite a bit farther away. The thing to remember is that in order to track a radio-collared lion, you have to ballpark it first using other methods. And you have to know what frequency the radio is transmitting on. Then, when you get a signal, you use the antenna on your receiver to home in."

"And you can't do that with a GPS collar?"

"Now who's getting ahead of themselves?"

Martha zipped her lips with a forefinger. "My bad. Go on."

"The short answer is no. A GPS transmitter gives you a precise location that you can access remotely, but you can't program the collar to transmit continuously or you'd run out of battery. So you set it to transmit two or three times a day, which will give you about three years of data before the built-in obsolescence. You can catch a wave on Maui, check your email on the beach, and see that your cat was at such-and-such coordinates as of three o'clock Mountain Standard Time. As far as catching the cat is concerned, you can direct the hounds to the last waypoint. That can be close enough, but only if you have a houndsman on call who can get his dogs on a hot track."

"Have you located a collared cat that you think is the Bangtail Ghost?"

"Is that what they're calling it?"

"It's what I'm calling it."

"To answer your question, yes and no."

"Start with the 'no.'"

"No, I haven't found a cat with either a VHS or a GPS collar that I think is your ghost. But I haven't gone through all the data yet—that's what I hoped you'd help me with."

"And the 'yes'?"

"I think I found the tom. The one that killed the hooker. In fact, I'm pretty sure of it."

CHAPTER TWENTY-NINE

The Making of a Man-eater

R eally?" Martha said.

"You're skeptical. I understand that. I also understand it's a moot point and can't make up for the loss of life. But looking at it glass half full, if I can study a bunch of maps for a few hours and find one killer, I—I mean, we—might be able to find the other, the one that killed the herder and, presumably, Buster Garrett. The one that's still out there hunting."

Martha gestured at the stacks of maps. "Shouldn't this have been looked into months ago?"

"As I said, this avenue of the investigation was quashed the day after the big tom was shot. Over my objection, if you want to know. I'm not supposed to be helping you out right now, not without going through the channels."

"I know," Martha said. "I appreciate what you're doing. It's just frustrating."

"For me, too. But here's what I've managed to dig up so far. With Carson Taylor's help, I should say. I called him late last night to run some of my theories by him. So when I say something about cat behavior, or how the radio receiver works, it's not just me talking off the top of my head."

"Gotcha. Not talking off the top of your head, what do you got?"

Harold pointed to the center and right-hand topographic maps on the wall.

"The dots are waypoints transmitted by a GPS receiver. The blue lines connect the dots in sequential order by time of transmission, showing the pattern of the animal's travel over time. Take, for example, this map." He pointed to the middle quad. "It details the movements of a female lion that was in the study for about fourteen months, before she was hit by a car on U.S. 89 near Willow Creek. As you can see, she was a homebody." He pointed to the maze of zigzag lines connecting the waypoints. "Looks like a Rorschach test or, as you suggested, Martha, something you'd see in a modern art museum. In the winter, she strayed to the southernmost part of her range to follow the elk herds as they migrated to the valley floor, and during most of April and May she was up around the eight-thousand-foot contour and didn't move far at all, which probably means she had kittens. Her territory covers about twenty-five square miles. That's typical for a female lion.

"Now, if we turn to the other map"—he pointed to the right-hand quad—"you see differences right away. One, this lion covers a hell of a lot more territory, roughly eighty square miles in the same time frame that the other covered twenty-five. Second, instead of so much back-and-forth travel, this one makes a circuit in a roughly oval pattern. It's what's called a beat. It has two advantages, according to Carson. First, the male can check in on the females that his territory overlaps and make scrapes and scent marks to broadcast his dominance to other males. Second, he doesn't overhunt any one area. He makes a kill and moves on. What you're looking at is the travel pattern of a male lion over a six-week period last fall. In the study he's listed as T-9. 'T' because he's a tom. 'Nine' because he was the ninth male lion collared for the study."

"Go on."

"He was GPS collared in the Bobcat Creek drainage on the Wall Creek game range"—Harold paused to glance at a notation he'd made in a notebook—"May thirty-first, 2014. At the time he was an adult, one hundred forty-two pounds, tooth wear indicating an age of around six. So that would make him about eleven years old this past November, at the time of Kincaid's death. Past his prime, but still a formidable animal and possibly the dominant male over a large area."

Martha began to interject a question and Harold held up a hand.

"Take a closer look now. What jumps out at you?"

Martha put her hands on her hips.

"It's a clusterfuck," she said. Then, holding Harold's eyes and furrowing her brow—"Is that where I think it is?"

Harold nodded. "The congregation of waypoints, the 'clusterfuck,' as you put it, indicates he was in the vicinity of the trailer where Clarice Kincaid was living for four straight days preceding the attack, and he'd visited this location a few weeks earlier as well. Now look at the other waypoint clusters and you'll see that this is a pattern. Stake out a residence—in this case, a trailer—leave, then return anywhere from a week to a month to maybe even a year later."

"How far back did you take this?" Sean asked.

"I looked at previous maps going as far back as last July. When I'd spot a cluster of waypoints near a residence, I'd cross-reference with ownership maps, find out who was living there. He staked out at least half a dozen residences, ranches, second homes, so on, the common thread being they're secluded. One of those clusters was up Bear Creek, near the home of Hunter Ross, the young boy who disappeared. Another was an old homestead-era cabin that was part of a dude ranch complex and the owners rented out to seasonal workers. Similar MOs for all. Stalk, linger, leave, return."

"He was working up his nerve," Sean said.

"He was working up to becoming a man-eater. I also think I might have found the place he crossed over. There was one cabin on the east side of the Snowcrests that he visited on five occasions over the last eight months. Resident a Viet vet, PTSD diagnosis, near recluse. When he didn't come into the town to pick up his disability check, his nephew got suspicious. Filed a missing persons. No remains were found. Dog gone, too. I think there's a good chance old Broken Tooth popped his cherry on him."

"The cat I treed with Buster wasn't wearing a collar," Sean said. "What happened to it?"

Harold nodded. "That threw me, too. Collars issue a fatality alert when the animal stops moving for a long period. Carson said that the mercury that acts as the sensing agent is so sensitive to movement that it can pick up exactly when an animal's heart stops beating. In this case, though, there was no fatality alert. The collar just quit transmitting. According to Carson, water seeping into the housing could be the cause. Then there's O-rings rotting, batteries dying, collars tearing off, electronics shorting out. Murphy's Law. But if you look at the map, you see a congregation of dots right here on these open slopes where the contour lines say the country is fairly flat. There's no dwelling here because it's in the national forest."

"Those slopes are where the herder pitched his tent," Sean said.

"Actually, they're about half a mile away. Probably where the sheep were at the time. The tom visited this general location three times, the last time about ten days before you killed him. Now what could have happened to make him lose his collar? I think it has to be the guard dogs. He got into a fight with them and the collar was damaged and got torn off."

"There were partly healed wounds on his body," Sean said. "I thought it was from fights with other male lions, but it could have been the dogs."

Martha made a sound between a grunt and a harrumph.

"I'm still not sure how this helps. We're looking for a different animal for the deaths of both the herder and Buster. Knowing where one cat was at a particular time, one that's dead and ready to be stuffed, I don't see how it helps us find the other one. Or am I missing something?"

"That's just it, though, Martha. You're not missing anything. I think it's all right here in front of us. When you've found one, you've found the other."

That was something to digest, and while Martha waited for Harold to clarify, there was a crunch of gravel outside and Marcus came in the door, a bag of groceries in each hand and a third hanging from his teeth. *When you've found one, you've found the other,* Harold had said. In another context, he might have been talking about himself and his son. Put gray streaks in his braid, add thirty pounds, and Marcus *was* Harold. He even wore a plaid flannel shirt with the sleeves cut off.

For a few minutes the business at hand was set aside and they talked about college—Marcus was in his first year at MSU and had been accepted into the prestigious film and photography school, with an eye toward applying for an internship with Lucasfilm down the road.

Harold could not be prouder and didn't try to hide it, and this was Harold, a man who presented to the world the mask of his stoicism and hid everything from everyone, present company included. Marcus asked what they were doing and said "Cool" and offered his help.

Martha said they'd appreciate his input and meant it, if only Harold would explain how following one cat's trail was going to lead to another.

"Okay," Harold said, "not to belabor the point, but just to make sure we're on the same page, we know from the maps that the big tom was in the habit of staking out potential victims. We know this because his collar told us so before he lost it. He is treed and killed in early January. Four months later, Cesar Rodriguez is killed by a lion. Obviously the same lion can't be responsible for his death. But logic tells us the two must be related."

He held up a hand as Martha began to object. "First," he said, "human attacks are so rare that the chances of them being unrelated are slim to none. Carson's words. Second, the lion chooses to kill someone who has been stalked on prior occasions. How would it know where to find the herder unless it had accompanied the big male when he stalked the herder on prior occasions?"

"That's a bit of conjecture, isn't it?" Martha said.

"I don't think so. In science, confirmation is determined by replication of test results. In this case, I think if we find any corroborating evidence that two lions were together in any of the places where the waypoints suggest a person has been stalked, then I think we have to assume that we've been dealing with two animals all along."

Martha put a finger in the slight dimple on her chin. Worked it around. "Sean, didn't you tell me that was Blake's idea, two cats, not one?"

"He thought the cat that confronted me the night Kincaid was killed might be a female, and that what I heard was the male calling to her after he had made a kill."

"But we're looking for a cat that was accompanying another for a long period of time. Not hooking up for a weekend. That seems to be stretching the bounds of species behavior."

Harold nodded. "You're right, Martha. It is, or rather, it used to be the common wisdom. Carson says that's changed, ever since everyone and his brother has nailed a game trail camera to a tree. He's seeing more and more videos of cougars being sociable: adult siblings traveling together, a male lion sharing kills with his mate and cubs, no longer that exceptional. He's even seen footage of a female traveling with four adult cubs."

"*Beowulf.*"

"Everyone turned to Sean at the word.

"Say what?" Martha said.

"Buster told me that he'd created a monster. Like in *Beowulf,* he said, as if I should know the story. When I went through his journals, I found that one of his clients shot the toe off a tom lion—this would be two and a half, maybe three years ago—and that the bullet had also broken one of the cat's teeth. Buster said he knew the cat had survived because he found his track again several months later. He also examined an elk the lion had killed and determined that the right upper canine was missing. Buster was convinced it was that same cat that went on to become the man-eater. That's why he was so obsessed with getting him. He felt responsible and knew the lion would kill again. You remember this, Martha. I told you."

"You told me. It seemed far-fetched."

"I've never heard of this *Beowulf*," Harold said.

"I know the story." It was Marcus. "It's Old English, an epic poem. Like really old. One of the professors talked about it, how there were parallels in the oral histories from our ancestors. Beowulf was a hero from a mythical land called in by the king of the Danes to slay a monster. Beowulf kills him, then finds that his job isn't finished, because by killing the monster, he has raised its mother from her sleep. He has to kill her, too."

"Really?" Martha said. Then, to Sean: "Was Garrett suggesting that this second monster was the mother to the first?"

"I asked him to be specific, but he clammed up."

"Humpff. So what now?"

Harold scratched his arm. "Well, assuming that the two cats in fact hunted together, related by blood or not, we have to assume that the remaining one will go back to the places where they stalked potential victims, just like it returned to the place where the herder was. We need to warn those residents. And if your nonagenarian shows up, he'll have a list of places to start searching for scent. Be a long shot, the cat being in any one vicinity, but better than waiting around for it to make another human kill."

"We need to get eyes in the sky," Martha said. "Get Judy McGregor up there with her receiver. Maybe she'll locate what Garrett couldn't. Or did and paid the price of his life."

"One problem, Martha," Harold said. "In order to look for a particular animal, you have to know the frequency that the collar transmitter is tuned to."

"Oh. Yeah, you said that earlier. So how do we winnow it down, the frequency numbers?"

"Well, first we got to find out what cat we're looking for. We start by going through those boxes." Harold gestured to four big cardboard boxes stacked against a wall. "Like I said earlier, some cats in the study were fitted with GPS collars. But the earliest ones had VHF, the older technology. No crumb trail, but each folder gives the specifics of the cats that were collared, and at least some of them include the frequencies."

"We're not even through all the GPS maps yet," Martha said.

They had started work sitting at the kitchen table, but by the end of two hours they had moved to the pine floor, each surrounded by stacks of paper.

"Remind me not to come back as a biologist in my next life," Martha said. "What would you like to come back as, Harold?"

"Never gave it any thought."

"Give it three seconds' thought."

"Maybe a wolverine."

"And eat carrion? Yecht. You, Sean?"

"A cow in India. They're treated like royalty and you can count on being reincarnated."

"Marcus?"

"I'd like to come back as myself, but better-looking and able to shoot a basketball. Then I could be a proper Indian."

"Me," Martha said, "I want to be a bluebird. Just fly around and eat bugs and be beautiful."

They had moved back to the kitchen, where they drank iced tea and ate "wild beast" sandwiches, as Harold called them, slabs of elk slathered in horseradish mayo on homemade sourdough.

"So what's the problem with Investigative Services?" Martha asked Harold. "I remember writing your letter of recommendation. You clearly wanted the job."

"I did, but I didn't know how much of it would be wiping the scum off my boots. Going undercover is a lose-your-soul proposition, and to what end? Put a dent in drug distribution? Poaching? Human trafficking? People selling their bodies for meth, their children's bodies, their children's children's? You take one black heart out of the equation and another starts to beat. The Smith thing last summer exposed me. Too many people know my face. I go underground again, I could be stepping into a bullet."

"And police work is different how?"

"It's a different degree of hope. You wear the badge. You're up front about who you are, what you believe in. Sometimes you can make a difference."

"You're serious, aren't you?"

"I've been giving it some thought."

"What would you do instead? Come back to the county? I'm sure we could find a place for you."

"I thought maybe run for office."

"What office?"

"I thought maybe sheriff. It's a position I'd be qualified for."

"You're kidding."

The table went silent.

"Like I said, I'm just thinking about it. I want to give back to my people. What I really want to do is find out what's happening to all our women. Indian females disappear at a rate higher than any other ethnic group in the country. Being an Indian sheriff, I could shine a light on the issue, maybe get a grassroots movement going, get the media involved, solicit funding for an investigation. And I'd be seen by the Native community as a role model. It could give kids hope that they weren't helpless in their own lives."

"You'd run against me," Martha said. It wasn't a question.

"I'd run for the office. It wouldn't be against a particular person."

"That's bullshit."

"It's how I see it."

They sat there, the silence working into the corners of the room. They were no longer friends at a table.

"Well, shit," Martha said at length. "What a hell of a time to tell me."

"What time would be better?"

"No, you're right. There's no reason you shouldn't run. I just . . . I don't know. Thanks for telling me, I guess."

"Like I said, I'm just thinking down the road, different possibilities. Wouldn't change anything between us."

"That's naïve. Of course it would." She turned to Sean. "If Harold ran against me, who would you vote for?"

"Before or after we're married?"

She gave him her dead eyes.

"I'd have to vote for my wife."

"Good answer. You got anything stronger than coffee, Harold? I feel like I need a drink."

"No," Harold said.

"That's right. You don't drink. Only your friend's blood."

CHAPTER THIRTY

A Body to Die For

The sun was riding its downward slant when they left Pony, the shadows dark on the hood of the Land Cruiser as they approached the T-junction with Highway 287.

"Can you believe that Harold?" Martha said.

"Like he said, Martha, it isn't personal."

"Sure feels like it."

"Do you want to know what I think?"

She grunted.

"I think Harold got a dose of mortality last summer. He thought he was never going to see his son again. You can't go through something like that without it changing you."

"I understand, but what's it have to do with him running for sheriff? And hell, if he's dead set on it, then run in Glacier County, where he has roots and there's an Indian voting base."

"Sheriff's safer," Sean said, not listening. "Than undercover, I mean."

Martha looked to knock on the closest wood, not finding any. "Harold scared? I never thought I'd see the day."

They drove in silence, gloom all around, streaks of dirty snow clinging to life in the barrow ditches, fields of tan stubble. Depression country. Eat-the-barrel-of-your-gun weather. Every now and then, someone did.

"So where to?" Sean asked. "It's just after three."

"Home, I suppose. No, the office first. I've got an hour of catch-up to do. Maybe two. You mind waiting for me?"

"Your two hours have a way of turning into three."

"We go home, I'll make it worth your while."

"I want details."

"Onion soup, that's the detail. Will you or won't you?"

"What?"

"Can't you follow a thought for two seconds?"

Sean smiled. "I'm just trying to get a rise. No problem. I'll drop you and go to the studio. I can get started on the rest of the boxes."

The cardboard boxes in question were in the rear cargo hold. They were three of the four that contained data that Carson Taylor had collected on the cats in the early years, those that had been fitted with VHF collars. They had managed to get through only the first box by mid-afternoon, all the time Harold could spare, having to change hats and drive up to Helena for a four o'clock meeting with state honchos. Martha, as always, was balancing too many plates to take the time, so Sean had volunteered. He didn't have high expectations that the data would lead anywhere, but he'd have a look.

But when he climbed the stairs to his studio, he found that the boxes would have to wait. He had no sooner cleared the fly-tying table to make space for them when he heard steps ringing in the hall. The cadence was unfamiliar, and when the steps stopped at his door, he preempted the knock.

"Come in."

A young woman stepped inside. She shut the door and turned to face him. In her teal puff jacket, loosely woven cashmere cap with blond fringe to match her hair, and glistening Chapsticked lips, she looked like a ski bunny, albeit one who had taken a few falls, in life as well as on the slopes.

For a long moment Sean couldn't place her.

She took off her hat and shook out her hair. "Connie Carpenter. You know, 'The Bare Necessities'? Me in my birthday suit? I left a message I'd be by."

"I haven't checked in a while. I'm sorry. It's been a long time, Connie. I thought you'd changed your mind. I just . . . Did you get your hair cut?"

"Yeah, and highlighted. But that doesn't let you off the hook. I guess you weren't looking at my face so much that night."

"If all I looked at was your face, you'd think I didn't find the rest of you attractive. I had to fall in love with your body to do the painting justice. It isn't the same as sexual attraction. There's an objectivity. You think in terms of body line and shading, not flesh and blood."

"Uh-huh. Sounds like a lot of gobbledygook to me."

"You got me, Connie. I peeked." He smiled. "I have the painting right here." He found the nude study in a stack of framed canvases in a corner of the studio. "I hope you like it."

"Thanks for not hanging it on your wall so just anyone could see it."

Sean propped the painting on his easel.

She drew her right thumb and forefinger across her lower lip.

"You don't like it?"

"No. It's great. I look great. Thanks for evening up my muchachas."

"Think your boyfriend will like it?"

"My ex-boyfriend. No, he's not going to have a chance to like it. He's not going to get to see it."

"I'm sorry."

"No reason to be sorry. He's a jerk. You know what he did? He held a level under my nipples to show me how uneven they were, said I should get a boob job to correct it and while I was at it to add another cup size. Bastard."

"If you don't want it—"

"No, I like it. Even if I can't, like, hang it up just anywhere." She took her purse off her shoulder and set it on his table and got out a checkbook. "Another thousand to settle up?"

"Yes, that sounds right. You're a very attractive woman, Connie. Some guy will come along who deserves to see it."

"Oh, he will. Some guy always comes knocking. My problem is the ones I open the door for are the wrong ones. You know what some guy said to me? After I found out he was engaged? He said that he felt like we'd been married in a previous life. Like that made it okay to cheat on his fiancée, because he'd loved me first. I had to give him credit for originality. I mean, I've heard a lot of lines."

She smiled and shook her head. "I guess that's my fate, huh? I never seem to learn."

She wrote the check. When she placed it on the table, she saw the Montana FWP label on the top cardboard box with the grizzly bear logo.

PUMA STUDY—VHF COLLARS, GAME TRAP VIDEO,
PHOTOS, MISC.

August 2009–August 2011

She raised her eyes to Sean's. "What's this about?" she said.

Sean saw no reason to lie. "Information about mountain lions in a study."

She nodded. "My old boyfriend, this was before the asshole, he ran lions with his uncles."

"What was his name?"

"Dusan. Danny Dusan."

Sean nodded. "I met them, the brothers."

"What are you doing with this stuff, trying to find the Bangtail Ghost? Or shouldn't you be telling me? I mean, you being a dick and all."

"No, it's all right. I'm helping the sheriff's department do some data crunching. Not as exciting as chasing lions."

"Yeah, they're still pretty pissed about their dog being killed. It was worth like a couple thousand dollars. Danny says it's in a chest freezer in his father's basement. Like the whole dog. They're going to give it a burial next week. Shoot off guns. Pretty redneck, if you ask me."

She looked up at him. "Strange, huh? I mean, you were sketching me from right where you're standing and I had, like, a mountain lion tenderizing me with its tongue. My heart was pounding like you wouldn't believe, but I wasn't really afraid of it. Just excited. I went home and I didn't sleep for one minute. My heart just kept racing. It wasn't until later I thought, if it had decided to kill me, who was going to stop it? I don't remember you having a gun or anything.

"Now there's this mountain lion that's terrorizing the whole valley and nobody wants to even open their door and here I am, living out of town in this old cabin on the ranch where the cowboys used to bunk, the ceiling's, like, so low you duck, and you have to park sixty-eight steps from the door. I know, 'cause I count them every night when I walk. I don't know whether it's best to keep the light on the porch on and use my flashlight, or sneak back and forth in the dark, or maybe just get another boyfriend. Jeremy was an asshole, but he had a shotgun. When I'd drive home after dark, he'd meet me and be my escort to the door. He'd kid me about having a body to die for, the cat choosing me 'cause I would taste the sweetest. But it wasn't funny. I was scared."

"Maybe you should think about renting someplace closer to town. One thing we've found out, this cat likes to haunt secluded places where it's stalked people before. We're still going through the data to locate those places. You haven't seen tracks where you live, have you?"

"No. Some guests on a horse ride saw two lions up behind the property line. That was last summer."

"Together?"

"I think so. Why?"

"We're looking into the possibility that there were two cats all along. I don't mean to tell you what to do, but the danger's real. This lion that killed Buster Garrett and the sheepherder, the one they call the Bangtail Ghost, it isn't going away. Really, you should think about moving."

"Would that I could, you know. The board comes with the job. I can't afford any other place."

Sean thought, *How can you afford the painting I made of you?*

She seemed to sense the question.

"No, don't you worry your head. I had a little bit of a windfall, like found money, and someday you'll be famous and I can say I was the hot babe in an original."

"If you change your—"

"Nope." She took two steps forward and put a forefinger to his nose. She was one of those women who are academically pretty at ten feet, but exert a magnetic attraction that increases as the distance closes.

"I'm a good judge of character, Mr. Sean Stranahan, my love life excluded. And you're a good person." She smiled up at him. "Hey, I have an idea. Maybe you could be my boyfriend, just until they catch the cat. You've already seen what you'd be getting."

She looked down at the table. Sean saw the color come into her cheeks. He thought she'd been kidding. Now he wondered if she had only been half kidding.

"I'm flattered you think of me that way," he said. "If I didn't have a fiancée . . ."

She laughed. "Story of my life."

The awkward moment passed.

"That guy who said you'd met in another life," Sean said. "What did you tell him?"

"I told him to walk and keep walking, or I'd tell his wife-to-be in the present day."

A few minutes later, Sean heard her walk and keep walking, her right hand clutching the painting he'd bubble-wrapped for her, her footsteps ringing off the travertine tiles.

"Be careful" were the last words he'd said.

"Yeah, sure," the last he'd heard.

CHAPTER THIRTY-ONE

West with the Light

Sean used his fly-tying scissors to slice open the packing tape on the top box. He didn't open it at once, but shifted his eyes to the half-tied fly in his vise. The pattern was called a Sunray Shadow, an Atlantic salmon fly that called for a Colobus monkey wing. Sean didn't have any monkey hair, preferring his monkeys alive and in trees rather than skinned for fly-tying materials. Instead, he used a substitute he got from his barber, who saved him long locks of hair cut from Asian customers. The black hair, unlike Caucasian hair, was round and strong, and would undulate in the water like a small eel. The fact that Sean had never fished for Atlantic salmon had nothing to do with selecting the pattern. That was part of why you tied the fly, not to catch the fish but to take the journey, in this case to the Gaula River in Norway, which Sean had fished many times in his mind, able to picture it from internet videos.

He picked up his thread bobbin to wrap on the wing, then set it down. No, he'd save finishing the fly as a reward after wading through the data. He blew bits of feather and fur off the table and lifted out the contents of the box, which consisted mostly of manila folders, along with several bulky VHS tapes. Sean opened the top folder. In contrast to the lions in the GPS studies, which were identified by a letter indicating sex, either a *T* or an *F*, followed by a number, the lions in the VHS study were identified by names. The first, a 160-pound tom, was named Gorgeous George.

"Hello, Gorgeous," Sean said.

FROM THE CONTENTS OF the folders, Sean learned that the lion study had begun as a shoestring project in 2009, when the first cat, a three-year-old female called Precious, had been collared in the Bridger Mountains. Each collaring team consisted of one or two houndsmen and a biologist, and in a few cases, a veterinarian. For the earliest collarings, Carson Taylor, who headed up the project, acted as both biologist and veterinarian, tranquilizing the cats, lowering them safely from the tree, taking blood samples, and fitting the collars. All but two of the seventeen cats fitted with VHS collars had been treed with the help of either Buster Garrett's hounds or the Walkers run by Ike and Jedediah Dusan.

The folders, one for each cat, included time, place, and details of capture, fading snapshots of the cats, both in the tree and on the ground as they were being collared, and the names of the participants, including, sometimes, the hounds.

That the cats were given names proved annoying, as most had later been recaptured and fitted with either a new radio collar or the more modern GPS technology, and from that point forward they were known by letter and number. In some instances the change-over was noted in the paperwork, but not always. Sean was marrying threads of information, trying to match names to numbers, when his phone buzzed.

It was Martha, calling to say he could pick her up.

"I'm barely halfway through the first box," he said.

"Well, I just got done. See you in ten."

"Yes, dear."

There was a heavy silence on the line.

Then: "I'm going to choose not to have heard that."

"Yes, dear." This time he only mouthed the words.

"I can read your lips over the phone."

"I'm not afraid of you," he said.

"You should be."

She was standing outside Law and Justice when he picked her up ten minutes later. She planted a quick kiss on his cheek and they were off.

"You can be difficult to read, you know that, Martha? Are we okay?" He really didn't know.

One of her secret smiles. "Nobody can ruin my day, not Harold Little Feather, not even you."

HE WAS CLEARING the soup bowls before the subject of the lion came up again. "I got a call back from Wilkerson on the blood that was dried on the VHF receiver," Martha said.

"Was it Garrett's?"

"Some was. Some was someone else's, which means he wasn't alone up there, which we already know. No DNA matches in the data banks. Whoever Garrett was with, he, she, didn't have a record. Gigi asked if I had taken down the band number that the receiver was tuned to. I had to admit I'd dropped the ball there. So she gave me the frequency, twenty-two. It was programmed into the receiver."

"That could help with an aerial search."

"It could." Martha fingered her chin. "The mystery is how Garrett knew to tune to that frequency."

"I'm not sure it's a mystery, Martha. I didn't have time to go through many of the files, but Garrett was listed as the houndsman for some of the captures. Either he or the biologist would have programmed in the frequency before fastening the collar. Garrett could know either way. . . . You look like you're somewhere else."

"I'm just picking at a nit. Someone, *some thing*, lit a fire under Garrett's ass, one that was hot enough that he went looking for the cat in the dead of the night. If he was called out by somebody who said he knew where the cat was, then it's logical to think that someone had picked up a signal on a receiver and knew it was the ghost because, like Garrett, he knew the proper frequency to tune in to. That means this person's name could be in the study and staring us in the face. Are you following me?"

Sean was. He felt tumblers begin to move in his head, not yet clicking into place, but beginning to fall into a loose magnetic alignment. "I'll drive into town and get the boxes," he said.

"No." Martha shook her head. "We've had a long day. The boxes will be there in the morning, and we have other priorities."

"You told me the only thing on the agenda tonight was onion soup."

"That was before Harold blindsided me about running for sheriff."

"I thought you said you weren't going to let that ruin your day."

"I'm a woman. It's my prerogative. I just want to go to bed and have you hold me while I fall asleep. Some nights a dog to curl up with isn't enough."

So they went to bed and Sean did as he was told. But as Martha's breathing steadied and deepened, he lay awake, unable to stop the tumblers in his head from turning. At four in the morning, he finally said the hell with it and eased his dead arm from under her side. He wrote a note on the kitchen table—"It has to be in the boxes." And looked up from his pen as she padded into the room in her slippers.

"What are you doing up at this hour?"

"I'm driving to the studio. I can't sleep."

"That doesn't mean you have to leave."

"You know me."

"I do know you. That's the problem. If we're going to have a proper marriage, then you can't go off in the middle of the night without telling me. I don't think that's too much to ask."

"It's not the middle of the night and I was leaving you a note. See?" He showed it to her.

"Were you going to kiss me before you left?"

"I was going to blow one because I didn't want to wake you up. Am I in some kind of trouble here?"

"Are you?"

"Oh, come here." Sean kissed her. "Is this going to become a regular thing, sharing plans and kissing each other every time one of us opens or closes a door?"

"You disapprove because you think it compromises your independence?"

"No. It's just new. Other relationships, we didn't kiss each other every time we turned around."

"How many times did you turn around in those relationships before you were out the door?"

"When you have your working face on, you don't exactly invite kissing, you know."

"Now you're saying I look hard. I have to look hard or I couldn't do the job. Men would walk all over me. You have no idea what it's like being a woman in this job."

"I can imagine."

"No, you can't. That's my point. I'm one of maybe forty female sheriffs in the entire country. You could fit all of us in a two-door garage. Just remember, though, when the clock strikes five, I'm Martha. I hang the gun belt up at the door."

"The first time I kissed you, I had to tell you to take it off."

"It was our fourth kiss, and I took it off, didn't I?"

"You took everything off."

"If that's the worst that can happen, then what's to worry about?"

She had him there, and he kissed her again and walked out into the night, and either they'd made up or they hadn't.

"Too many rules to the game," Sean said, when Choti came to his whistle. He climbed behind the wheel, she turned around twice in the passenger seat before shutting her eyes, and they drove away with the road ahead bathed in the lambency of a three-quarter moon.

BACK AT HIS STUDIO, Sean made himself a cup of instant and finished tying the Sunray Shadow. "I'd eat it," he said aloud. Then he withdrew the folders that he'd transferred to the whiskey drawer. Working on Harold's assumption that you find one cat, you find the other, he began leafing through the folders for a male lion that had originally been radio-collared and then a number of years later been treed again and fitted with a GPS collar. It was slow going, but he finally struck gold, in a very literal sense. The folder he turned in his hands was for the male mountain lion that was identified as T-9, the big tom that killed Clarice Kincaid. There was a notation that the cat had originally been radio-collared as a three-year-old in the Gold Creek drainage of the West Pioneer Mountains, entering the study under the name Simba. The second capture, when he was fitted with the GPS collar, had occurred in the Madison Range in 2014, when he was six. No mention of a broken tooth. That must have occurred later.

The logical reason for the venue change was that lions are territorial, especially males, and that a larger tom had driven the young Simba from his original range, and he had traveled east to establish a home of his own.

Sean felt a thrill race up his spine as his mind made a connection. Fly tying requires steady fingers and Sean had them, but as he pawed through the remaining folders, he noticed a tremor. He was halfway through the folders in the last box when he found what he was looking for.

A female lion, also estimated at three years of age and given the name Zahara, had been treed and radio-collared in the East Pioneers, in the Lacy Creek drainage. Sean tapped up a USGS quad on his laptop. Lacy Creek fed into the Wise River no more than five miles from Gold Creek, where Simba had been fitted with his collar. The interval between the two captures was three days. The lions were of similar age. Was he looking at brother and sister? It seemed likely.

Sean shook out the contents of the folders for both cats. There were several photographs. One showed a younger Garrett, wolfishly masculine, a hound's butt intruding into the lower right corner of the frame, the tranquilized male lion lying at his feet. Another showed the female having a blood sample drawn by a kneeling man wearing a green-and-black-checked shirt. The last photo was of a woman taking the man's place and fitting a collar. She also was wearing a green-and-black-checked shirt. Sean didn't have to turn the photos over and read the notations to know he was looking at younger versions of the lion couple, as he'd come to think of them, Drick and Scarlett Blake.

On the back of one photo were jotted details of the female's capture.

> *Zahara*
>
> *April 11, 2011*
>
> *Lacy Creek, junction with Skull Creek,*
> *East Pioneer Mountains*
>
> *Biologist, D. Blake*
>
> *Accompanied, S. Blake*
>
> *Hounds, B. Garrett*
>
> *VHS frequency 22*

Sean pushed back in his chair. "You're the guy who doesn't play well with others," he said under his breath.

So Buster Garrett and Drick Blake, Scarlett as well, had been present at the capture of the young cats, both of which, if Sean's thinking was right, had gone on to become man-eaters. Had the two cats been together all along? If so, had the female become injured and the male provided for her until he was killed? Had killing one monster in fact loosed another, as told in the poem?

Sean knew that the coincidence of Buster Garrett and Drick Blake sharing the cats' history could be just that, a coincidence. It didn't mean they were guilty of anything except a desire to join teams and

rid the countryside of a menace. Who had called who on the day
that Buster Garrett died didn't really matter, though, Sean thought,
of the two, it was more likely that Blake had placed the call, telling
Garrett that he had located the cat. Garrett had the hounds. Plus he
was the loner, and Sean saw no reason for him to ask for Blake's help,
or anyone's, and take a chance on losing the cat while waiting for it
to arrive.

Another possibility, that the mysterious second man was not
Blake, could not be dismissed. In that case, Sean was trying to force
pieces into the wrong puzzle.

One thing he did know. He wasn't going to find answers to his
questions tying flies.

Mindful of his recent admonishment, Sean punched in Martha's
cell number, though a glance at the graying sky told him that she'd
be feeding chickens or mucking out Petal's stall after turning her
out to pasture, and it wasn't her custom to buckle her phone onto
her duty belt until she'd traded her overalls for her khakis.

He waited until the answering service kicked in and left a message, telling her where he was headed and why, adding a postscript
not to worry, that he wasn't. He left an identical message on her office landline, minus only the "I love you."

Blake might well be a vain man, Sean thought, an arrogant, con-
descending, overbearing man. Even a zealot. His sister had called
him mad. But Sean had not seen him as sinister, and on his visit to
the yurt, he had been drawn in by the force field of the man's unde-
niable charisma. Blake's offer to help hunt down the man-eater had
come across as genuine.

No, Sean thought, the worst thing Blake could be guilty of was
cowardice, if in fact he had fled from the ridge when Buster was

attacked. That he had not reported the incident meant to Sean that he'd been embarrassed to do so.

So he told himself as the day came to life, and so what if the telephone wires were strung with blackbirds that should have arrived weeks ago and stared with cold pebble eyes as the Land Cruiser passed, heading west with the light?

CHAPTER THIRTY-TWO

Secrets of the Heart

When Martha drove in to work that morning, a blinking light on her office phone vied for attention with a manila envelope and a white cardboard box on her desk. Martha opened the envelope first, which carried the letterhead of the county coroner's office. It was the preliminary report on Buster Garrett's cause of death, strangulation from a crushed windpipe—no surprise. Ancillary to the primary cause was blood loss due to puncture wounds consistent with those from a cat's teeth. Measurements of the bite marks indicated an animal with a skull the approximate size of a grown mountain lion's. A formal autopsy, conducted by the medical examiner, Bob Hanson, was scheduled for the following day.

Martha put the letter back into the envelope and turned her attention to the box, which was from the regional crime lab and carried its seal. She used the blade of her Swiss Army knife to slice through the tape. Inside was a note from Georgeanne Wilkerson, saying that the enclosed items were personal belongings found with or near Buster Garrett's body. The box also included the claw pendant Sean had found near the sheepherder's body and the bullet he'd found under the skin of one of the guard dogs. Each piece of evidence was encased in its own resealable bag. Martha was free to open and examine the effects in any order, as they had been fully processed, with a noted exception. She was to call the lab before opening the sealed bag marked #7.

Martha pulled on blue latex gloves and followed the protocol. The first bag held Garrett's wallet, which he wore Western-style, on a chain affixed to his belted jeans. The wallet was bloodstained and contained Garrett's driver's license, credit cards, medical insurance information, currency. It also included two facing photographs in a plastic sleeve, with a frosted surface meant to keep the photos from slipping out of the wallet. One was a sepia-toned snapshot of a woman with severe features standing under a cracked cowboy hat by a sign that read GARRETT CATTLE STATION. The land behind her was desolate and faded nearly white. *Garrett's mother?* The other photograph showed Garrett's wife standing with what Martha presumed were Buster's two sons, the boys wearing Little League uniforms that read ACE HARDWARE BLUE JAYS.

Another bag contained the lion's claw pendant and another the bullet. An enclosed note supported Sean Stranahan's conclusion in the field. The rifling marks on the base of the bullet were a match with the bore peculiarities of Garrett's .45/70 rifle.

None of this was anything to elevate the blood pressure. The box was now empty but for item #7. It was a matchbox, about three inches long by an inch wide, with a sliding cover. A snarling red lion, similar to the one on the Scottish national flag, was embossed on the cover. Through the clear plastic, Martha could read the lettering.

WILD AND FREE SYMPOSIUM

North American Felid Society
Workshops, Conference, Banquet
Salt Lake City Convention Center
SALT LAKE CITY, UTAH
August 24–August 27, 2018

Martha shook the box to see if she could hear matches shifting. She couldn't, and she called Wilkerson's number. She twiddled her thumbs one way, then the other, until Wilkerson picked up.

"What's with the box, Gigi? Can I open it or not? I have gloves."

"Good morning, Martha. No gloves necessary."

"Why don't I hear matches shaking?"

"Because they're flammable and we have travel restrictions. And they aren't what's notable."

"Isn't that for me to decide?"

A beat of silence. "What side of the bed did you get up on?"

"The wrong one, like most mornings. Sorry, Gigi."

"That's okay. We love you for all your warts and graces, as Bob Hanson says."

"Kind of him. I'm sliding the cover back now."

On the white inside of the box was a heart outlined in blue ink, with an arrow through it. It was signed with the letter S. The S was scrolled, like calligraphy. Underneath was a number—407.

"Where did you find this, Gigi?"

"It was in the butt stock of Buster Garrett's rifle. You know how you can remove the butt plate and ream out the stock to lighten up a gun or change its balance point? Well, it looks like he used a drill bit to make three overlapping cavities. The opening was just long and wide enough to fit the matchbox. I got a confession. I would have never have noticed it, but the screws holding the plate on were marred by the wrong-size screwdriver. I got curious and unscrewed the plate. I'm guessing 407 is a hotel room number. And whoever drew the heart was who was waiting for him in bed. Looks like Garrett wasn't getting all of his pussy out of trees."

The remark struck Martha as crude and out of character for Wilkerson, but, she thought, possibly accurate.

"I got a number for the North America Felid Society," Wilkerson said. "Guess who was listed as a speaker last year?"

"Scarlett Blake," Martha said.

"She's one of the weirdo lion people?"

"That would be the one."

"No, it was Buster Garrett. He spoke about the role of the houndsman in predator studies."

Martha let this sink in. "Did you specifically ask if either of the Blakes was there?"

"No. I had no word from your office that they were of interest. This is my argument against strict compartmentalization. We need more back-and-forth with your people."

"This isn't the time to get into that. Who did you speak to?"

"A woman who lives in Salt Lake. She was the program organizer. You think Garrett was having an affair with this cat woman? Scarlett starts with an *S*."

Martha grunted. *Buster Garrett and Scarlett Blake?* They were an odd couple at first glance, at second glance, too, but both were wildlife advocates, even if Buster's advocacy sometimes came with a bullet. Sean had told her about the friction between Scarlett and her brother. Perhaps Buster was an escape, or a way at getting back at her brother's own indiscretions. Or maybe it was just old-fashioned romance. The heart wants what the heart wants.

All speculation, and Martha speculated while she waited for someone to pick up the phone. The organization woman said hello. Yes, she told Martha, Scarlett had been both a presenter and a panelist. Everyone knew her—she was a rock star in the world of wildlife advocacy. Wore her scars like jewelry. And no, her brother had not attended. He was invited, but the organizer's understanding was that he had a conflict with a conference of the World Wildlife Federation held in Berlin. Couldn't really blame him. The WWF had a lot more trees to shake money out of than the Felid Society.

"How about Buster Garrett?" Martha asked her.

"Oh, he's a controversial figure, that one. But as he points out, houndsmen need lions in the hills or they're out of a job. The real enemies are the only-good-cat-is-a-dead-cat people. The ranchers, mostly."

"Would Garrett know Scarlett Blake?"

"Oh, sure. It's a small community. Everybody knows everybody."

Martha asked what hotel the presenters had stayed at and thanked the woman for the information.

"If I can be of any more help . . ."

Martha saw that she had not yet picked up her messages and tapped the button. The first was from Cecil Flowers, saying he was at a rest stop on the Colorado/Wyoming line and should arrive the day after tomorrow. Did she get the perfume?

"Yeah, and you owe me fifty bucks, mister," she said to the room.

She punched in the second message and listened to Sean's voice. An odd tingling sensation flushed over her face, as if her skin had contracted around a thousand pinpoint icicles. The tight feeling left and she replayed the message just to hear his voice again, then switched off the phone with his last words echoing—"Don't worry. I'm not."

And she wouldn't have, if not for a heart inked inside a souvenir matchbox.

CHAPTER THIRTY-THREE

A Soft Spot to Fall

The last time Sean had crossed the bridge over the Wise River, he'd had to go four-wheel to negotiate the snowed-in road that wound up Swallowtail Creek. The snow was a month gone, but the rig fishtailed in the mud, and finally he set the brake and got out to lock the hubs.

It was while squatting by the left front tire that he noticed the tread marks in the mud. He had assumed the tread pattern he'd been following belonged to Blake's Land Rover, for even from behind the wheel he had noted that they were similar to the pattern of tread he'd seen on his first visit to the yurt months earlier. He had not automatically made the leap in judgment to conclude that the tread looked similar to the tire tracks that he and Martha had seen at the trailhead only two days earlier. Those tread marks had been rained on and were largely washed out.

Now, though, his eyes were closer to the ground, and he noticed that the Rover's tread partly obscured narrower tire marks left by a trailer, and that the tires were distinctly mismatched. This confirmed that it had been Blake's rig at the trailhead.

Sean should have stopped then. He should have turned around and driven back into cell range to consult with Martha. He told himself to stop, even told Choti to stop him. But he had never listened to his own advice. Knocking on the spider-cracked dash, an old habit for luck, he drove to the locked gate and left Choti in the Land Cruiser with the window cracked. He began to climb through the trees. The yurt came into view. He saw the Rover parked in front, where it had been on his first visit. No horse trailer, though. It must be around back.

No smoke pigtailed from the chimney. The aspen tree that had been skeletal on Sean's first visit was newly minted with leaves. The only sound was a faint flapping from the tattered prayer flags fluttering from the branches.

He knocked, feeling the emptiness within that he had felt when standing before the herder's tent.

"Hello—it's Sean Stranahan. Anyone there?" Echoing silence. He turned the knob. Inside, the tidy ship that had been the Blakes' home was not in evidence. The vestiges of a breakfast congealed on a plate on the couch, a half-full mug of coffee set on the arm, begging to be tipped over. Seam dipped an index finger. The coffee was as cool as the morning. The acrid sage odor of the lynx permeated the room. Books, magazines, clothes, whatnot, all strewn across the floor.

Sean lifted his eyes to the shelf that ran the perimeter of the room. The skulls were there, including the tigress's skull in the plexiglass cube. Also a dead soldier that had been a bottle of rum.

One hard day's night? Or a life falling apart?

Sean riffled through papers stacked on the end of the table that served as an office. Business dealings, records of sales of Scarlett's wildlife videos, nothing stood out. The laptop was shut, asleep but not turned off. Sean touched the space bar. He needed either the right fingerprint or the password. He keyed in *lion*. The little round icons shook their heads. He played around with words—*Scarlett, Tatiana, Zahara*—as he tried to recall his time with the man. What was it that the guides in India had called him?

"Keeten"? Something like that. "Keesan"? Closer, Sean thought. "Kessan." The icons vibrated. No cigar. "Kesin"? He was in.

In, but where to go? Documents? Photos? That would take time he didn't have. He found the email and dragged it up. The most recent messages were innocent enough—correspondence with wildlife organizations, a request for a radio interview, nothing that caused Sean to pause. He scrolled down to see if there were any emails during the window of Garrett's disappearance. He told himself it was too much to hope that he'd find a correspondence with Garrett, and he was right. Nothing popped up. Sean took a long shot and opened deleted messages.

And there it was. Blake had deleted an email correspondence with bgarrett45/70@troubadour.com on the night that Garrett had gone to his wife's house to pick up his best hound. Blake had moved the message to trash, but had failed to empty his trash folder. He had written:

Zahara called 8 p.m. Receiver places her in vicinity where Simba killed the prostitute. She has come into estrus and is looking for love in all the old places. If you can get a nose on her, we still might be able to end this before the next one.

Garrett had responded at 10:07 p.m.

Ninety minutes out. U need a horse?

The response came a minute later.

Already saddled. See you at the turn-around.

The next one, Sean thought, must mean the next victim. Going
back to the in-box, Sean found that the two men had checked in
with each other irregularly, dating back to the previous November.
Mostly it was a where-to-meet-up-and-when kind of back-and-forth.
The gist Sean took away was that the two men had teamed up to
search for the cats, starting shortly after Clarice Kincaid's death,
with Garrett doing most of the hunting and Blake checking in with
advice and asking for progress reports.

Sean had left the door open so that he could hear anyone approaching. He felt like he was pressing his luck, and closed the
screen of the computer. Feeling hyperalert, as if he were walking on
a cushion of air, he went around to the side where the galvanized tub
squatted on the deck. He stepped onto an overturned crate that
served as a stool. A skim of ice rimmed the tank. Peering at the surface, he saw his face in the reflection of the water, his visage as shaky
as his nerve.

He straightened up. Where to now? Behind the yurt was a large
barnlike structure he'd noticed on his prior visit. Tire tracks skirted
the yurt, passed by the horse trailer, and headed toward the sliding
double doors. He'd check it out, but the enclosure was closer. As Sean
approached it, he half expected to hear Tatiana greet him with a snarl.

The chain-link door was closed, but the padlock's shackle hung loose. *No reason to go inside,* he told himself. *None at all. And perhaps one good reason not to.*

"It's just me," he said aloud, as he stepped into the enclosure. "Anybody else here?" His voice had a quaver.

He began to walk toward a copse of trees where he'd seen Tatiana disappear when carrying away the rabbit. Beyond the pine saplings, and striped by their tightly spaced trunks, something white was lying on the ground. A patch of old snow? But the only snow he'd seen had receded to the peaks. Here and there were great boulders of white quartz colored with rose lichen, and as Sean stepped past one of the rocks, he felt a puff of wind and felt a prickling sensation that made his right thigh momentarily tighten. Then, in front of him, an apparition rose from the ground. The apparition was white, and as it was covered with pink blotches, he at first took it for one of the quartz rocks. But how could it be a rock if it moved? It looked like the shrouded figure of a woman. She was swaying in a breeze. Sean found that his mind was traveling in circles and then the circles began to slow and then to slow some more. The apparition was coming forward. At its side, he saw a blue-white creature the size of a dog.

"It's you," Sean said.

He felt a second puff of wind and a sharp sting like a bee. He turned his head. Two small pink flowers had blossomed on the back of his right thigh. Again he saw the apparition, but this time it was behind him and had taken the form of a man. The man was animal-like, with one long arm that looked to be made of leather. Points of light glinted from the hand. A mane of dirty hair fell across the face. Sean's nostrils drank in a heavy odor. He turned back toward the first figure and stumbled, almost falling. It was as if an oxen's yoke had settled onto his shoulders. Gasping for breath, he put his hands on his knees.

"Who are you?" he said. "What are you?"

Sean's mouth was dry and it was hard to form words. He craned his neck to see what had become of the flowers. They were still there. He heard a scream then. It seemed to reverberate off the rock walls of the canyon. Far away. Some other world.

"Do you hear her, Sean?"

Was someone speaking? Or was it in his head? Then he heard the scream again. But fainter, like echoes fading.

And once more came the voice. "That is your Bangtail Ghost. But you will see soon enough that 'ghost' is wishful thinking."

Sean stumbled forward. One step. His knees wobbled. Another.

"Go. Run if you can, but take my advice and find a soft spot to fall."

CHAPTER THIRTY-FOUR

The Language of Love

By the time Martha reached the Wise River, the blackbirds that had strung the telephone wires had flown, though she was lost in thought and wouldn't have seen them had there been thousands.

A quick phone call had established that Buster Garrett and Scarlett Blake had indeed stayed at the same hotel during the symposium, and that Scarlett's room was in fact 407. That plus the matchbox was strong if circumstantial evidence that the relationship between the two went beyond the professional. Then, too, she recalled Sean's description of the scars on Scarlett's body and her cryptic warning to be aware of all predators, which he'd taken to include her brother.

Well, it certainly could be possible. A possessive man who was blind to betrayal, perhaps, until he wasn't; a proud woman who had taken too much abuse at his hands; and a flawed rogue who took her heart and hid it in the buttstock of a rifle. A love triangle. A story as old as the mountains in the window. A story, and this she knew well, that could precipitate into violence.

"Sean," she said aloud, as she followed the directions he'd given her in his message. "You don't know the trouble you've driven into."

SEAN STRANAHAN HEARD the scream as if from a great depth. He seemed to have traveled to the bottom of a lake that glimmered with lights, like the phosphorescence of a cresting wave. He tried to move toward the lights, and then pulled back into himself, where all was dark. Again he heard the scream. This time he tried to bend to it, but was restrained. He couldn't lift his arms and something rough was pulled over his face. It itched and made him feel like sneezing. Then the roughness was gone and the phosphorescence danced closer as his pupils drew to points in the glare.

Vaguely, he remembered being half carried, half dragged from the enclosure, remembered his head banging off stones and downed timber.

Where am I?

He opened his eyes and found that he was sitting with his back to a tree. He saw movement. Then the same apparition he'd seen before loomed over him. Not the woman's image, but that of the man. The image was shot with sun, hazy, and then, in a heartbeat of resolve, he saw it clearly.

"I know you." Sean's voice was thick. "Your sister says you tried to grow whiskers."

He became aware of a burning sensation and looked down at his legs. On the side of his right thigh toward the back were the two pink flowers. He could see now that they were tufts of fiber on thin metal shafts. He tried to grasp the nearest and found that his hands were bound behind the trunk. He bent forward from his waist, trying to reach the tufts with his teeth.

Blake's voice cut through the fog. "You are quite flexible, Sean. But here, let me help you. The dart is barbed. It takes a hard yank." He reached with his right hand, which was thick with hair, and Sean felt a sharp, jabbing pain.

"You shot me," Sean said.

Drick Blake moved a few feet away and squatted down. He rolled the dart in his fingers. "The dosage is the same as I use for an adult mountain lion. A combination of zolazepam, ketamine, and xylazine. You needed two. The first didn't take the proper effect, and then I had to sedate you for the drive up here. It will be undetectable in your bloodstream in a few days, should you have a heartbeat."

"Where are we?"

"At the beginning, Sean, if you must know. Where the circle started."

"You mean where you collared Zahara."

"Yes, near enough. Simba too, not far from there. How did you know?"

"It's in the paper trail. Buster kept records. Don't do anything stupid. I'm not the only person who knows what you've done. The sheriff knows, and she knows where I am."

Blake smiled. "You and I, we are men who follow our gut. We do not pause to inform others." But the smile seemed forced.

Just keep him talking, Sean thought. *This is someone who likes to talk, who wants to be noticed, to be flattered.*

"Here, I have something to show you." Blake began to paw through a backpack. He pulled out a takedown rifle, then a recording device with a small bullhorn.

"Is that what you shot me with?"

"No, I shot you with a gun that uses a CO_2 cartridge. That is why you didn't hear the shots. This rifle makes more of a bang. It shoots the same darts, but at a much higher velocity."

He began to thread the recording device onto the bullhorn. "I taped the mating call of a female cougar a few years ago," he said. "The recording can be broadcast at a hundred and forty decibels. That is louder than the loudest scream registered by a human woman. Some biologists believe that only the fairer of the sexes is capable of caterwauling. That is only because they haven't heard it. I assure you tomcats can and will scream, if not as often as females, and in a lower register. Scarlett can imitate the caterwauling using only her vocal cords. Uncanny. Of course her rendition is not so loud. My opinion is that regardless of Zahara's interpretation of the call, she will respond. She will come to the call of a male cat, but she is just as likely to investigate the call of another female, thinking that if that cat is coaxing a male, she might steal him away. Imagine her courage, as damaged as she has been by man and nature."

Sean heard the first distant chimes of Blake's intentions toward him.

"How has she been damaged?"

"I have not physically seen her for some years. Her track shows that her right foot is turned inward. I have my suspicions as to the cause, but we shall see shortly enough."

"What happens to me? What will she do when she finds me instead of a mate?"

"That we find out."

"Is this what happened to Buster? You tied him to a tree and the cat killed him? I know you had a hand in it."

"If you know, why did you come alone? No, you came because you *thought* you knew something, not because you did. Soon you will be departed from this Earth. The least you can do is leave it with dignity. Buster did, almost until his last breath."

"The sheriff is on her way."

"I'll make you a promise, Sean. If you quit asking so many questions, I'll tell you some of what you don't know. Promise?"

"Yes." *Anything to keep breathing,* Sean thought.

"FIRST, I CAN ASSURE YOU that Zahara had nothing to do with Buster's death. It was his own guilt that sealed his fate. He and I go back a long way. Very early on, I recognized the ruthless qualities that made him valuable. Let no bleeding heart tell you otherwise— but a good houndsman is more important to a predator study than the biologist drawing blood. Without the houndsman, there is no lion to collar, no DNA to test. Buster was like other houndsmen I knew, rough and ready, not really giving a damn about how he came across to the world. But where others drew lines, he saw opportunities and stepped over those lines. I had use for such a man. I, too, was a crosser of lines, although for different reasons.

"You asked me if I had ever considered returning Tatiana to the wild. I did, though briefly, as she has a genetic condition that compromises her vision, and would have made her ability to secure prey doubtful. You saw how long it took her to spot the hare. But the concept of rewilding has long fascinated me. I have a far-seeing eye and my travels studying the big cats of the world have revealed one indisputable fact, that they are vanishing from the Earth at a startling rate. I foresee a time when they disappear completely from former habitats, and that when those habitats are restored—*if* they are restored—there will be a need for rewilding captive-bred predators into their former ranges.

"Specifically, what will be required is a blueprint for introduction. You can't just open a cage door. That would be sending an animal to certain death. The rewilding must be gradual. You introduce the animal to its new environment, keep it safe from other predators, and supplement its diet as it learns to hunt. You have to wean it from its dependence upon you, and yet at the same time encourage its instinct. You must refrain from interference. A tall order. If the animal imprints upon you, or begins to view humans solely as providers of food, the line you walk becomes fine indeed. It is, in fact, possible that the cat would come to see humans as more than providers of protein. It would begin to see them as composed of it. That has happened. A tigress in the Dudhwa Tiger Reserve, in India, that was raised from a cub and rewilded ate two dozen people before she was killed."

Blake shrugged. "Personally, I am willing to sacrifice lives to the experiment. After all, man has been persecuting the cats for thousands of years. Why should he not suffer for his acts, when the cats suffer so greatly for theirs?"

"Is that what you have done," Sean said, "rewilded a cat that turned man-eater? Created a monster?"

"That word, 'monster.' I refuse to acknowledge it. Only humans are capable of monstrous deeds. A man-eater is simply an animal that has been forced to prey upon the one species that can feed its hunger. It has not broken any law of nature, only of man. Did Buster tell you that he sold Zahara to me, when she was only a cub? Or that she had a brother we named Simba, and that I rewilded both of them, starting when they were three? No? Buster told me that you knew. But then I think he was trying to postpone the inevitable. Those who are staring at death will say anything. It is what you are doing now. Keeping me engaged, wondering where the key to your escape may be found. I will give you a clue." He touched his breastbone. "It is under my shirt, safe and sound." Then he laughed. "There is no key. You are tied by a rope with Boy Scout knots. I have a leg iron and shackle, but it is being deployed elsewhere."

He paused, a finger in the air. "No, nothing. I thought I heard her call." He turned an ear. Then shook his head.

"As I was telling you about Buster, that hard core he presented, it grew softer with his age and his abstinence. He grew a conscience. Having stolen the cubs from their mother's den and so been an accomplice to their rewilding, he felt responsible for the human kills. It was bad enough when the male had turned to man-eating. When the herder was taken by Zahara, his remorse was compounded. It was Buster himself who had killed Simba, who was her provider. And it was his client who had wounded the tom and turned it maneater in the first place. He came to the yurt a broken man and told me that he could no longer stay silent. He had blood on his hands that he could not wash away."

"Like you could."

Blake frowned. "If you wish to put it that way. I couldn't let him talk, of course. When my role in the buying and training of these animals became known, I would lose my position. Rewilding captive animals is against federal law. I could go to prison. Wrongful-death suits could be brought against me and my foundation by the families of those who'd been killed. Most important, I would no longer be able to raise money, and I would lose my voice as an advocate for the cats. You do understand I could not let this happen. There is a greater good to consider than the collateral sufferings of a few people. And there was another matter, a personal one, concerning Mr. Garrett and myself. Leave it at that."

"You saw a way to bury a murder and cast blame on the cat. What did Buster do that you hated him enough to kill him?"

Sean saw rage boil up in Blake's face. He had touched a nerve.

"That is none of your concern."

"How did you do it, Drick?"

A pause. The dark blood flushed from his cheeks, and for the first time Sean noticed that his face was heavily bruised. He had seen the signs of a struggle on the ridge where they found Garrett's body. He must have fought back before the sedative kicked in.

Blake collected himself before speaking.

"I lured him with the one bait he could not resist—Zahara. I told him that I had located her by her calling and that we could find her with the radio receiver. He would buy it. It was in fact the truth."

"What did you use to kill him?"

Blake laughed. "You may find you do not want an answer to that question. It's time. No more words. We will speak Zahara's language now."

There was a clicking sound as Blake turned the recorder on, a long moment of static, and then a scream, startling in its intensity. And again, one long note rising and falling, pulsing in echoes, as if the canyon itself had taken up the call.

He switched the recorder off. Silence. That vast stillness of the north. Then, somewhere far away, the faintest response, whispered on the wind.

Blake tapped his ear.

Sean worked his bound hands, searching for a weakness in the knot, anything to give him hope. But his hands were almost useless now, the circulation all but cut off.

Minutes passed.

"Maybe she won't come," Sean said.

"She has been searching for a mate for days, maybe weeks. She will—you will see. I will tempt her."

He played the recording again. Then, from the mountain, the answer. Closer? Sean thought so.

Blake gave him his smile. "She will come now. She has already started."

CHAPTER THIRTY-FIVE

Monster by a Different Name

It was the lynx, finally, that led her to the body. Martha had checked the yurt and the grounds in that order, finding no sign that anyone was near. Sean had told her about the rabbit chase with the lynx, and as she passed the open door of the enclosure, she hesitated. She unsnapped the safety strap on her bear spray and did the same with her holstered revolver, tapped the hammer of the .357 for assurance, took a breath, and entered.

The enclosure was so large you could walk through the middle of it without knowing you were inside fencing. Martha could feel each of her footfalls, could feel the pulsing of blood in her throat. As she approached the back of the enclosure she saw the lynx. The animal was crouched beside a white cloth or sheet that appeared to be bloodstained. The lynx flattened her ears.

"Good kitty." She had forgotten the name that Sean had told her.

She took a bold step and the cat, rising to full height, turned and bound away in a fluid motion.

Martha steeled herself, flashing back to the dogs that had eaten the herder's body. But then she saw a corner of the cloth flutter with no wind to make it move. The shape shifted and a woman sat up. Her face was filthy, her hair caked with mud. The entire front of what Martha now recognized as a robe with a sash tie was soaked in blood. Some was crusted over and dark, almost black. Other patches were crimson.

The woman spoke. Her voice was unexpectedly calm. "I've lost blood, but the bleeding has stopped now. Tatiana has been cleaning me with her tongue. Please do not hurt her."

Martha squatted down. She saw that the woman—she knew it was Scarlett Blake, though she had never met her—had a shackle on one ankle, and that she was chained to a small tree.

"Let me see how badly you're hurt."

Martha tugged the sash open. The right half of the woman's torso had swirls of raised white scar tissue that resembled scrollwork. The left side, what she could see, for the skin was sticking to the cloth, had the same pattern of deep lacerations, but they were fresh and raw, raking from the collarbone to the woman's abdomen. Sean had told Martha about the scars. Still, she was not prepared for the oddly beautiful horror, and gasped involuntarily.

"Who did this to you?"

"He did." A pause. "As he has before." Her eyes never quite settled, but roamed, seeking one cloud, then another.

"Your brother, you mean?"

Scarlett brought her head down. She seemed to see Martha for the first time. "If you wish to call him that."

"Sean Stranahan, is he with him? Are they together?"

A hesitation.

"I know he was here. His rig is parked at the gate. His dog is inside."

"He was here. When we met in the winter, I found him . . . attractive. Someone who knows where his feet are planted on the Earth. He had kind eyes."

"Where are they, Scarlett?"

"I tried to warn him. I told him, 'Never turn your back.'"

"Where have they gone?"

"Earlier, I could hear her calling."

"The lion?"

"Zahara, yes."

"Where? Can you direct me?"

Again, a hesitation.

"You do understand that if you withhold information and anything happens to him, then you could be implicated. You could be abetting a crime. You could go away."

The eyes that had been roaming again relinquished the sky. Her gaze fell on Martha.

"Go where?" she said. "I'm already gone."

"Go to prison."

"Where do you think I've been?" She stood, her body shaking, and tugged on the shackle. "Where do you think I am now?"

SEAN FELT CAUGHT IN that nightmare where feet turn to cement as a demon in diabolical form draws closer and closer. He heard a scraping noise and turned his head. Blake, who had not spoken since the second call of the cat, was climbing into a tree some twenty feet away. His boots showered down the rough, scale-like bark. The tranquilizer gun he had drawn from his pack was slung over his shoulder. He reached a crotch in the trunk and sat down on one of the heavy lower branches.

Sean's eyes searched the forest. Shadows upon shadows. The cat's last call had sounded close, closer than any before. He strained his eyes. He saw a smear of tan in the trees. One glimpse and it was gone. Was it the lion? Or maybe an elk? Their coats were similar in color. But wouldn't an elk have run off upon hearing the lion's scream?

Sean had that wincing feeling of waiting for a big gun to go off. But there was no sound except for the whispering of a Canada jay in the forest canopy. Then Sean heard the caterwaul of the cat. It seemed to come from all around him at once.

"IS THERE A KEY to this damned thing?" Martha said.

Receiving no response, she opened the saw blade of her Swiss Army knife and got to work on the sapling. Five minutes later she had accomplished little beyond rubbing the skin off her hand where it gripped the handle. She knew there would be an ax somewhere on the property, probably a chain saw as well, but the work acted as a stimulus and seemed to loosen the woman's tongue. Martha kept sawing, and as the sawdust began to accumulate, she coaxed the story of the affair out of Scarlett Blake.

Scarlett initially feigned ignorance, but when Martha told her about the matchbox, the woman's face had collapsed.

Buster, she told Martha, had not been physically attractive to her, not the persona he presented the world. The five o'clock shadow. The scar. The machismo. But she had admired his struggle, the fact that he had struggled when so many of his nature would succumb to their baser instincts. Buster changed, and change, real change, was as rarely found in the human animal as it was among the cats.

But what he could not change were the sins of his past, and he suffered for them. When he was thrown together with Scarlett, they had circled each other warily before becoming each other's port in the storm that was Scarlett's brother.

The sapling was cut halfway through.

"Did he know about it?" Martha asked.

No, she said. Drick was too arrogant, too vain to consider that she might find comfort elsewhere. In the end, she had confessed to the affair, though not to the name. The name had come out after the claws dug in.

"Did Drick kill him?"

The green eyes had begun to wander again and Martha held up two spread fingers. "Look at me. I need to know what happened."

Drick, she said, told her he'd arranged to meet Buster in the Pioneers, near the drainage where Zahara had first been introduced into the wild and where she had returned before to find a mate. Said that he had located Zahara by the radio transmitter built into her collar. When Drick came back the following day, he told her that they had found no trace of Zahara and he assumed that Buster had gone home. Scarlett hadn't believed a word, starting with the location where he said they had met. His explanations seemed pat and overly rehearsed. Drick didn't have to tell her that he'd killed Buster. She'd seen the murder in his eyes. She'd seen the signs of a struggle on his face, too, the bruising and cuts that he explained away by saying that his horse had ducked under a branch and scraped him off. She'd seen the blood on his clothes. Blood persists. Having been ritually cut by her brother as a sign of his ownership, she knew a thing or two about that.

"I saw his body," Martha said. "Buster was killed by a cat. I saw the teeth marks in his throat."

"That is only what you think you saw. He makes . . . contraptions."

Martha was almost through the sapling. She made a cut on the other side of the tree, an inch underneath the facing cut, so she could control the direction that it fell in. She pushed against the trunk. "Timber," she said.

Scarlett was wobbly, but strong enough to walk with Martha's assist, the chain dragging in her wake. At the yurt, she hobbled over to the shelf with the skulls and opened the jaws of one of the smaller ones. She turned with a key in her hand and unlocked the shackle.

Martha looked at her.

"I just remembered," Scarlett said. "I was a little woozy, but I'm all right now. If you want, I can take you to my brother."

The drive was no more than half a mile, but a long grind in second gear up switchbacks to the open country of the snow line. Scarlett had brought a radio receiver from the yurt and said the range would be extended in the high country.

At the end of the trace road, Martha parked and wedged stones under the tires, an old habit in steep country. Martha asked Scarlett again if she was okay to wait in the rig. Scarlett said she was fine, that the blood made the wounds on her torso look worse than they were. Just follow the contour, Scarlett told her. And keep your ears open.

She drew her fingers down the scars on her face. "Remember," she said, "it is not Zahara you need to be afraid of. The monster goes by a different name."

CHAPTER THIRTY-SIX

Zahara

Sean heard the light padding of the footfalls. They seemed to be coming up from behind him. He craned his head to his right as far as he could.

Zahara.

The cat had managed to approach without his seeing so much as a hair. She was fifteen feet away, her stomach pressed against the forest floor, her rear legs tucked under her belly. Sean felt the hairs on the back of his neck stir against his jacket collar. The cat pinned her ears back and growled deep in her throat.

"Hello, Zahara." He tried to strike a conversational tone, but the words sounded strangled.

Again the cat growled.

"Let me have a look at you, Zahara."

As if on cue, the cat stood. Low, her belly brushing the dead grass that poked above the thin snow cover, she circled the tree trunk. Sean's eyes never left her. *Never turn your back.*

Zahara opened her mouth in a silent hiss. Her muzzle was wrinkled back. Sean could see the long canines.

"My, what sharp teeth you have." His voice was not his own.

What did he know about the proper response to lion aggression? Hold their eyes. Make yourself appear larger. Pick up a stick, any weapon at hand. Don't run. A lot of good that did. The rope that tied his hands behind the tree trunk prevented him from standing, and even had his hands been free, the only debris within reach was leaf litter and pinecones.

She was facing him now, no more than ten feet away. Sean could smell a faint odor. Something like sawdust and sage, but darker. She circled back behind him.

In the next few minutes she circled him three more times, her posture aggressive, but each time the circle was larger, the cat a few feet farther away. Then she inexplicably turned her back to the tree, glanced once at him over her shoulder, and, her ears no longer folded flat, began to walk away. It was only then that Sean noticed the pronounced limp in her right foreleg and heard the moaning she made with every other step.

He heard a sharp cracking sound from somewhere above. A bloom of pink appeared on Zahara's left haunch. She whipped around and tugged at the dart with her teeth. She caught Sean's eyes and spat at him. She took a step toward him, then, seeming to lose focus, stopped and looked around curiously. She glanced skyward, as if looking for a singing bird. Her eyes fixed on the man in the pine tree. A low growl came from her throat. She walked over to the trunk and stood against it, reaching high with her front paws and clawing at the bark. Twice she leapt up into the lowest branches, but well short of Blake, whose hands gripped the tranquilizing rifle. The third time the cat leapt up, she fell back onto the ground. Her legs quivering, she began to walk away. Her path took her directly in front of Sean, so close that he might have touched her with a stick, but she did not appear to even see him. A few yards away, she sat down. The muscles in her forelegs fluttered. Then she lay down. Her head drooped and she rolled over onto her side.

"That was intense. I was afraid I might have to give her a second dart."

"What?" Sean's eyes were on the cat.

"It would have been dangerous for her, one dose on top of another." Blake set down the rifle on a stump. He began to dig through his backpack. He spread a space blanket over the ground. Standing on one end of it, he half lifted, half dragged the drugged cat onto the reflective fabric. He draped a cloth game bag over her head. Then, with a businesslike approach, he arranged tools from the backpack onto the blanket—fisherman's hemostats, a Vise-Grip with pointed jaws, several sheathed scalpels, a bottle of some solution, and a tube of ointment.

"She didn't attack me," Sean said.

"No. She came here to find a mate, not a meal."

"What's wrong with her leg?" The right foreleg was scarcely more than half as big around as the left.

"Porcupine quills, as I suspected from her tracks. Actually, as I've expected for some time. Had she been taught to properly kill by her mother, she would have known better than to get stuck. It is hard to say how long she has been in this condition. If she was unable to rely on her brother for meat, I'm sure she would have died years ago. We'll see how many we can extract. She's bitten them off short, so they're not going to be easy to grip. Each quill is barbed like a fish hook, which makes it work deeper into the flesh. I've known quills to migrate a foot or more, pierce the heart. The good news is she doesn't have them in the pad of her paw and I don't see obvious signs of infection."

"You plan to release her."

"If you mean to give her a chance to survive on her own, then yes. Of course. That has been my mission since she was a cub."

"She'll kill again."

Blake shook his head. "That is the common wisdom, but where is the data? If she recovers, she can just as easily turn back to killing her natural prey. You've seen how reluctant she is to attack people. She may be guilty of eating the bodies that her brother provided her, but to my knowledge she has only killed one person, the sheep-herder. And on that occasion she was driven away by the dogs, which must have left a bad taste. Those scars you see are from fighting dogs, not other cats."

All the time he talked, he was using pliers to remove the quills, the largest of which were as long and almost as big around as pencils. When the shafts came out, they were smeared with a thin film of blood and dotted with a globular, puslike substance. Blake traded the pliers for hemostats and began removing the smaller quills.

"Sometimes I have to use a scalpel to expose the base. I try to make the incision as small as possible and still grip the quill. You pull a hundred and eighty degrees from the direction it went in. Then you wipe with antiseptic and put on a topical antibiotic and hope for the best." Lecturing Sean now.

"What happens to me?"

"Why, she kills you." His voice was matter-of-fact.

"How will you manage that trick?"

"The same way I did with Buster. Think about it. It will come to you. Here, I'll give you a clue." He reached into the backpack and removed a mechanical device about two feet long, a sort of artificial forearm made from leather and metal and armed with what looked like cat claws. Sean had seen it in the enclosure, but not clearly, and, only half conscious then, he had not divined its purpose.

"The claws are real," Blake said. "They belonged to a man-eating lion killed in the Tsavo district, in Kenya, in 1954. It was my father who shot it."

"So that's what happened to your sister. You raked her body with this . . . robot."

"It's not a robot. It is an apparatus to manipulate the claws. I will show you."

He pulled the sleeve of metal over his right arm and inserted his fingers into the leather fingertips that held the claws and metal hinges. He opened his hand and the claws emerged from their sheaths and flared out. He squeezed and they folded closed.

"We made a pact, Scarlett and I. We would cut each other with the claws, then press our bodies chest to chest as we made love. Blood brother, blood sister. I used the claws first. Scarlett passed out from the trauma and developed an infection. By the time the antibiotic treatment ran its course and she recovered, our pact no longer held an allure for her. I offered my chest, but she couldn't bring herself to cut me. Now she wears the scars as witness of her love for me, and I reciprocate in other ways. Our relationship is instinctual. We try to do exactly as we feel. That can create drama. It recently has. She had done something that required another session, one that was not performed in love."

He nodded. "There now, I think that's the last quill. I'll apply the antibiotic. I call it the purple nightmare. The hope being it tastes so vile she won't lick it off. She'll be under another half hour, or another half minute—you can't be sure with a cat. Of course I can give her an antidote, but I prefer she comes to on her own time."

"What happens then?"

"She will be groggy. One moment she will be struggling to her feet, the next she will be up and gone. I have tranquilized many cats. Aggression, upon recovery, is not in their nature."

"You'll sit here beside me?"

Blake laughed. "She is not *that* tolerant. I'll move away a bit. She needs to see clear avenues of escape. But there's one last thing I must do for her." He drew his belt knife and slipped the blade under the tight leather collar mounted with the radio transmitter. The leather was rotted and cracked and the knife sliced through it easily. Blake put the collar in his pack. "Now she is untraceable."

"It's the skull, isn't it?" Sean said. "What's left in your bag of tricks. Hiding in plain sight on the shelf in your home. You took it before we came up here."

"Excellent, Sean. But as you might have noticed, that cat had only three canine teeth, and the wounds in Buster's throat had a fourth puncture."

"You could have improvised the fourth puncture."

"I could have. But that is a tiger's skull, not a cougar's. It is much too large. A cat of such size bites with a force of more than a thousand pounds per square inch. The depth of the wounds and the spacing of the teeth would have raised suspicion. No, I had to make another model specific to the task." He brought a skull out of the pack and set it on the stump where he had placed the tranquilizing gun.

"This is the skull of a mountain lion that one of Buster's clients shot. It is similar in size to Zahara's skull. But the jaws work on a different mechanical principle than the tiger's jaws. With the tiger's, you had to screw the jaws together one half-turn at a time. Messy. It was not pretty to see the effect. This model is much more efficient."

"You've killed with it before."

"I tested it on a deer carcass. I am not a sadist, Sean. The jaws are made of aircraft aluminum and exert compound leverage. You simply crank this lever." He tapped it. "A jaws of death, if you will, so user-friendly that a woman could operate it. Not that the details of its operation will be your paramount concern. After the next injection, you won't feel anything, and if your body is ever found, and that I doubt, then you will be simply the latest victim in the career of a man-eating cat."

CHAPTER THIRTY-SEVEN

The Ninth Life

Martha was hoping to hear it, had her rifle in her hands. But when she heard the caterwauling of the cat, as if floating down on some hellish wind, she had to fight the urge to run either away from it or toward it. Toward it because it sounded like the cry of the dying, and someone in desperate need of succor. Away from it because it sounded like the breath of the devil, the most horrifying sound that Martha had ever heard. That it was a mating call was hard to fathom. No human being in the throes of passion screamed like that.

In the confined walls of the canyon, the caterwauling reverberated and echoed out. Martha switched on the radio receiver and pointed the antenna in the direction she thought the sound had come from. Deliberately, she turned in a three-quarter circle, sweeping the antenna in a smooth arc, as Scarlett had instructed her. Nothing. Again she swept the receiver, holding the wand out in front. She moved the antenna back and forth.

At first, the blips were so faint she couldn't be sure she'd heard them. She adjusted the volume knob, turning it a little to the right. She could hear the blips fade out, then get stronger. Below the tree line? She began to pick her way down the steep mountainside.

SEAN SAW ONE of the cat's rear legs stir. Blake hadn't noticed; he was smearing the purple ointment up and down the withered fore-leg. Now both rear legs were stirring, pumping the pedals of an invisible bicycle. *Surely he can feel the movement,* Sean thought. But Blake was looking away from the cat into Sean's eyes, his mouth was smiling, he was saying something, listening to himself expound.

Sean saw the heavy tail lift an inch, then twitch against the snow. Past the cat, at the edge of the trees, something else moved. It was a tawny color, and for a long moment Sean thought that there was a second cat, that Blake had called in a male, too. Then the color shifted and Sean saw the figure of a woman. The woman was swallowed up in a heavy canvas coat, and he could not believe what his eyes were seeing. It was Scarlett, walking toward them with effort, limping as the cat had limped minutes before. Her eyes were trained on the ground and she did not appear to understand what was happening. Sean wanted to shout at her to turn and run, but said nothing. Blake was still speaking as he worked on the leg of the lion.

"What do you mean?" Sean said. He didn't care what the man was saying; he only wanted his focus to be anywhere but on Scarlett or the cat.

"Well, it really goes back to the Bible," Blake said.

Sean would never know what went back to the Bible. For abruptly, without warning or sound, the cat drew her foreleg back from Blake's treatment. She crouched. Then she sprang. Sean saw an amazed expression on Blake's face, saw his head jerk, and then felt the air rush as the cat flashed by, a tawny streak, no more than a foot from the tree he was tied to.

As she sprang past, her body elongated, her tail high, she made a splash of tan against the pines. The cat leapt again, stretching like a rubber band, and then once more, clearing a pile of downed timber. In three heartbeats she was gone.

MARTHA SAW THE FLASH of color and knelt on the forest floor. She eased the fore-end of her rifle over a branch of a Ponderosa pine and looked through the scope. It was the new Leupold Vari-XIII that Sean had bought her for Christmas, after their ordeal on the Smith River, where Martha had found her old K-4 Weaver lacking in both power and clarity. By comparison, the Leupold was the eye of God, and with the power knob at nine, its highest setting, she could see Sean's face in profile and his upper chest. He was at least two hundred yards away. Ground cover obscured the rest of his body. Nothing of Blake. Where her chest pressed against the trunk of the tree, she could feel the pounding of her heart.

Where are you, you bastard?

Then, at the edge of the scope's field of view, she saw something that could be the bare trunk of a tree. She shifted her rifle so that the patch of color was centered in the scope. She was looking at Scarlett. Was but could not be. She would have to have hiked here from Martha's Jeep, there was no other explanation. How could any person whose body had been tortured the way that hers had been manage such a feat of strength and endurance? But then Martha had seen determination before. She knew that people under duress were always sold short, and that when the adrenaline kicked in they were capable of the impossible. She was looking at an example now. She checked the loads in her rifle to make sure there was one in the chamber and rested her thumb on the safety. She began to toe down the slope.

SEAN'S EYES HAD FOLLOWED the cat and now they returned to Blake, who still had a stupefied look on his face. He was clutching at the collar of his jacket. He brought the hand in front of his face. It was slimed with blood.

"Why isn't it pumping?" he said. There was a note of wonder in his voice. "Why, it's hardly a scratch." He looked into Sean's eyes. "She caught her dewclaw on my jacket. That first jump. She couldn't have missed my carotid by an inch. If I believed in God, I would take it as a sign."

"Forgive me if I don't care," Sean said.

Beyond Blake's left shoulder, Sean watched Scarlett. She was stepping in line like a cat. In ten steps, Sean judged, she would reach the stump where Blake had set down the tranquilizing gun beside the skull.

"Hurry!" Sean wanted to shout. Instead he dropped his eyes. *Do not look past him,* he told himself. *Don't give him reason to turn his head. Keep his attention.*

"Tell me," Sean said. "Since it won't matter anyway, there are a couple things I've wondered about. The bullet I found in the dog, and the claw Buster wore around his neck. They placed him where the herder was killed. I can't understand how they got there. It's never made any sense to me."

"Ah, that would have been me." There was a note of pride in the voice. "A bit of misdirection. Buster was dead, you see. I knew his body might be found, that it was only a matter of time before his truck and his horse trailer were spotted. But the longer the interval between his death and his discovery, the better. Rain would fall, perhaps even one last snow. It would sweep the evidence of his death like a broom. Any possible connection to me would be erased. So I fired his rifle into a dirt bank and dug out the slug. I was going to make a show of finding it where the herder was killed, but then you took me to the dogs. The first one had been eviscerated and it was easy to tuck the bullet under a flap of skin. The claw I placed where you found it. If you hadn't spotted it, I would have drawn your attention to it. It would concentrate the search where he wasn't, you see. Later, I thought I was being too clever by half—the bullet or the necklace, either one, would have served the purpose."

"You said there were two things you wondered about. What is the other?"

Sean searched his mind. There was no second question. He had been lucky to have thought of the first.

"The DNA," he said after an interval. "There was lion DNA found on Garrett's body. How did you manage that?"

"So there was." Blake nodded. "If you bother to compare it to samples of DNA taken from the lions in the study, you will find that it matches the DNA collected from a female lion whose collar quit transmitting three years ago. We always took blood and saliva samples for future studies. Carson kept the main data bank, as it was his project, but I took samples, too. For safekeeping, in case one was degraded or lost. All I did was smear it in a few places on Buster's body."

"You thought of everything."

"No, I did not anticipate you would come to the yurt so soon, or find me engaged in a domestic spat."

"If that's what you call ripping a person apart."

"It was necessary. Now, I think, no more talk of the past. We return to the present. Unfortunately for you, it will be a brief return."

As Blake rose from his crouch, there was a sharp cracking sound and Sean saw his body flinch. Blake swatted at the small flower that had bloomed between his shoulder blades. He couldn't reach it. He twisted his torso and swatted with his other hand. Then he saw his sister for the first time. She stood, her arms at her sides, the muzzle of the tranquilizing gun dragging on the ground.

"Scarlett, my darling, will you please give me the antidote." His voice was calm and measured, though his hands, Sean saw, were trembling. "It is on that space blanket. I love you, my darling—you know how much I love you."

Sean saw her collect the syringes off the space blanket.

"Thank you so much, my angel." Blake was moving toward her, a little drunkenly, his legs seemingly unable to track in a straight line.

Scarlett put the syringes in the pocket of her coat and picked up the skull. She looked at it curiously, then dug her fingers into the cavernous eye sockets and began to walk away, the skull in one hand, banging against her thigh, the gun in her other. She did not appear to be in a hurry, or even to acknowledge the staggering figure in her wake, or his pleading declarations of love, which now had a desperate quality.

"Please," he said.

She stopped and turned to face him.

"I can't live without you, Scarlett."

"But I can live without you." She turned and walked into the trees.

Blake began to reel. Sean saw him place his hands on his right leg and move it forward. Then follow with the left. He staggered a few more feet and fell. He got to his feet and fell again. The second time he fell, he began to roll down the slope where Sean couldn't see him. He was behind the trees where Scarlett had disappeared. Sean heard him and then he didn't.

After that, nothing for a minute. Then Sean faintly heard a grinding noise that went on and off intermittently, and much louder, a gagging, guttural sound that seemed to go on forever, but probably for no more than half a minute. He had an awful moment of realization, when he knew what he was hearing.

"Don't do it," he called out. But it was too late for that, and he knew that if Blake was not dead already he soon would be, a victim of his own medicine in the end, his self-described jaws of death.

Sean heard Scarlett begin to wail then. First it was a woman's wailing, then she was screaming, caterwauling like a cat. Sean recalled Blake saying that she could duplicate the sound using only her voice. This was a cry from the wilderness, a last lament, calling out not for Drick, to whom she had been bound by tortured love, by blood, and by hate, but for Buster, Sean thought, the lover who was now forever beyond the sound of her voice.

The caterwauling died away.

Sean craned his head. He'd heard something behind him, and for just a second he thought it could be the cat, that it was returning, drawn to Scarlett's call. But this was something heavy, coming quickly, branches breaking underfoot. He heard a voice call out, a voice that he knew.

"Martha, I'm over here!" Sean shouted.

She came into the opening. "Jesus," she said. "What the hell happened here?"

He pointed with his head. "In the thicket. I think she killed him."

"I'll cut the rope."

"No time," he said.

"You're my priority. I'm cutting the damned rope."

Sean's circulation had been cut off so long that his hands were numb. They lay on his lap like lobster claws. Martha tried to help him to his feet, but the tranquilizing solution was still in his system and he sat back down.

"Go," he said. He told her what to expect, and Martha began to walk toward the thicket, her rifle held at port arms. When she was just out of sight, he heard her say "Jesus."

Over the next ten minutes or so, Sean heard voices intermittently, the words garbled by the wind moving through the trees. More time passed. The burn began in his fingers and he finally managed to stand up and stay up. Martha was slogging back up the hill.

"Where's Scarlett?"

She unshouldered her rifle and blew out a breath. "She's with him. She won't leave him. And he's not going anywhere."

THAT EVENING, after Scarlett had been ambulanced fifty miles to the hospital in Dillon and the usual suspects had arrived, including a coroner from Anaconda to state the obvious and four deputies from Beaverhead County to tape off the scene and remove the body on a litter, Martha told Sean the rest of the story. She said that when she reached Scarlett, she was bent over her brother's body and her right hand was cranking a handle that operated the jaws of the cat skull. It reminded Martha of churning ice cream with her mother's bucket maker, how you really had to bear down to turn the crank. It wasn't the teeth that killed Blake but the pressure of the bite, the crushing of his trachea. That gagging sound Sean had heard? It was the ninth life leaving the body, as Scarlett put it to Martha. After that, she'd just kept killing a corpse.

They were sitting down to a late dinner and Sean's face betrayed a brief smile.

"I'm not sure what about any of this is funny," Martha said.

"Something Drick said up there. He said the jaws worked more efficiently than his first model, that it was so user-friendly that even a woman could operate it. Turns out he was right. Poetic justice."

"I guess," Martha said. She looked like she was going to say something else, then shook her head. "I don't want to nag you, Sean. I don't want us to have that kind of relationship, and I've been holding my tongue until we were alone. All I want to say is that you could have told me where you were going this morning. You could have done that one little thing."

"I did. I left a message."

"I mean, you could have waited to leave until you were sure I knew about it. If your message hadn't come through, you'd be dead up there, and Scarlett would have died of exposure, probably wouldn't have endured the night."

"You're right, Martha. I'm sorry."

"I don't know what to do with you sometimes."

"Well," Sean said, "you could marry me."

CHAPTER THIRTY-EIGHT

Catnip and Roses

Though it was deliberate homicide, and no question about it, Scarlett Blake would never stand trial for killing her brother. There were mitigating circumstances—her abuse at Drick's hands, the imminent threat posed to Sean Stranahan. Neither of those was the real reason, of course. The real reason was that Buck Collins, the newly elected district attorney, would never agree to prosecute a loser. And this one had loser written all over it, in blood, no less. All a defense attorney needed to do was show the jury Scarlett's scars. The DA would object on the grounds that the photos were prejudicial and inflammatory. But they were key pieces of evidence pertaining to the defendant's state of mind, and the judge would of a certainty overrule. And she'd walk. And in fact she did, only a few weeks into her recovery, leading Tatiana on a leash down a sidewalk in Pasadena, while attending a symposium for an environmental group called Panthera.

It was early in the summer then, what in Montana was called a bluebird winter, what with snow still falling in the mountains. In the valley, the forecast called for a 50 percent chance of rain. That didn't threaten the wedding, which, as the couple had agreed, was a civil ceremony conducted indoors: a judge, a witness—Sam Meslik did the honors—and the bride and groom. Sean had dressed in a crisp white shirt with pearl snaps, his best black jeans, and a turquoise stone bolo tie in the shape of a grizzly bear's claws. Martha wore a cream silk shirt unbuttoned to reveal a bit more décolletage than she was comfortable showing and a calf-length skirt that showcased her cowboy boots with the red roses. Her right hand clutched a bouquet of wildflowers that Harold Little Feather had picked from his sister's garden.

"I'll take care of you," Sean said, taking her free hand.

"I'll take care of you," Martha said.

Walking out into the gloom of clouds, both felt a little like they'd just stepped off a cliff.

The rain started a little after the kickoff of the party that Patrick Willoughby threw on the grounds of the Madison River Liars and Fly Tiers Club later that day. For a time the fifty or so in attendance crowded under the big canvas tent rented for the festivities.

But a day of overcast skies, off-and-on drizzle, and mild temperatures is a great day if you are a mayfly looking to mate, or a trout fisherman with a mayfly imitation tied to the end of his tippet. As the hatch intensified and swirls began to mar the surface of the river, a number of the partyers abandoned the canopy and donned waders.

Sean had promised Martha he wouldn't fish and that he'd try to make friends with her father, whom she adored even though she suspected he was on the spectrum, and whom Sean had met on only one prior occasion. Mr. Ettinger was the type of man who exhausts subjects as quickly as a Scandinavian farmer, which he was. Even dressed in his best, he looked like a man who carried a pitchfork to work.

Conversation was difficult until Sean asked him about stock car racing. Martha had told Sean that her father had driven Montana's dirt tracks when he was younger, and he had an endless supply of stories. After telling a few, he took a couple of harmonicas from his pocket and taught Sean to play "Autumn Leaves" in G minor.

"You keep it," Mr. Ettinger said, when Sean tried to hand back the harmonica. "You learn to play with my Martha. Couple that plays together, stays together. Me and the missus are going on fifty years, been together since we was in kindergarten."

Sean pocketed the harp and saw Sam crooking a finger.

"Kemosabe," he said. "Got a little something for you."

He led Sean to his truck and withdrew a green Cordura rod case from the rear bench.

"Uh-uh," Sean said. "I promised Martha."

"Hey, did I say anything about fishing? Just listen to your uncle Sam. Go on now, pull it out of the sock and swish it a few times. You know you want to."

The big man smiled, revealing the grooves in his teeth. Sean pulled out the graphite sections and assembled the rod. He touched the tip to the ground and whistled. "This is the longest rod I've ever seen," he said. "You could pole-vault with it."

"Damned straight," Sam said. "It's a Bruce and Walker. Fifteen-footer. It's the first half of your wedding present. Only the best, Kemosabe. Only the best."

"Thanks, Sam, but there isn't a trout in Montana that could put a bend in it. Besides, I'm heading off on my honeymoon."

The honeymoon would be a cruise down the Rhine River through Germany and the Black Forest, where some of Martha's people on her mother's side had lived, to be followed by a few days in Donegal, in Ireland, where she'd learned that Sean's great-great-great-grandparents had burned peat for warmth before being driven out by the potato famine and emigrating to Nova Scotia. Martha had caught the genealogy bug as others might catch a cold, and had planned the honeymoon with an eye toward killing several birds with one stone.

"Of course it isn't a trout rod," Sam said. "It isn't meant for no pipsqueak trout. But it's just what the good doctor ordered for the Gaula River."

"That's in Norway."

"I know where the fuck the Gaula is. We got a week on one of the best beats on the river. That's the second part of your gift. After you're done deflowering your bride in the land of fairies, you're hopping on a puddle jumper out of Dublin. I'll meet you in Oslo and we'll be in fucking Lapland before nightfall. If there is a nightfall. Which I don't think there is. It's the fucking Land of the Midnight Sun."

"I've always wanted to catch a big Atlantic salmon," Sean said. "I just thought I'd have to rob a bank for the chance."

"Yeah, well, I know some people who know some people. Only thing you got to do is tie the flies."

"I've been tying salmon flies for years."

"Then we're set, aren't we? Go on back now and mingle. I just might have to prick a lip before this hatch is over and the fish put their brains back into their heads."

The plaid-shirt band Willoughby had rented showed up an hour late, four twenty-something Oregonians who couldn't fix a flat if they were handed the tools, and they didn't know where the tools were. A passerby finally did the deed. They held an umbrella over his head while he used the tire iron to screw the nuts back on, and gave him a doobie for the road. "We got soaked," the bandleader said. They laughed as they told Sean the story. They were still stoned.

They were good, though, and Sean and Martha danced the night away, or the first part of it, but who was counting steps?

"We could have just stayed lovers," Martha said, as they danced to "Moon River." "Couples who share dogs, it's the new marriage, I hear."

"I like the old way," Sean said. "You know the first time I kissed you, we were dancing just like this. Your cousin's wedding, remember? Before I asked you to take off your gun."

"I'm not wearing it now."

Nor was she wearing it later that night, after they had excused themselves from the party and driven to the Old Faithful Inn in Yellowstone Park for their first night as legally betrothed. Martha covered the bed with rose petals, and it was midnight when she came back to the darkly paneled room from the bathroom down the hall. Sean had lit a candle and she untied the sash of her bathrobe and took it off. Underneath she was wearing a cream silk camisole. She slipped a finger under one shoulder strap and then the other, and pulled the camisole down to her waist, led him to the bed, and, as she moved above him, her breasts swaying in the candlelight, Sean was enveloped in her warm, intoxicating scent, at once familiar and yet subtly foreign.

"What are you wearing?" he said.

She smiled. "Just a little something from a bottle."

"Is that Calvin Klein's Obsession?"

"A woman never tells."

The houndsman from New Mexico, Cecil Flowers, had been delayed by car trouble and finally arrived in Bridger three days after

Drick Blake died on the mountain. But by then the trail laid down by the cat had washed away in rain and wind, and though he stayed on for close to a month, putting his Walkers' noses to the ground in all the places that the cat had been known to visit, he never cut the track of a female whose track showed an inturned right foreleg. He told Martha that it was likely that she had either died of starvation or recovered and found a mate who had led her to parts unknown, and that he was wasting her time and the county's money. He turned the nose of his truck around and headed south, leaving her a promise that he would return if there was another human kill. Martha had kept the bottle of eau de parfum.

"Do you like it?" she said. "They say it's catnip to mountain lions."

Sean started to speak, but she put a finger to his lips.

"Shh now. That's enough. I know the answer to my question."

And as she smiled down at him, the odds she had given for them staying hitched rising with each intake and exhalation of her breath, no further words were spoken.

CHAPTER THIRTY-NINE

They That Believeth

Schools in Montana opened for the fall semester on August twenty-eighth. At three o'clock that afternoon, the woman whose name meant Sea of Sorrow, who had worked the day shift at the Ennis Public Library, drove a few blocks out of her way to watch the children streaming out of the elementary school on Charles Avenue. Miriam Ross was in no hurry to return to the shell of her existence that less than a year before had been a life, before her five-year-old son, Hunter, had been taken by a mountain lion. For months, she had clung to the hope that Hunter was still alive, that he had been kidnapped that night by his father, her estranged husband, and not killed by tooth and claw. After all, her ex had disappeared from the grid, and though cat tracks and sign had been found in the ranch vicinity, the only human body parts ever recovered that could belong to a child were regurgitated toes that were too degraded to DNA-test. Sure, the toes were small, but then all children had small feet, and there were always lions prowling about. *Weren't there?*

Such is a story you tell yourself to keep breathing, to keep putting one foot in front of the other in your shattered life.

"You'd be six now," she said, as the last of the children came through the double doors. "You'd be going into first grade."

She smiled. It was a wan smile, one her lips fought to remember. The smile faded when she put her truck into gear and began to drive south toward the ranch. As she turned off Highway 287 onto the mile-long gravel road that led to the house, a truck she didn't recognize was coming the other way. As it passed by, the driver touched the brim of his hat in a two-finger salute. Miriam returned the gesture. Probably some crony of her father's. The driver's face had been in shadow, chin down, the hat brim pulled low.

"You'd have been somebody," she said, not even aware that she was speaking. "You would have made your mother proud."

Why chin down? Hat brim, Miriam understood. But chin down, like you're saying a prayer? She knew only one person who did that, who sat in the driver's seat like dinner was on the dash and he was saying the blessing.

Feeling her heart pounding as the house grew larger in the foreground, the porch coming into view, she couldn't believe what she saw. No, she couldn't believe it, she wouldn't. Not and draw another breath ever again. No merciful God would do that to a person. And then she was out of her truck and running, and she scooped him into her arms and hugged him to her chest until she thought her heart would explode.

"Oh, God," she said. "Oh, Hunter, we thought you were dead."

The boy's voice was muffled against her shirt. "Daddy said to tell you he didn't have what it takes."

"To what, be a father?"

"I don't know. Stop it, Mama. Stop it. You're breaking me."

She'd looked at the line of dust raised by her truck driving in and the other going out, the vehicle just a glint now in the distance. It was Earl, it had to be. Finally doing the one good thing he could.

The next day, Hunter Ross was enrolled in the Ennis Elementary School. Martha Ettinger took the call from the principal, who'd got the story from the first-grade teacher, who'd got it from Hunter's mother, who hadn't yet notified the authorities. Martha set down the receiver and punched in the number for Harold Little Feather, who was still stealing an hour now and then to compile the data for the last interagency report on the two lions that had terrorized residents of the valley.

"There is a God," Martha told him. "I wasn't sure."

Though Harold's god was the sun and never in doubt, he rejoiced with Martha, which meant he spoke more than a few words before clicking the phone off.

He told her that there had been two developments since Blake's death. The first was that an antler hunter had come forward to say that he had shot the guard dogs. They had charged at him and it was self-defense, but still, he felt guilty and had been a coward for leaving the scene without informing the herder. One mystery solved.

The second development concerned the regurgitated toes that Martha had suspected belonged to Hunter Ross. Harold's son Marcus had told his father that a fellow student in Native American Studies said that his kid brother had died in a car accident the past November, and that they had constructed a scaffold to bury him on,

as his ancestors had been buried in the Sioux tradition. The student
told Marcus that when he had visited the site a few days later to pray
and scatter a few keepsakes for the departed, he saw that the toes
from the boy's right foot had been eaten, apparently by coyotes or
other scavengers. No other part of the body had been touched, except by birds. Marcus, knowing that the date was only a week or so
before the toes were found in the regurgitation, asked where the
burial had taken place. The Gravelly Range, the student told him.
On the QT, as the practice on Forest Service land was prohibited.

"Maybe the cat was put off by the taste and only ate the toes,"
Martha mused.

She hesitated. "Tell me something, Harold. Have you thought any
more about running?" A short silence. "If you have, I just want you
to know those things I said, it was heat of the moment. I was wrong
to say it. You have to do what you have to do. I'm not part of the
equation. And it won't affect our friendship. I just want you to know
that."

"We're more than friends, though, aren't we? There's more to lose.
But thanks, it's been bothering me. I don't know if I'll run. If I do,
you'll be the first to know."

After they'd hung up, Harold limped to the map on the wall behind the desk. His eyes moved over the colored magnets that identified the locations and dates of lion confrontations and attacks. He
found the sparkly magnet painted with fingernail polish called
Starry Night, which marked Hunter Ross's disappearance on the
family ranch up the south fork of Bear Creek on October 31, Halloween night.

Many times over the past year, Harold had thought to remove the
magnet and replace it with a cross to mark the boy's death, but each
time he had refrained from doing so. Not because he held out hope

against hope, as Miriam Ross did. No, Harold was not a man who clung to threads. It was the family dog, the one that didn't bark that night. That was what bothered him. When Martha had first told him the details of the boy's disappearance, that one inconsistency was what had struck him. If there had been a lion prowling about that night, surely the dog would have barked, or in some other way betrayed its unease. But if it was Miriam's ex coming to abduct the boy, then perhaps not. Perhaps the dog would have stayed silent.

Harold removed the magnet and went into the kitchen. He looked at the refrigerator door, which his sister had peppered with magnets to pin down her favorite Bible verses. Harold chose one that she had altered to be more inclusive of women and placed the magnet on it.

ALL THINGS ARE POSSIBLE TO THEY THAT BELIEVETH.

MARK 9:23

CHAPTER FORTY

The Lovely Dark

In the hour of the dying light, on a day savaged by thunderstorms and lightning, the cat left the shallow cave where she had been nursing her three cubs and took up a position behind a log. In front of her, two game trails formed an X where they crossed a creek that sang a quiet little song. Here she crouched with her belly to the pine needle floor of the forest.

The two trails, in addition to being used by mule deer and elk, were traveled by backpackers, hikers, and, in season, hunters. Archery season had in fact begun the previous Saturday, a week after Labor Day, and in this last of the twilight, the lion watched a bow hunter hurrying down one of the trails. The hunter was dressed in camouflage clothes and had approached to within twenty feet of the lion when the sky was lit up by a bolt of lightning.

Abruptly, the man stopped. As he did, the lion pumped her legs, and her tail switched from one side to the other. She drew back her lips in a silent snarl.

Throughout the summer, as her old wounds healed, the lion had lain in ambush along many trails. Though the game she sought was no longer safe from her, humans she remained reluctant to confront, in spite of having eaten the flesh provided by her brother.

Their relationship had always been uneasy. It was unusual for siblings to travel together, let alone to share kills. And the tom was a reluctant provider. But she was the dominant cat, perhaps because she was the more desperate, and, as with wolves, the alpha is not always the biggest or strongest animal. She had shadowed him from the time they had been released into the wild. For eight years she had left his side on only a few occasions to follow her instinct and mate with other males. It had been after one of those liaisons that she had swiped at the porcupine.

As the quills drove into her muscles and her foreleg twisted and wasted away, she came to rely more and more upon her brother's teeth and claws. They slept side by side and hunted together when the nights came on, with him leading the way, her following, lamps to each other in the lovely darkness. She had been only a little distance away when he claimed his first human victim, a man who lived alone in a remote cabin. He was the first of three, the woman who lived in the trailer the last, before her brother was taken from her by a bullet through his heart. She had been close enough to hear the shot, and in the middle of that night she had followed the trail he'd taken as he was pursued by the hounds. Coming to where he lay dead, his body already stiffening, she had sniffed at him, walked around him, and eventually lain down, nudging him with her head. She had left his side only when she heard humans approaching in the morning.

On her own ever since, she had taken to revisiting human habitations where her brother had stalked their possible victims. One, a sheepherder, she had lain in wait for and killed, but had been driven away by his dogs before she could satisfy her hunger. Another, a woman, spoke in a cadence, counting her steps from her car to a small log cabin. Yet another followed a routine, parking a truck at a ranch gate in the middle of nowhere, then standing alone by the road in the morning darkness, waiting to catch a bus. As these and other humans approached and passed by her, she had gathered her legs, her muscles as taut as steel coils, prepared to spring. And might have, if one had stopped and bent over suddenly, or coughed, or in some other way had broken routine. But they did not break routine, and they never knew how close they had come to triggering her attack.

This hunter was different. He had stopped only yards away and switched on his headlamp, had then provoked her instinct further by bending down with his back turned to rummage through his pack. He stood up, and as he zipped up the jacket he had retrieved, he turned his head and the beam of his light searched through the undergrowth. For a second, two jade orbs pierced the darkness. The orbs were blazing in their intensity and then they were gone.

The hunter must have seen them, for he hurriedly shouldered his pack and began to walk down the trail, breaking into a trot, then a run, his pack bouncing off his back, his flashlight beam jerking crazily, illuminating the pines. The arms of the trees whipped at him as he fled.

As for the lion, she had shifted her gaze just as the beam of the man's light swept over her face. The impulse to give chase was strong, and she had followed down the path the hunter had taken with narrowing focus, tracking the firefly glow of his light. But even as she closed the gap, her aversion to humans began to reassert itself, and her attention flagged. A month before, perhaps, the chase wouldn't have ended in this manner. A month before her hunger was greater.

But she was strong now, and humans were no longer the only animal slow enough for her to catch, nor weak enough to kill. With only curiosity propelling her forward, she followed to a break in the trees where she could see the carpet of lights in the valley. A magnetic force field seemed to pulse from the lights, repelling any further pursuit. Turning, she padded back into the reassuring dark of the forest, where she resumed her ambush behind the log.

An hour later, a young mule deer buck picked his way down to the creek where the trails crossed. When he dropped his nose to drink, the cat sprang. In one leap she was on him, her right paw sweeping the hind legs from underneath his body. As the deer tripped, she caught him by the throat.

She stood over him, her chest heaving from the exertion, as lightning flashed on the top of the ridge. Perhaps, then, the deer, like the hunter, saw the fire in the eyes of the lion. Or perhaps by then the last light in the world had gone out, leaving the Bangtail Ghost as a shadow in the night.

ACKNOWLEDGMENTS

This book is dedicated to Kathryn Court, the former publisher and president of Penguin Books, who has been my editor for the Sean Stranahan series since its inception. It is also dedicated to Dominick Abel, my literary agent, who, as my wife puts it, is a knight riding his white horse to the rescue of this Montana writer, and to that of many others. Without Dominick, there might not be any Sean Stranahan books to publish. Without Kathryn, they might not have found a home, let alone at such a respected publishing house. I am honored to consider them friends and to have been the beneficiary of their wisdom in the shaping of this novel.

Also, I especially want to acknowledge associate editor Victoria Savanh, who took the reins on this project after Kathryn Court's retirement last year. Victoria's guidance and suggestions made this a better book. For shepherding the novel through its final stages, and for his infinite patience in indulging my many last-minute changes, I am greatly indebted to senior production editor Bruce Giffords. I also want to thank Amy Edelman, who is the most thorough and spot-on of all the copy editors with whom I have worked.

A book, if the author is lucky and has the support of a dedicated team, enjoys both a private and public life. For bringing my books to the readers, I want to thank associate publicity director Ben Petrone.

For the layout and striking jacket design, I thank book designer Alexis Farabaugh and senior designer Matt Vee. It is Matt who is responsible for the jacket, and it is my hope that the novel will live up to those bright and penetrating eyes.

The Bangtail Ghost of this book's title is a mountain lion, and I am fortunate that a reader of my previous books, Jim Williams, just happens to be one of the foremost mountain lion researchers in the world and the author of the bible on mountain lion biology and behavior, *Path of the Puma*, which I recommend to anyone who finds these great carnivores as fascinating as I do. Jim, who is the Region 1 supervisor for Montana Fish, Wildlife and Parks, was kind enough to review this book from the perspective of a biologist who

Acknowledgments

has studied lions from Glacier National Park in Montana to Patagonia in Argentina and Chile. Any errors of fact or animal behavior in the story are mine alone.

I'd also like to recognize my friend Julie Cunningham, a biologist for Montana Fish, Wildlife and Parks, who taught me how to radio-track game.

It is hard to exaggerate the role that houndsmen play in the study of big cats. Without hounds there are no lions to collar, and without collared lions there are no digital trails to follow that reveal to us the lions' life stories, so that we might better understand them and help them coexist with us. Among houndsmen, Orvel Fletcher is legendary. I treasure the week I spent with him, riding horseback through the rimrock canyons east of Trujillo, New Mexico, on the trail of a cattle-killing lion.

Halfway around the world, in the foothills of the Himalayas, a much larger cat rules with tooth and claw, the royal Bengal tiger. I want to thank Sid and Choti Anand, who run Blaze a Trail Adventures (blazeatrailadventures.com), for making my dream of spending time with tigers in the wild a reality.

As for the writing of the book, I thank my son, Tom, for his scrupulous reading of early drafts of the novel, and my counselor daughter, Jessie, for providing insight into character and motivation. I also thank them for social media and tech support, and for operating and updating my website.

Last, and most of all, I thank my wife, Gail Schontzler, for her years of support and guidance. She is my companion on this journey and my last and best editor. Her skills and patience were never more needed or appreciated than in the writing of this novel.